THE DOMINO QUEEN

'Again, slave,' she says, very quietly.

Alexandra takes a deep breath. Her breasts rise. She moistens her lips with her sweet pink tongue.

'The condition of a slave,' she says, 'is a condition of quietness and tranquility. The bondage of a slave is threefold freedom.'

'What are the three freedoms?' asks Josephine, her voice hard as a whip across the stillness of the group.

Alexandra is ready now to answer. They have been over this and over it, the training punctuated with the necessary punishments and rewards.

'Freedom from motion,' says Alexandra, 'freedom from thought, and freedom from will. The duty of a slave is to remain mindful at all times of her own humility . . .'

A NEXUS CLASSIC

THE DOMINO QUEEN

Cyrian Amberlake

This book is a work of fiction.
In real life, make sure you practise safe sex.

This Nexus Classic edition published in 2006

First published in 1991 by Nexus Books
Thames Wharf Studios
Rainville Road
London
W6 9HA

www.nexus-books.co.uk

A catalogue record for this book is available from the
British Library.

Typeset by TW Typesetting, Plymouth, Devon
Printed and bound in Great Britain by
Clays Ltd, St Ives PLC

ISBN 0 352 34074 6
ISBN 978 0 352 34074 0

Prologue

In the first weeks of June, Auvergne reclaims from the twentieth century most of its antique, rugged character. The last skiers have gone, the first spa-takers are only just arriving. Spring here was quick and vital, all over, so it seemed, in a few days of May. The cattle are afield, browsing in the tender new grass. The *couzes* are still swollen, white and turbulent with meltwater. Only one lone fisherman stands in hip-high waders in a sky-blue pool below Lac Pavin, his wicker creel slung from his hip, his battered woollen hat pulled low over his eyes. He will catch nothing today, or tomorrow; he is here for the solitude, the silence, at once tranquil and electric with the potency of the infant summer.

Already the light, translucent greens of the woodland are thickening, growing richer and deeper. All across the slopes of the ancient volcanoes a haze of orange-brown and green is spreading, blurring and softening the cruel prehistoric outlines of basalt and granite. Up at the crater this morning, the mist thins quickly from the mysterious, vivid blue lake, as if the pines were inhaling it, drawing it into themselves. This was the lake the ancients feared; its very name means 'frightening'. They believed that here was the place the thunder slept. To throw a stone into its horrid depths was to invoke Jupiter and bring tumultuous storms down upon one's head. Nor is Lac Pavin without its sunken village, its sonorous peal of bells still tolling from beneath those ominous waters.

From Besse-en-Chandesse to Le Mont-Dore, the traveller takes the tortuous mountain route (but here, all routes are tortuous and mountainous) through Murol and on to the Col de la Croix Morland. His vintage Bentley tourer, noble and noisy as a passionate steed, shoulders around the bends with an imperious clamour, stones from under its heavy wheels flying over the edge, spinning into space. The traveller thinks of the welcome awaiting him at the manor, the woman who is surely out of doors on such a grand, rejuvenating morning, taking the sun on her skin. He thinks also of the servant girl, who will be about her business in the house and the outbuildings: so near home, and yet so far. Then he turns the wheel in its glove of pale kid's leather and masters another bend.

Poised airily alone on a promontory of rock, the low church of St Nectaire roosts above the valley. Here too there is a legend, of a Greek missionary ferried across the Tiber by the Devil himself but protected by an angel; dying on his journey but resurrected by St Peter in person. Even in the bright arc of early summer, there is an autumnal colour to the modest building, strengthened and redoubled by the red rocks of the gorge, the rosy mass of Puy Ferrand. The Couze de Chambon hurtles by below among the pines, into the peaceful lake where, says the writer, 'the bourgeois placidly exercise their copious meals away'. Today the lake is vacant, the pedal-boats still being fetched from under canvas for their annual coat of varnish.

Unhindered, the Bentley sweeps though the village. Between the cottages of fawn stone a melancholy lingers in the air above the prospect of the lake, flashing and flickering though it is with young sunbeams. This location's pious legend is of the Leap of the Virgin: a young girl who, to save her virtue, cast herself perilously into the water and was saved by miraculous intervention. The traveller knows another, grimmer version, in which, egged on by disbelieving friends, the maiden foolishly repeated her leap, and drowned, as is only reasonable. These legends of damnation and salvation barely mask a strong and dangerous truth. Impatient now, the traveller floors the accelerator, risking hidden obstacles, a lumbering farm cart, a flock of sheep, that could lie around the next bend or the next. He still has some way to drive.

At the manor at this hour all is silent. The fields are empty, the grass in the orchard grows ungrazed. On the roof two rooks strut and preen, spreading their indigo feathers to the sun. On the lawn a woman reclines on cushions and a soft alpaca blanket.

She is young, still, comfortably in her thirties. She is not tall; her figure in repose is sleek, if not as trim now, perhaps, as when she once exercised regularly and energetically every week in a private gymnasium, in a city across the sea. Her hair is straw blonde, cut boyishly short in anticipation of the summer heart. Her lips are pink as a fresh shrimp, her eyes like the sea seem to change colour with the weather, now blue, now grey, now almost as green as the hills of St Nectaire. At this moment they are hidden behind a large pair of Tenoshi-Hi sunglasses with upswept frames of marbled pink plastic. She wears a fraying, broad-brimmed straw hat with an Indian silk scarf of blue and pink batik knotted carelessly around the crown. On her feet are slave sandals, flat soles of tan leather laced up to the swell of her calves with slender thongs of soft calf's hide. She wears nothing else.

She reads, it may be, a slim novel by Marguerite Duras. She reads about Hélène Lagonelle, who is seventeen, who has no memory, whose body is the most beautiful of all the things given by God. Her breasts are as white as flour, says the narrator, and she walks naked and innocent through the dormitory, carrying them before her like a gift. The woman smiles, and almost unconsciously runs her hand over her own breasts, which are large and loll outwards across her narrow chest, flattened by their own weight. In the cleft between them is a small black tattoo: a domino mask, such as one might wear at a Venetian carnival. Her nipples are thick and dark, and soft as fruit. She runs her hand down the curve of her ribcage, feeling the supple warmth of her skin in the sun, the moist sheen of her perspiration, down past her flat belly to the firm edge of her hipbone, down to the junction of her thighs, where the hair is brown and profuse as it curls over her mound.

Her hand pauses. Her lips, pink as shrimps, part slightly and the tip of her tongue hovers expectantly in the opening.

The manor house is no great size, though it is nine and ten times as large as any of the houses in the villages hereabouts. It is built of stone, with plain and solid wooden beams, doors and window frames, and a cruck roof of orange tile. Around the chimney stacks, the rooks peck among the proliferating clumps of moss and weeds.

Inside these thick walls the house is cool, and not well lit. The luxurious furnishings of the drawing room and master bedroom seem to belong to another house, another age. In the scullery, a young woman in a plain black frock and cotton apron kneels up on the massive, white-scoured draining board to peek out of the window, over the net curtain. She places her skinny white knees carefully, balancing among the various pots and pans stacked there to dry. Though she is alone in the house, she does not wish to make a sound.

Her name is Yvette. She is not yet twenty, though poor diet and a severely encompassed childhood have made her look younger still. Her hair is a mousey grey-brown, parted in the centre and pulled straight back either side of her round face, and fixed firmly with corrugated hairgrips. Her nose is straight and long, but not absurdly long. Together with her thick, bold eyebrows it gives her face a rather serious, disapproving expression, even in repose. She does not, in fact, disapprove, or approve, of what happens here at the manor, to her and to others. It never occurs to her that she has the right or ability to do either. She accepts all equally because it is inexplicable, whether pleasant or unpleasant, or that strange, turbulent sensation which is a mixture of the two. She feels this sensation now, as so often when she spies on the lady of the manor, the woman her master brought home one day and introduced to her as her mistress.

The lady of the manor shifts her leg, opening her sheer sun-brown thighs to the indifferent sun, and to her own somnolently exploring fingers. Though her eyes are covered by the pink Japanese sunglasses, the angle of her head shows she is not looking at what her hand is doing. She has no need to look; what her hand is doing is too familiar. In the swelling heat of the clear June day, she exists in a universe of touch and sensation. The moisture on her naked thighs is now not only perspiration.

The servant girl sees her raise her hand to her face as if to adjust her glasses; but that is not what she is doing. The first two fingers of her hand are extended, the others curled in on her palm, in the gesture of the saints made in the church where Yvette once went with her brothers and her sister, and her mother of course, every Sunday. Yvette sees her mistress bring the fingers delicately to her nose. She is smelling them. She tilts her head back against the pillows. Now her hand returns to her crotch. Perhaps she has an itch there. She seems to be rubbing herself, slowly, gently.

As if in imitation, like a monkey, Yvette reaches beneath her own black frock. She encounters no underwear. Except once a month, when she is bleeding, and in the winter, the master gives her none. Nor did she wear any when she lived at home in poverty with her family. She did not do this either then, this, that she begins to do now, for she did not know why she should. Her pale lips part at the feel of her fingers. Her mouth opens wide in an O.

On the lawn the mistress's hand ceases to move. She raises her knee, bringing her sandalled foot nearer in to her bare bottom. She lets her leg lean sideways, tilting from the hip. She lifts her hand to her book and turns a page. Her hand falls back into the open vee of her thighs.

The mistress reads about the Chinese millionaire who lays bare the girlish body of the narrator and washes her slowly under the shower, with cool water from a special jar, then carries her, still wet, to the bed beneath the slowly turning fan. The mistress's hand begins to move again upon herself.

Behind the scullery window, inside the silent house of grey stone, the movements of Yvette's hand are diffident, without certainty or rhythm: a faint echo of her mistress's. All the same, there is a little moisture on her fingertips now that is not water, or saliva, or perspiration. Yvette makes a tiny noise of sensuous apprehension, a gasp as small as the squeak of a mouse. Her shoulders tense and quiver beneath her plain black frock.

In a nest of pasture below leafy uplands lies the spa town of La Bourboule, still sedate if no longer quite as chic as it was in another age, another lifetime. The palatial Hotel Metropole, where Queen Victoria used to stay, is now a mundane block of flats. The white cupolas of the majestic Bains Grands shine as serene as ever in the clear, tangy air; but the crowds jostling in and out of the august doors beneath are no longer the well-to-do and the gracefully decrepit, but herds of schoolchildren. For childish complaints of asthma and eczema they come, dispatched by elderly doctors who put their trust in these arsenical waters. The Bentley must stop and growl sulkily in a neutral gear while a slender, harried-looking young schoolma'am shepherds her charges across the road, their heads swathed in bandages.

As soon as the crocodile is past, the traveller is away, spurning the café terraces, the bonbon kiosks and shadowy photographers' studios with the dust of his wheels.

Yvette is gone from the scullery, from the draining board. She is on the toilet, the skirt of her black frock hitched up to her narrow waist, her legs, skinny as sparrows', dangling from the enormous antediluvian throne. Her little feet in their button-strap sandals barely touch the red-tiled floor. Yvette pees in spurts, uncomfortably, her bladder excited by her clumsy fingering. She has not locked the toilet door. A blazing wedge of sunlight intrudes dazzling into the gloom.

On her rug on the lawn, Yvette's mistress is still busy. Her legs sprawl wide, one knee raised, swaying to the motion of her fingers that dip and stroke and slide, perhaps a little quicker now, in and out, in and out, round and round and round. The rug is crumpled beneath her legs, rucked up between her feet and her buttocks. A tiny puddle of stickiness has begun to soak into the fine material. Forgotten, needed no longer, the book has fallen to the ground at her side. It lies open, face down, the sun drenching its cream wove paper cover, the grey print of the insouciant face with its thirties Cupid-bow mouth, its mannish coiffure. The lady of the manor arches her back, her own lipsticked mouth open wide. Her hat slips from her head and rolls, wobbling, from the pillows.

A shadow falls across her nude body, coming between her and the beautiful sun.

A young man's voice asks, 'Did I tell you to touch yourself?'

'Leonard!'

She opens her eyes, startled, her hand arrested at her crotch. She smiles, happily, her free hand lifting her sunglasses to look properly at the man who has come silently across the lawn from the house.

He is younger than her, by seven or eight or nine years. He looks like a boy, like an angelic boy in a painting by Caravaggio. His cheeks are pink from the heat of the day and the rushing of the air in the open-topped tourer. Wild blond curls tumble luxuriantly down the back of his neck and over the band of his loose, collarless, snow-white cotton blouson. A pair of silver reflective aviator sunglasses are perched up on top of his head among the chaotic curls. His hands are on his hips, his thumbs tucked through the loops of a pair of soft jeans in washed-out blue denim. His belt is broad black leather, old, cracked and creased; on his feet he wears short black boots that could do with polishing.

'I didn't know you were back,' says the woman who sprawls at his feet. She takes her hand slowly from her crotch. Silver strings of mucus trail after it, flashing in the sunlight. She tilts her head back as though expecting a kiss.

He does not kiss her.

He looks at the neglected novel. He leans over and picks it up. 'Is this how you look after my books, Josephine?'

Josephine squints against the sun. 'It's my book,' she says.

He looks her steadily in the eye, saying nothing. She does not move. He stands over her and reads a paragraph. When he reaches the end of the page, he turns over and continues for a moment or two; then he riffles through the rest of the book, as if gauging what interest it might hold for him. None, to judge by his face.

Slowly the sunbather lowers her sunglasses back onto her nose. He shuts the book one-handed, with a snap.

'Kneel,' he says.

At once the woman gets up on her knees on the alpaca rug. She faces him, but bows her head.

'Things here have become lax in my absence,' he observes.

Josephine's heart is loud in her own ears; 'I expect so,' she murmurs.

'I didn't hear that?' he says.

'Yes,' she says, slightly louder. 'Master.'

She is aware that he is taking something out of the pocket of his jeans She feels his fingers at the back of her neck, lifting her short hair out of the way. He slips a collar around her neck. It is slim, made of shiny black leather, with a buckle at the back and a silver ring at the front, in the middle. His fingers are cool on her hot skin.

When the buckle is fastened, he lifts her head, not gently, with a finger under her chin. Their eyes meet.

'Would you prefer to be whipped before lunch,' he asks softly, 'or after?'

Her lips, pink as prawns, part slightly and the tip of her tongue moistens them.

'After, master,' she says. 'If it pleases you.'

Yvette, who heard the approach of the Bentley at a great distance across the stony fields, lies on her own narrow bed with her apron off, her frock pulled right up to her modest, shell-like breasts. She is rubbing herself with a will now. She has heard the master come in the door from the yard and go straight outside again. They will be wanting their lunch soon, so she has little time to finish, wash, and return to the kitchen. She imagines the master, how he looks when he comes to the door of her room in the middle of the night. With her left hand she presses the folds of the counterpane into her mouth, gripping it between her teeth to stifle her panting gasps. She imagines the mistress, naked in bed, her arms wide in welcome. With a little lurch, she heaves her thin hips up off the bed, rubbing hard.

Yvette has been with the master more than a year now, nearly two. Everything in her life has changed since that day when her cousin Marie-Claire ran in from the top field to fetch her, to show her the big old car sailing serenely past along the village road. It was the colour of oxblood, and the man in the driver's seat was an angel.

Neither of the girls had ever seen anything so wonderful. Abandoning their farmwork, they ran at once into the village, where they found the marvellous chariot parked outside the inn with everyone standing around it at a cautious, respectful distance, and the angel sitting, in a pair of blue jeans with mirrors over his eyes, drinking a glass of wine with the corpulent and unsavoury old *patron*! Confused by the bustle and the excitement of the event, old Aimée, blind in one eye and lame in her right hindleg, had hobbled over to bark at the whispering girls; and fat Bernard, calling her to him, had eyed the pair and given the stranger a word and a nod.

Yvette had nearly died when later that day the blood-red car came grinding slowly up the stony track from the big house and stopped at their cottage. Sometimes, late at night, and when the master is away, she wonders what price her father set upon her; and why her mother would not leave the chimney corner to bid her adieu, but only hide her face in her apron. For now, she thinks of them and of her runny-nosed starving siblings not at all. They are far away, beyond the Livradois mountains; which is to say, on the other side of the world. One day she will learn to write, and then she will write them a letter. For the present, she thinks only of the angels, her master and mistress, and rubs herself harder, grinding the counterpane between her teeth.

Alone in her room Josephine finishes washing herself, wiping the sweat and the suntan lotion and the mucilage from her body. She dips the flannel in the bowl again and wrings it out, looking at herself in the mirror. She cups her breasts in her hands, feeling the weight of them. She likes the way she looks, her healthy colour from the hot sun, her breasts bare, the slim black collar around her throat. She admires her black tattoo.

She towels herself. Her skin is soon dry in the heat. She puts on old-fashioned underwear: a stiff, boned white brassière and a pair of high-sided white knickers; a heavily elasticated corset with dangling suspenders. She pulls on black stockings, sheer, with a delicate pattern of chevrons up the side. The clothes feel firm and good, enclosing and supporting her everywhere. She covers everything with a full-length white cotton slip; buttons up a soft grey blouse with a white shirtcollar; steps into a thin skirt of charcoal-coloured corduroy, calf length. In the mirror she see a good *bourgeoise*, modest, neat, about to go down to lunch with her husband at their weekend house in the picturesque Auvergne. She smiles at herself and straightens her collar.

Yvette knocks at the door. 'Lunch is ready, madame.'

'Thank you, Yvette.'

Leonard has washed too, and changed into black: black open-necked shirt from Aron Valois, back chinos. His black boots have been polished. He and Josephine greet each other cordially. They drink Clermont-Chanturgue, she asks him how was his trip. Yvette serves them crisp baguettes, a good Cantal fresh from Salers, thinly sliced sausage, tomatoes, sweet green peppers. Josephine thinks the quiet maid looks a little flushed, and hides a smile in her wineglass. Leonard tells her of a new television series, a traffic accident, the face of a dignified young lady in the pharmacy at Nantes. Between their eyes, only one who knew them very well might detect discourse of a different kind.

Finishing his coffee, Leonard rises. He is going out to take a stroll around the estate. Josephine puts her cup in her saucer, props her chin on her hands, looks up at him attentively, with a grave smile. 'I shall see you upstairs,' he tells her, 'in –'. He consults his watch, an elaborate chronometer designed by an Italian architect. ' – fifteen minutes. Have Yvette prepare you.' He kisses her then, lightly on the cheek. She holds up one hand and he takes it in a trailing caress, letting her fingers slip through his as he goes.

Josephine lingers over her coffee. She would like to take it outside in the sun; but outside is Leonard's territory now, for the moment, and inside is hers. She finds her novel and reads a few more pages. Then she looks at the ancient clock on the dining room wall and rings a little handbell.

Soundless as ever, Yvette comes in. She bobs the merest trace of a curtsey. 'Shall I clear away, madame?'

'Yes, Yvette, thank you. Then I shall require your assistance, upstairs.'

In the bedroom Josephine stands and looks out at the wild and rugged scenery, the rich June green of the heartland, almost violent in its vividness. The sun is high now, and the earth seems to throb with its powerful light. She is glad that they are not in a city, where it is sometimes necessary to draw the curtains in the middle of the day.

Yvette is taking the fat, goose-feather pillows from the top of the bed and piling them in a bank at the foot. She plumps and pats them with her hands. One slides from the pile. '*Zut!*' she mutters under her breath, and makes haste to replace it.

At last she is satisfied. She stands back from the bed, her hands folded patiently in front of her.

'Madame?'

The mistress turns from the window where she has been standing gazing, smiling at nothing in the world. Now she smiles at Yvette, who drops her eyes in modesty.

The mistress comes to the bed. She stands at the foot. She bends her knees and places her hands on the foot of the bed, either side the bank of pillows; and she lies down, across the pillows, on her face. The pillows raise her hips above the level of her head. She folds her arms behind her back.

Yvette comes up behind her. She curtseys again, though it is a mere reflex, in this position Mistress Josephine cannot see her. Yvette takes hold of the hem of Mistress Josephine's skirt and lifts it, pulling it up to the middle of her back, just below her folded arms. She pulls the slip up after it, and folds both up together so that they lie there, across the mistress's back, out of the way.

Not stopping to admire the severe white lingerie, Yvette inserts the tips of her fingers in the elastic waistband of the long-sided knickers. She stretches it out and lifts it up, over and down. She draws the knickers down over the taut white suspenders and settles them just above the black stocking-tops, leaving a few centimetres of bare flesh between the full swell of the cheeks of Josephine's bottom and the lowered knickers, the way the master prefers. She fusses a moment with the knickers, straightening them around Josephine's thighs. Then she stands back.

'Cuff me, please, Yvette,' says the woman on the bed.

Yvette goes to the drawer where such things are kept and finds a pair of handcuffs which close with a spring, without a key. Josephine puts her wrists together behind her back, and Yvette fastens the cuffs on her, clicking the ratchet down until they fit around those slender wrists.

She glances at the drawer. 'Will you require an implement, madame?'

Josephine considers. 'No, thank you, Yvette ,' she says. 'I think today he will use his belt.'

Yvette finds herself blushing slightly. She knows that belt, the weight and power of it. She makes haste to shut the drawer, hurries out of the room.

Josephine feels the sun coming in the window, falling across the bed. She feels its warmth on her bare bottom. She is glad Leonard is home at last.

Fifteen minutes stretch out to twenty, to twenty-five, as she knew they would.

She shifts her hands, easing the pressure of the cuffs on her wrists, feeling and hearing the clink of the chain that joins them. She waits, patiently, across the bed.

At last she hears his tread on the stair. Her heart sets up a low clamour in her breast. Her face is turned away from the door. She hears it open, hears him come in and softly close it behind him.

He seems to stand a long while looking at her. It has been some time since they were last together like this.

He says: 'How many?'

Josephine has thought about this. She answers readily. 'Twenty. Please, master.'

He lays his hand gently on her right buttock. She shivers in apprehension. 'Twenty-five,' he says. 'Five extra for answering back.'

She hides a smile, remembering about the book.

She is right about the belt. She hears the chink of the opened buckle, the slither as he pulls it free from the loops of his trousers.

With the belt, he is a perfect master, as he is with all forms of discipline. Downstairs, washing up again, Yvette hears the fierce, methodical crack of broad leather on bare flesh. When she hears the mistress's high, clear cries, Yvette presses her pelvis against the deep sink, moving her hips in time to the rhythm of the belt.

When the belt stops, she imagines the master lowering his trousers, stripping the mistress's white knickers from her legs, taking his penis in his hand and pressing himself firmly and deeply into the haven of her red welted bottom and thighs.

Another cry rings through the stone chambers of the ancient manor.

Afterwards, lying together in bed, the couple murmur sweet nothings, little confidences to each other. Josephine brushes his smooth cheek with her lips. 'She was spying on me from the scullery,' she says.

He smiles, caressing her heavy breasts, her burning flanks. He asks, 'Did you punish her?'

'No . . .' Josephine breathes deeply, riding on the ache of her bottom, her stiffening shoulders. He is spent, soft, drowsy, but she has come only twice and is ready for more. Still she defers to him, because she loves him, because she is reluctant to feel this mood pass from him. 'Will you see to her or shall I?'

'Oh, I think you must,' says Leonard, rolling a little apart from her in the bed. 'She is not yet altogether familiar with your hand. Anyway, it was against you, the offence.' Leonard is half Swiss, he has an accent which you can hear only when he is completely relaxed, as he is now. He kisses her.

Josephine levers herself up and out of the bed. She stands with her back to him. His gentle hands trace the flaming marks his belt has left across her high round bottom. She breathes deeper and deeper. 'Take my cuffs off,' she tells him at last, and he does.

Naked but for her collar, idly massaging the red marks around her wrists, Josephine Morrow goes to the bedroom door and opens it a crack.

'Yvette,' she calls.

Beyond Paulhac, dominated by its spectacular sixteenth-century château, and across the high plateau west of Brioude, lies Blesle, a pretty little town. It sits snugly beneath a cliff that seems to protect it from the weather, from the ruin of 'development', from time itself. Down by the swift and lively river, among houses of stone as dark as gingerbread, one may pass an hour of ease, reading a book or simply watching the ever-changing play of sunlight though the willow shade. Here, it is said, some time in the ninth century, the Comtesse d'Auvergne founded a convent; and not content with that, gave the whole town over entirely into the rule of women. It is a charming legend, to be sure. Even the wizened, pot-bellied churchwarden will not admit the existence of a secret book, copied from contemporary manuscript records, of the practices and prescriptions of the Abbess of Blesle.

Josephine Morrow has read the book. There is much in it that she finds useful, dealing with Yvette, and with Leonard.

She wonders what methods will be suitable for Cadence, when she comes.

1

Cadence Szathkowicz is in L.A., in Willow Brook, taking the corner of Latham and 27th a little too fast in her daddy's Toyota. Cadence is going hospital visiting, and she doesn't want to be late. She sees no willow, she sees no brook. She sees Burger King, Dunkin Donuts, she sees Photo Op, she sees Toys 'R' Us. She sees brown automotive emission haze, she sees kids with brutalist haircuts and orange and acid green shorts hopping the kerb on skateboards, she sees an old black lady skinny as a match, a scarlet beret topping her dazzling ice-white cotton candy hairdo, stalking muscularly across the lights in her scarlet high heels, walking a poodle that matches her hair. Man is it hot. 105 by the McKendrick Savings Tower display. Cadence flaps the white scoopneck T-shirt between her boobs, revs the engine for the sheer pleasure of it, Cadence is in the *city*, down in the hot and stinking hell of it. She's cutting classes again, she's got Bon Jovi on the radio, she turns it up *loud*, blow that poodle right off the street. She throws back her head and laughs. Cadence Szathkowicz is hot and horny and she's going to do something about it right now.

The U.S. Army Hospital is over on 32nd, a block of long low buildings always as white as if they'd just been painted, with lawns all round and shade trees and a yellow brick wall. She parks the car, swings her long, slender, bare brown legs out of the door and slides her shades down on her sharp little nose. She walks into reception like she was fixing to buy the place. A Mexican cleaner in olive drab fatigues stands back to watch her as she strides by, he looks worried, a little sad, like he thinks she's going to steal his mop.

Little Mexican nurse on reception gives her a clear-eyed California smile, how may I help you today? Cadence leans on the counter, letting her tits swing forward under her tee, pushes her shades up into her

1

hair again, which is curly today, sand-blonde with a pale pale green highlight. 'Have you seen Bob Baskind? Is he at work today?'

'Baskind, he's the orderly?' This little chiquita knows exactly who Bob Baskind is, and Cadence *knows* she knows, Bob makes it his personal goal to shoehorn as many of the employees as he can get, the female ones, the pretty ones, into a compromising position, and he's been aptitude testing this one all week already. 'I think he's cleaning in Theatre Three right now,' she says. 'Oh, but you can't go down there,' for Cadence has already pushed open the double door with the round glass windows. Cadence looks back and smiles reassuringly. 'It's all right, honey, I used to be a nurse.'

Like in grade school at recess, you used to be a nurse, Cadence Szathkowicz, she says to herself, walking fast down the antiseptic corridor and taking the stairs because she's in too much of a hurry to wait for the elevator.

Here is Theatre Three, and here is Bob Baskind, crazy black man with a face like a chicken, beaky nose and big pouches for his eyes, army regulation haircut sneaked up into a peak along the top of his long square head. Bob Baskind also has a floor mop, but it can go to hell, it clatters to the floor the instant he sees her. 'Cadence, what are you doin' here?'

She walks up to him, her heels clacking on the grey marble oilcloth floor, she puts her arms round him and kisses him like she didn't have no breakfast.

'Just passing through,' she says.

Bob Baskind is fast, he's got his hands up under her dangling T-shirt and he's squeezing her nipples with his big square fingers and thumbs, hard, the way she likes it. She presses those babies up against his chest and he's cuddling them one in each hand, this is an unscheduled leisure break and he's going for every second of it. He feels the heat of the day on her skin, sniffs her perspiration, her perfume.

'Oh Bob,' suggests Cadence, 'can we go to the storeroom?' He hears the lust roiling in her voice, hears it directly on some cellular wave length that bypasses his ears entirely.

'Storeroom, shit,' says Bob eloquently, in his golden tenor voice, 'we got us a bed right here.' And he removes his right hand from Cadence's left boob to wave with all the suggestive grandeur of a furniture salesperson at the empty white operating table.

2

'Bob, honey,' gasps Cadence, laughing, 'we can't do that!' But she's already got her hand down the front of his regulation orderly white drawstring fatigue pants, and the way she's dragging at his non-regulation hard-on, she isn't really advocating any delay, any removal, any withdrawal to conditions of enhanced security. And Bob Baskind's right hand, returning at once to the magnet of her body, has relinquished Cadence's left breast to invade the inner reaches of her flouncy Greek skirt, where it is even now fondling the curve of her left buttock, appreciating how the lightweight cotton fabric spreads across the warm flesh in a way that suggests the hand will very shortly be sliding beneath that fabric to experience the warmth and the flesh itself. There it goes now. Man it is hot down under there.

Cadence wriggles against him, arching her back and squeezing her bottom into his hand. As she reaches up and kisses him again, hungrily, she feels those reliable square fingertips come right around into the cleft of her ass and tickle the button of her anus, which Bob knows is sensitive as hell, and the little pinky finger is already working its way forward between her legs, just following the groove.

'Oh, oh, Bob, come *on*!'

And Bob is coming on, he is coming on just as hard and fast as he knows how, and he knows how. He pushes her tee up out of his way, exposing her breasts to the sterile air of Theatre Three and to the fertile suction of his lips, which are so sensitive and muscular he could be a trumpet-player, Cadence thinks to herself, lifting her left leg and rubbing her thigh on him, pressing her crotch up against his right hip. Then, just like magic, just like some routine they learned from an old Astaire and Rogers movie, Bob scoops her up, sitting her on the palm of his right hand as he tips her weight back into his left, spread behind her right shoulderblade, and at the same time he takes a big long step forward, sliding across the freshly-waxed floor to toss Cadence lightly onto the taut white sheet of the operating table.

She laughs and lies back, kicking up her legs, displaying her sunshine yellow panties to him as an unambiguous invitation to remove them, which he swiftly does, loving the way they slide up her smooth brown legs, which too are freshly waxed. Then he pulls the regulation drawstring at his waist, which is not as trim as it might be if he ever took any exercise other than this, but it is supple enough, it bends in the right places as he skins down his pants and his undershorts together and releases the meat of Cadence's delight to swing out into

3

the air, into her grasping hands as he kneels up on the table between her welcoming legs.

It is a tableau of black and white: Bob's black skin, Cadence's dark tan, his white uniform, her white tee, blonde hair, the white sheets and walls. The chrome finish of the big lights and the anaesthetic fitments reflects faithfully and without comment the supple movements of their bodies, his gleaming black buttocks driving down between her golden-fudge thighs, her skirt a high and irrelevant frill crushed up beneath her bare tits.

'Oh, Bob! Oh, *Bob*, oh, *oh*!'

The first rush of their pleasure sweeps them up to a plateau of erotic sensation. Bob's left hand brushes Cadence's hair back from her face, then adroitly massages her round, sound, right breast while they kiss, all the while the right hand is delving under the table itself, to the clips on the underside where one of the anaesthetists showed him they keep a sneaky little cylinder of nitrous oxide. It comes with a mask already fitted.

'Where did you get that?' Cadence laughs with pleasure and surprise. The device is already hissing in his hand, she reaches for the first hit, sliding her hips up against him in a way that ensures that a man whose attention is already fully engaged cannot say no. She presses the mask to her face and inhales a full measure of silly bubbly wiggle, a grin that goes all the way down to her belly. 'Dinky!' she squeals, and giggles as she wraps her arms and legs around him.

He breathes, she breathes, they snort laughter into one another's hair and dive into one another again, rocking wild and juicy on the buoyant suspension, state-of-the-art surgical technology, nothing but the best for our wounded fighting men.

'Oh Bob, hey — like this —'

She shows him, swinging his hips left and right as he thrusts, feeling the one-eyed head butt blindly against her cervix, alternate sides. 'Now put your finger — no, no, give it to me, here — oh yes oh, *god*, oh I like that! I love that when you do that to me . . .'

'Yeah?' says Bob, cheerfully, but there is an edge in his voice. 'Did we do that before?' He is in a high craziness of the gas, he doesn't quite know what it is she is having him do, he realises she has pulled ahead of him somewhere here along the track.

She laughs at him, he is laughing, but confused. 'We never did that, Cadence.' He's still doing it, and she's still grooving on it, but she's lost

4

him. He lifts his head and tries to focus on her face. Something hard has come to sit between his wary chicken eyes. He says, 'Where did you learn that?'

'Around. Oh don't stop, don't –'

But Bob Baskind pauses in his pleasuring of her.

'You been sleeping around again? Have ya, huh? Huh?'

'Quiet, Bob, someone will hear.'

But he says, 'Answer me, Cadence.'

She is sweaty, horny as hell, irritated, she scowls up at him. 'Maybe,' she says. 'Goddammit Bob –'

'Goddammit what? What?' He thrusts into her again, harder, challenging her with his cock. He feels her impatience, her anger with him.

The blonde beauty on the operating table glares at him. The gas hisses away, unattended. 'It's my body,' she says, undeniably. Pointedly she grabs hold of his prick with her left hand, holds it still and begins to frig herself with her right.

'You're my girl, Cadence!' says the orderly, kissing her. This usually sets things straight with ladies, when they're out of line.

But it's not a good thing to say to this lady right now, it turns out. She says, 'I'm not anybody's *girl*, Bob Baskind. I'm a free woman, I fuck who I want to. I want you, come here, baby.' And she hugs him tight, grinding her pelvis against him.

But Bob is jealous. Bob is cooling. Bob is thinking maybe he should get back to work. He pulls out of her hard and fast, still erect, that'll show her, gets down off the table and pulls up his pants. 'I'm real busy. I got to get back to work now. I'll see you later,' he threatens as he goes for his mop.

'Maybe,' she says, her green eyes flashing lightning like a summer storm.

Cadence is angry, she strides out of the building and drives off fast, gunning the car, leaving black zigzags on the white lines. She is going back up north, where she belongs. Little Feat on the radio now. *'Gonna boogie my scruples away.'* She smiles, nastily, she doesn't want to leave the city, she loves it, the stores, the cars, the crazy people, the rock music all hours of the day. Northern California is so boring, so quiet, nothing ever happens. She jolts and squeezes through the traffic up to the freeway and then puts Bob Baskind firmly behind her, shaking the dust of her chariot wheels over his stupid head. Screw Bob

Baskind, it's time she got back to college, she needs to do some study, see her professor for Christ's sake.

She kicks back and drives all the way up I-5. Traffic is mortal bad, but she doesn't mind. She looks at the signs, she loves these names of the places up the Golden State Highway: Buttonwillow, Lost Hills, Devil's Den, Tranquillity. Tranquillity, that is the word. Tranquillity, right, that is it, that is — these hills. L.A. is a burned-out memory, just another bum morning. Already she feels San Francisco spread its penumbra of graceful and forgiving light before her wheels. She's been driving without a break, just not thinking, man, just on automatic. Maybe she should stop off awhile here, along the road. Maybe that would be good for her, for her feelings, maybe that is what she needs, right, a few days' tranquillity at the Ormerod Ranch. Rise early and go for a run, fly a kite, ride a horse along the trail — do some meditation, you can really get into some good meditation up here above the fog, really get in touch with yourself. She can really get her head together here.

Cadence is filled with love and enthusiasm for San Fransisco, L.A. gets right on top of you, it's because of L.A. she was so mad and freaked out, she can see that now, in the clear air. She sees a turnoff, Los Banos and Chowchilla, she pulls out straight across the traffic in a blare of protesting horns — hey, she is feeling so mellow already she doesn't even give those assholes the finger. A pure, invisible line, like some thread of cosmic destiny, is pulling her heart straight to Marin County, the *beach*, man, but no, she's going to stop here first, take it slow, centre down on the Ormerod Ranch.

The Ormerod Ranch is the home of her classmate and soulmate, Nick Snyder. He's not jealous, he thinks it's cool she has other lovers. He respects her sincerely, Cadence feels, and he wants her to fulfil herself as a woman. A woman. She thinks fleetingly of a woman's body, sex with a woman. Then she thinks of Nick, slows down, drives with one hand, the other under her skirt, loving herself, bringing back those good feelings from before. She hates all the bad feelings she experienced on the table with Bob but hey, it's ok now, no hassle. Whatever's right. In her mind Bob turns into Nick and her fingers feel good.

She drives slow along the country turnpike, hits a new age music station, grooves with the afternoon breeze that blows the oily crap of L.A. out of her hair, out of her *mind*. Wow.

6

The drive down to the ranch-house is paved with shells, white oyster shells or something, the whole drive, like some ancient Indian site. Cadence is into it. She can smell that medicine in the air, that hunting wolf medicine. Rr*rowff*. Cool down, Cadence. Chill out, girl.

Nick is on the deck, studying. 'Hey Nick!'

'Hey! Cadence!'

He gives her a big hug like he hasn't seen her for a million years, she smiles into his eyes, giving him her pure love, then kissing him like she means to stay.

'Oh baby,' says Nick. His hands explore her back. She knows that funky tantric massage, he's visiting her chakras, energising each in turn, pretty soon they'll be calling up the kundalini, she hooks her foot behind his ankle, strokes his calf with her heel.

'What a nice surprise,' Nick says. He is fit and golden, dark brown hair waves sensitively across his high forehead. His neck is like a horse. He wears a white sun-kilt, a sweatband around his head, tiny diffraction crystals in his earlobes. When he becomes serious, which he easily does, he goes cross-eyed. Cadence and Nick are really in touch, they *know* one another. In another lifetime they were together.

'I got your message, Nick.'

He lifts his eyebrows a quizzical fraction. 'Message?'

Cadence puts her heead back, spreading her breasts against his chest. 'I saw the sun in the sky and I knew you loved me.'

'You've been reading those Hallmark cards again, Cadence.'

'Oh Nick.' She pouts. The wise Sufi master teaches by making fun of his disciples. She punches him on the arm, he winds himself around her like a world-snake. She can feel his genitals through the kilt, the feel of his soft cock makes her dizzy, she calls to it with her mind, she sings to it with her yoni. She's just melting in the sun like she's taken peyote or something, wow.

'Do you have any dope?' she asks.

'Dope? Sure!' His smile is wholesome, his gesture generous. He is the spirit of the good Earth itself. He rolls a spliff of this just incredible Michuocan.

'Oh man.'

The sun is the source of all being. The sun is an apple on the Tree of Life. The sun is a purple Studebaker.

'You want some yogurt?' Nick asks.

'Later . . . .'

7

'During,' he says. They have become very entwined.

'Oh, wow,' says Cadence. 'Hey man, I have to ask you something.' She kisses him, sloppily but intricately. 'You want to get in the jacuzzi?' I've been on the road *all day*, I'm all gritty and shitty . . . and sweaty.'

Nick makes a soft yowl in the back of his throat like a cat, kisses her, comprehensively. He takes off her Greek skirt, she takes off his Turkish kilt. The crotch of her panties is stiff where she's been dripping all day. He kisses it, pulls off her panties there on the deck, his folks are down in New Mexico, there's no one for miles but cows.

His cock is still soft, she kneels down a moment in her clammy T-shirt and blows gently on it, with her lips pursed up, then with her mouth open. She nibbles the end with her lips. Nick looks down at her back, the ridge of her spine, the minty highlight in her hair. He rests his hand on her shoulder. When she looks up at him and smiles, he gazes right down the neck of her tee, down between her tits to the soft brush between her thighs. It does look a little sticky down there, a little matted.

Cadence stands up. In one complex, definitive, mammalian movement, she pulls off her T-shirt. She kisses him briefly, as if she is about to depart on a mission of great importance. Then she jumps sideways in the water.

Nick Snyder pulls off his sweatband, his Bickerstocks, his solar watch that shows the night sky from twenty-five different cities, and leaps in with her. For a time they just float in the swirling water, immersing themselves again and again, easing out the kinks, soothing away the strain you incur simply by getting out of bed in the morning. Cadence embraces him. 'Be one with the water,' she murmurs, licking his ear. No chlorine here, his folks fitted an ionizer. He kisses her throat, moistly. Her slender body shivers eagerly up and down him. She is very still, *being* without *doing*. Nick is fitting his erect penis into her open vagina. It thrills her like a douche of starlight. 'Oh, mmmmm . . . Ommmm . . .'

'The ancients . . .' says Nick, swirling around with her in the centre of the tub.

'Boy, those guys really knew what they were doing,' agrees Cadence.

'What were they doing, Cadence?'

'This.'

'Oh, ah, um, heeeeeyyyy . . .'

'No but —' A pause, a minute or two long. ' — what were you going

8

to say?'

'I don't −' Another pause, of similar duration by the clock, but here, clocks count for nothing. Dig, the rhythm of the rotation is like, the rhythm of the tide, that's our water nature. In here it's sex time. Womb time. Did I say that or did you?

'− remember.'

They fit together like yin and yang. They are baptised. Their senses merge in the spiritual Cuisinart.

Cadence floats, suspended from the pivot of his cock. The water sustains her, spins her gently. Her head is full of stars.

He submerges his head, fills his mouth with her nipple. Bubbles come out of his ears. Then, just as Cadence is beginning to see colours, he surfaces, blowing and splashing wildly. She steadies him, but he slips from her honeypot.

'Nick −!'

An expression comes over his face that makes him look like Mickey Mouse. 'I forgot the yogurt,' he says.

'Later. C'mon. C'mon. Here.'

'No, Cadence, I have to study.'

He is climbing out of the − she doesn't believe this: he is climbing out of the tub. Can you believe that? He is crouching on the deck, naked, warm, wet, erect, kissing her ear and saying goodbye.

'I remember what I was going to say,' he tells her. 'The ancients believed the unicorn could be caught only by the pure of heart.'

'By *virgins*, Nick.'

'No, Cadence: by the pure of heart.'

She swipes at his bare ankle. 'It was fucking virgins, Nick, come back here, oh, *Nick* −'

'You can *be* a virgin, Cadence. Our Lord and Saviour Jesus Christ promised us that. You can do it, if you come to him like a little child to be born again.'

She gazes at him out of the water. She had forgotten the problem with Nick. The flesh is willing but the spirit is aloft. Nick Snyder has been transcendental since birth. He wasn't born, he levitated out. 'Nick, you smoke too much of that stuff. Now c'mon, lover, get *in* here.' She is hopping up and down in the water with frustration. Her breasts bob enticingly, she spreads her thighs and draws her feet up to her bottom, she stretched up her hand, trying to reach his cock.

He smiles at her beatifically. 'No, Cadence. I have to study.'

And he goes *away*. Back to his book.

Cadence Szathkowicz thumps the wet deck with her fist. She climbs from the whirlpool and dries herself swiftly and fiercely. She pulls on her knickers, her sweaty peds, her trainers. She pulls on her slavegirl skirt and her limp tee; her beads, her bangles. She walks past Nick, who is still naked, still erect, sitting in the lotus position drawing his sexual karma to his higher centres.

What a waste of *meat*.

He cracks an eye open as she passes. 'You feel like making us a cup of Red Zinger, precious?'

'Fuck *off*, Snyder. You know you really depress me, you know that?'

'Jesus loves you, Cadence.'

Cadence stomps off to her daddy's car. She forgot to put the top up, the upholstery scorches her thighs. 'You really depress me, Nicholas Snyder!' she yells at the top of her lungs. Then she stands on the pedal and burns rubber out of there, dusts a few thousand oystershells, abalone, clam, whatever the hell they are. She hates the ocean, hates anything that crawls up out of it. She hates Northern California, the rocks, the majestic soaring redwoods, the mighty eagle, the *men*. They're all faggots anyhow.

But the spirit of Northern California is still on her, for Cadence *relates* to her anger. She screams her way up the freeway, finds Bon Jovi again, in California someone is always playing Bon Jovi somewhere, every minute of your life, she turns it up to the max and screams over the top of it, all the way to Lodi. She goes screaming across the Sacramento River. Man, it feels so *primal*.

She's calm by the time she rolls onto campus, just a little spaced out from the dope, maybe. There are two guards at the post. They stop her, want to see her pass, even though she balled one of the guys last semester after a party, what *is* his name. Cadence wiggles her tits, gives her best dumb smile, says hi, then screeches past and rides over to the library where she left her stuff. Catching sight of a clock on her way in, she starts to run.

From her locker she picks up her file, her schedule, and her copy of Plato's *Republic*. Then she drives on to Professor McNeil's, where she parks in a staff space. She runs up the stairs to the deck and knocks, rather breathlessly, on his door.

Professor McNeil is dark. He looks like what Cadence thinks D.H. Lawrence must have looked like: craggy, soulful, phallic. He smokes a pipe, for Christ's sake. And he isn't that old. He comes to the door in his Gustav Mahler sweatshirt and windsurfer shorts. He seems very happy, and rather surprised, to see her.

'Professor,' says Cadence, 'did we discuss my grades yet this semester?'

He looks at her fondly. 'Yes,' he says, in his deep smoky voice. 'Twice.'

She pats him on the arm. 'Of course, I remember. So tell me, they getting any better?'

He squints at her in the blazing sunlight. 'D'you wanna discuss it?'

'Professor McNeil,' she says, crowding him back inside and kissing him in the hallway, 'I'll give you two per A.'

But one is all Professor McNeil can ever manage. He's very comforting, in a sweet kind of way, but he only looks like a satyr. He always talks about his wife all the time; and he does come so soon. Cadence sits, nude, dissatisfied, beside his sleeping form and makes a resolve. She is writing something on a pad with a picture of Bart Simpson at the top, saying, 'Don't have a cow, man!' Cadence is not interested in the *bons mots* of Bart Simpson, others of which are distributed cyclically through the remaining sheets of the pad. She is composing. Tonight she will phone England.

Naturally this is a call she prefers to make from her father's house, so she borrows a T-shirt, throws her peds in the trash, and scoots on back down to father's house, all the way to Laguna Beach. After she has disarmed all the security she triple-locks herself in her apartment with all the lights out, pulls off her clothes, orders a pizza, then checks her messages. There are several. They are all from her father. Click. *'Hi sweetheart it's me. How you doing? Studying hard? I thought I'd see you this weekend but it doesn't look like that plan is going to materialize . . . .'*

She turns it off, calls international enquiries, gets the number, calls it, what the fuck time is it there anyway? A woman answers, sounds like somebody off Masterpiece Theatre.

'Hello? Is that the London *Times*? I want to place an insert in your personals.' That seems to upset the woman for some reason, who knows with Brits? Cadence talks right over her. She picks up the sheet she tore off Professor McNeil's pad. 'This is the ad, right? "Don't have a c–" Oh no, here it is, excuse me. "Desperately seeking Josephine." '

11

|2|

Josephine. Josephine Morrow. She was Cadence's first lover, the one who woke her up, the one who taught her what went where. Since then, Cadence has been experimenting. She's been partying. She's gotten pretty wild, frankly, what with Bob and Nick and Luis and Jake, and some other guys on campus, oh, and Professor McNeil, and — well, the list goes on.

But in the middle of the night, she remembers Dominica and Josephine: her touch, her mouth, her scent. Her beautiful body. Her firm thighs straddling Cadence's face. The electric, animal taste of her cunt. There's been no one like Josephine since. In the middle of the night sometimes Cadence longs for Josephine and touches herself. In her mind it is Josephine touching her with her fabulous, telepathic fingers, and she cries out when she comes.

Cadence never discovered who Josephine was or what she did or why she was there at the hotel on Dominica. She was kind of a mysterious person, like she was on some secret mission. She went off without saying goodbye, just disappeared. All Cadence knows is she was English, she liked to walk around naked, she had a beautiful round bottom and wonderful breasts. With this funny little tattoo, right here in between them.

Cadence thinks maybe she fell in love with Josephine, kind of. But she's not thinking about her today, because today she's working for Kelly and Scott. They have this really neat suit for her to wear, real forties, in dark purple material with a box-line skirt and high-waisted jacket, slim lapels, shoulder pads. There's even a little pillbox hat they perch on the side of her head, with a little bitty veil. Her hair is black today, still curly, they have her spray this goop all over it to make it stiff and shiny. And all the make-up — blusher and mascara and killer crimson lipstick, the whole works. Last thing Kelly ties a curly satin ribbon bow at the neck of her starched white blouse. Cadence looks in the mirror, she doesn't believe it. She sees the guy in the mirror, he's just sitting there in his overalls reading a magazine at this point. Pretty hunky, though.

Kelly says, 'Okay, Cadence, you ready?'

She nods. She rubs her lips together, trying to make the gluey stuff more even.

'Go outside, count to ten, then in you come. Don't forget the packages.'

Cadence steps out of the room, shuts the door. She looks out the window, sees a little kid riding a tricycle down the street, a brown delivery truck stopping at a house down the way. There's a whole normal world out there, it's kinda funny. She's forgetting to count, Kelly said to count and she's forgetting. Oh, eight, nine, ten, ready or not, here I come.

She picks up the paper sacks, one under her arm, the other one balanced as she opens the bedroom door and goes in. Shuts the door behind her.

They have the lights on now, real bright. Hard to think you need light like that when the sun's shining down, but she guesses they have to see every detail. So she stands a moment in the doorway, letting them get a good look at her. Old-fashioned housewife home from shopping. She sets the bags down on the dressing table, stretches her arms up behind her head. She makes quite a thing of this, pressing her breasts forward against the suit jacket, which is buttoned tight. It's a little small, maybe, but that's no bad thing.

She swings herself around a little, walking aimlessly round the room, letting them get the full effect. Then she stops in front of the dressing table again, reaches up and unpins her hat.

She holds her left leg out straight in front of her, pulling her skirt up to show a couple of inches more black nylon, and slips off the shoe. Then she lifts her right knee, keeping her leg close to her body — a flash more thigh there — she takes off the second shoe.

She unbuttons the jacket, pushes it back off her shoulders, keeping her tits well forward as she slides her arms out of the sleeves, wonderful lining, is that real silk? She hangs it on a hanger on the wardrobe door, stroking it, they like that for some reason, maybe because they imagine she's stroking them. She lifts her chin and winds the end of her ribbon tie round her finger. Nail polish, matches the

13

lipstick, she feels like a piece of art. Well, that's what she is today, she's a piece of art. And with that thought she teases the bow slowly undone and pulls it out from under her collar. She drops it on the dressing table and opens the top button of her blouse. She opens the second button. She opens the third.

Then she unbuttons her cuffs. All the while she's moving her body, like a slow dance, Scott will put music in, and like she's really loving every minute of this, like she's in love with her own body. Somebody has to be, she thinks, and she ducks her head because she feels sad for a moment and she doesn't want that to show. She pretends she's concentrating on untucking her crisp white blouse from the waistband of her skirt. The sheer material slithers upwards, outwards, free. Scott doesn't say anything so it must be okay. She untucks the blouse all the way around.

And she unbuttons it all the way down. Doesn't take it off yet, lets it hang there, she knows if she leans her shoulders forward here the blouse will only gap a little way. A little glimpse, a little tease. Scott is pleased, he's crouching down now, moving around to get her from the side.

Cadence flips the blouse round behind her hip. She swivels her waist, brings her hands down smoothly to the skirt hook.

She's doing good today, she knows, he hasn't stopped her once. And she's into it, in a strange kind of way, it's better like this, everybody knows what they want and there's nothing to freak you out.

She opens the hook but leaves the button done up. This is a little refinement so that when she lowers the zipper, now, it gapes open and shows just a sliver of skin, two sections of sheer black nylon. Another little tease. Then she opens the button and gracefully dips forward, sticking out her butt and sliding the skirt down, stepping out of it, lots of display there, lots of leg movement.

She gets rid of the skirt, then stands upright to shuck off the blouse. Scott moves around to the front and back, Kelly's making notes on her clipboard, directing him with her pencil. This is like what they call the first climax, not that anything's happened yet, but this is a big revelation, Cadence standing there in black nylon lingerie, brassière, skinny little panties, black nylon garterbelt with two tiny red roses on the hip and black stockings. Not the old-fashioned housewife at all, but if that's what they want to think, well fine. If she has to do it again, maybe she'll leave the hat on, that would look pretty cute now, wouldn't it?

14

She gets lost a moment, hesitating, touches her hand to her hair, but nobody says anything, maybe they didn't catch it. The little red light is still shining. Anyway she moves straight back into it, unclips the left stocking, slides it down her leg, lifts her leg to pull it off slowly by the toe. Then she sits down at the dressing table, sideways on. From where Scott is now the packages are behind her, she really thinks she should have left her hat on. She lifts her right leg, points her foot right up at the ceiling and pushes the right stocking up as far as she can reach, then bends her knee to take the stocking off, keeping her left leg right out of the way so they can get lots of her right thigh and her panties.

She stands up, feet together, brushing her hair back out of her eyes, and looks down at herself. She undoes the garterbelt and loses it. She runs her hands over her body, like she's saying hallo. Like she's pretty horny and can't leave herself alone. She touches herself through the panties, starts to make sighing noises, mmmm.

When she takes off the brassière it's a whole drama, it's Shakespeare, Michelangelo, my God, those are the stars of this second climax: not her and the guy, who doesn't even come in yet, but her tits. Cadence doesn't have to wonder why some people go crazy for a pair of tits. She's pretty keen on tits too. She remembers Josephine's tits. She wishes it was Josephine here today, not this guy, she's forgotten his name already.

Cadence loves her tits, rubbing them, stroking them, lifting them in her hands, throwing her head back, oh oh. She squeezes her nipples hard, it feels good, shivers right the way down to her crotch. Speaking of which.

She stands up, turns her back, like she's admiring herself in the mirror, leaning over towards the mirror to get a good look at her tits. And she slips her thumbs in the elastic of her panties and pulls them down. Down to her thighs, down to her knees. Scott is having a real good time with her ass, she knows. She looks at them in the mirror: Kelly standing there looking neutral hugging her clipboard to her bosom, her arms crossed over it; Scott leaning sideways to get some kind of angle on her peachy ass; and the guy in the overalls, rubbing his eyebrow with his fingertip, he's seen everything, he's looking at his watch.

Well screw him.

Cadence whirls round, not fast but dramatically, her right hand spread over her hip, coming down to her crotch, massaging herself, her middle finger stuck out rigid so it digs right down the middle, oh boy, pouting and gasping, really humping that hand.

'Okay, cut,' calls Kelly.

Scott eases up, lowering the camcorder. 'Pretty good stuff there, Cadence,' he says. Scott is from the south, not far from where Cadence's momma used to live. He's easy, he don't crack much of a smile ever, he's so laid back. If he says it's pretty good, you know it's excellent.

Kelly had rushed over with a wrap, folding it around Cadence's body, Cadence doesn't know why she does that, it's not cold in here even with the air-conditioning. Some kind of symbol, she thinks vaguely. Taking care of the star. Or maybe Kelly just likes the excuse to touch her body, hug her, rub her as if she was cold. 'That was terrific, Cadence.'

Cadence feels cool, detached. 'Yeah,' she says, aimlessly. 'You want me to do any of it again, just say.'

Kelly is conferring with Scott, resting the lights, rewinding tape on a monitor. She lifts her pencil in the air, signalling to Cadence: 'Just a moment, sweetheart . . .'

Cadence looks at the guy. He looks at her. He smiles, a smile of professional approval. She smiles back, distantly. She feels kind of tired suddenly. 'Can I have some more coke?' she says.

'Sure thing, hon, just help yourself,' says Scott, looking at her on the screen, not looking at her in person. Cadence sidles over to the table, takes a couple of good snorts from the jar. 'Want some?' she says to the guy, offering him the spoon. He shakes his head. He looks pretty stupid, Cadence thinks. All muscle, no brain. Why should she care?

She sips Coke from a can, looks over Scott's shoulder. It's pretty funny to see her body all cut up that way, the close-ups, the intimate angles, shot of just her legs, shots when Scott was practically on the floor. It seems more than ever like a dance, like something she did just now and now it's over, what's on the tape is just traces. But these guys are good, she guesses, and what's on the tape is real too, real enough to please a lot of horny people. She doesn't know who sees these things, she only knows she makes them and then she gets paid. Oh, oh, right, that reminds her.

'Kelly?' she says. 'I have to ask you something.'

'What, sweetheart?'

16

Cadence toys with the edge of her robe, running her fingers up and down the nap. She doesn't like talking about money, money bores her, the credit cards her dad gives her have always been as much as she needs to know about money. 'Did you pay me yet for last time?'

Kelly looks concerned. She and Scott look at each other. 'Scott, you did send Cadence her cheque, didn't you? I remember you said you'd mail it.'

This is already more fuss than Cadence can be bothered with. She's losing interest. Anyway she doesn't want the guy to think she's hustling, or broke or something. It's cool. 'Probably I got it already,' she says, her head full of snow. 'Probably I forgot.' She thinks of the mail she hasn't opened at the house, she can't be bothered with anything that's not from England, even though it's too soon yet, probably. 'Probably it got in with the junk mail and I threw it out,' she says, and laughs.

She drinks some more Coke, then a slug of Jack Daniels. She stares at the screen, at her own bare bottom. 'Is it okay?' she asks.

'It's great, Cadence,' says Kelly, 'a milestone in motion picture history. You ready to go?'

She takes the wrap. Cadence sits back on the stool and cleans off her make-up. A couple of shots will do for that, that's not what the punters want to see. Then they move the lights into the bathroom and start again. Cadence turns on the shower and nothing comes out. They've turned the water off to make like it's broken. She makes a lot of mileage out of writhing around naked in the shower stall, pulling faces. Her boobs bob up and down as she wrestles with the control.

Cue doorbell.

Cadence wraps herself in a towel, real Doris Day stuff, she's getting bored. She tucks the corner of the towel in between her breasts so it hangs down around her like a little shift dress, walks with tiny steps to the door and opens it.

'Morning, lady. Plumber.'

Cadence looks surprised, then smiles. 'I guess my husband must have sent for you this morning,' she says. 'He's gone out of town on a business trip.' They don't write scripts for these things, they just tell her what to say and she says it, pretty much.

Now she's looking the guy over like she can hardly keep her hands off him, he's got this smirk on his face, she tries not to look him in the eye. 'You look like a strong guy,' she says in her best husky voice. 'I

17

think you'll need to be strong to fix the problem I'm having!'

The guy comes into the bathroom and plants his toolbox on the floor. Cadence acts dumb, gets in the shower with her towel on, tries to turn the control again. 'It seems to be stuck here! Are you good with things that get stuck?'

'Let's see if I can help you out, ma'am,' he says, and he squeezes in the shower with her, reaches around her to get at the control.

'This knob is so hard!' she says, rolling her eyes.

Then Kelly turns the water on and it splashes down all over them, they're both soaked.

So of course Cadence says: 'Here, let me help you off with those wet things.'

She undresses him on the bathroom floor, very attentively, runs her hands over his chest, touches his hairy thighs like she's afraid she might get an electric shock. Takes his shorts down, looking shocked at what she sees. 'I don't think any of my husband's things will be big enough to fit you!'

'We'll see about that, lady,' says the guy, reaching for her.

They break, towel off, Kelly has wraps for both of them. Cadence does some more coke, Kelly and Scott both have some too this time. Then they go straight to the bed, no sense in hanging about spinning the wheels anymore.

They always have really big guys. Cadence doesn't know why; like it says on the bumper sticker, It's not the meat, it's the motion. Still, meat is what the people like to see. This guy is really big, like eight, nine inches easy. He sits back against the headboard while Kelly slaps a lot of Vaseline on it and he grins, a little sideways macho grin, he thinks he's Sly Stallone. Kelly rubs Vaseline on Cadence's crotch. 'Oh baby do it to me,' says Cadence distantly to no one in particular and reaches for the bourbon. She wonders what Kelly is like in bed. Right now it's hard to care. Work is work. Kelly ducks her head and whispers to her: 'Be nice to him, sugar.' Cadence swivels her head, looks him up and down like she's seeing him for the first time, smiles like she likes what she sees. She grabs hold of Kelly's hand by the wrist, rubs herself with Kelly's greasy fingers. She's really flying now.

She lets Kelly's hand slip from her grasp, turns towards the hunk, reaching for him.

'Whoa, whoa,' says Scott, picking up his camcorder.

The lights are on, the camera's ready.

18

'Okay now, Cadence, Angelo —'

Angelo! 'Is that your real name?' Cadence asks.

'Cadence!' wails Kelly.

'Okay, okay, I'm sorry.' She sniffs. 'Is there a Kleenex there?'

Kelly wipes Cadence's nose. The hunk's grin is like he's thinking he never worked with anyone so stupid. The hunk's hard-on is as hard and as on as ever.

'And action.'

Cadence kisses the hunk, lingering and slow, then hard. She rubs her hand over his chest, playing with his hair. He's stroking her hard, not much feeling in his hands, or maybe it's her, she's hitting on the coke. He strokes her side, down onto her thigh, round to her butt. She swivels in the bed, sits up astride him.

They cut briefly, moving on the bed so Scott can kneel up behind Angelo's head and zoom right in on what Cadence is doing with his cock. She's pressing it against her belly, bowing down over him, scrooching down so she can rub his cock between her tits, rub her nipples with it until they go stiff. He lies right back, just grooving on it, letting it happen, then when Scott gets off the bed for a side shot, he lifts his head and kisses her. He puts his tongue in her mouth. Cadence nips it lightly with her teeth, comes down on his mouth with hers like he was a drinking fountain. Then she hotches up and squats astride his chest, sticking her butt up in the air, letting him rub that big monster up the crack between her cheeks.

Then she lies down for a while, on her back, and he covers her, rubs that thing all over her, she holds her legs straight up in the air and he plays with her pussy, Scott gets some good footage of that, you can be sure.

Angelo kneels astride her head, put his cock to her lips. It smells of Vaseline and hot man. Cadence runs her tongue over the head. Angelo spreads his hand on his thighs, throws back his head: 'Oh man!' Then he takes a fistful of her hair, moving her head around on her neck. He lifts himself up for Cadence to stroke his balls. He pushes his cock into her mouth.

Cadence chews on it awhile.

After that she gets down on her hands and knees again, legs apart, looks pleadingly back over her shoulder, her lips open. Angelo comes in and rubs his cock between her cheeks again like he's fixing to get inside her ass. Cadence doesn't think they're doing that today, unless

19

Kelly wants to cut and get out her Vaseline again.

The guy's dork is so big and stiff it's like an appliance, like it's not a part of him at all. Like a tool. A plumber's friend, she thinks. She's really out of it. Then she remembers her next line. She rolls over on her back and spreads her legs.

'Do it to me, big boy. Fix my leak!'

They fuck forever. They fuck until the tape's all gone. The guy is gasping like he's going to come, but he never does, and Cadence surely doesn't, though she fakes it a few times for the camera. Fucking is good, Cadence likes it, and this guy is really a major stud, but all it is is just a workout, really — as many push-ups as you can do, some lateral rolls and stuff. She hasn't the stamina to stay interested, she just goes limp and drifts off, lets him drag her around. It's easier that way. 'Oh, baby,' she croons. 'You're so good to me . . .'

'That's it,' says Scott, and he puts down the camcorder.

The guy pulls right out. He takes Cadence's face in his big hands and gives her a friendly kiss. Then he says something non-commital to the others and lopes off into the bathroom, his wet cock still red and hard, still bouncing in front of him like a salami.

Cadence hears the sound of the shower.

She stretches. 'That's it?' she says. She take a hit of Coke, squishes it round her mouth to take the taste away. Kelly is there with the Kleenex. Cadence mops herself up with a languid, half-hearted motion. 'I thought he was going to come for sure.'

'We can't afford it, sweetheart,' says Scott.

'They charge more for coming,' says Kelly, and she glances at the bathroom door with what looks like a wistful expression.

Cadence didn't know, she doesn't know much, really, this is only the third of these things she's done.

Cadence wonders why it isn't equal pay, not that she's ever come on tape. She takes a last hit of the Jack, feels its glow burn through the faded anaesthetic. She's glad Angelo didn't come in her mouth anyway. *She* would charge more for *that*, she reckons.

Scott is shutting down the equipment. 'You want to take a shower when he's done?' asks Kelly.

Cadence shakes her head.

'You don't?'

'I'll shower when I get home,' says Cadence. She's down from the coke, if she was horny before it was a long time ago, now she just wants

20

to get out of there fast, get home. Kelly hands her her T-shirt and shorts.

'You mail me the check?' she asks, doing the Velcro on her trainers.

'Sure thing,' says Scott. He straightens up, shakes her hand. 'Good to see you, Cadence. Y'all take care on the freeway, now.'

It is morning at the manor house in Auvergne. In jeans and a hunting shirt, Leonard sits comfortably in the window-seat balancing a croissant in the saucer of his coffee cup. Josephine sits at the table in a floor-length robe made several years ago by Sonia Rykiel, in a lightweight black pierced brocade.

She is barefoot. The sun shines in her short blonde hair, picks out triangles and lozenges of bare brown flesh through the gaps in the fabric of the robe.

Josephine is oiling a dildo. It is eight inches long, carved from ivory, curved thoughtfully in the appropriate places, and equipped with ribbons at the base, enabling it to be tied around the top of the thighs. It is quite yellow, and very old.

'Is that for Yvette?' Leonard asks.

'Yes,' says Josephine, continuing to lubricate it.

Leonard stirs. 'What's wrong with mine?' he asks.

Josephine purses her lips. She lays the venerable artifact down gently on the table and gets up, wiping her hands.

She comes over to him. She squats down easily between his knees, her legs apart. The robe falls open either side of her thighs, revealing that she is quite naked beneath it.

'The trouble with yours, Leonard,' she says, opening his fly and slipping out his penis, 'splendid though it is – ' She bows her head and kisses it, the sleek pink length of it. It rises in her palm to meet her lips. ' – is that it comes,' she continues, 'with you on the other end of it.'

He laughs shortly, setting his cup carefully on the windowsill, and leans forward from the seat to kiss her on the mouth.

She looks lovingly, arrogantly, into his grey-blue eyes, then casts a glance back to the table. 'Whereas our friend from the orient may be rather rigid and – unimaginative,' she goes on, 'but with him securely lodged in place, Yvette's bottom will be completely available. For the strap,' she says, sounding the plosive p most precisely.

Her explanation concluded, she closes her fingers lightly around

Leonard's cock and leans forward, seeking his mouth again.

They kiss. Leonard reaches down to fondle her crotch. He finds her warm, and dry, and closed. She is saving herself for Yvette. She expects some stimulation from the encounter.

She lets go of his penis. She smiles into his eyes and stands up, turning away from him. Before moving more than an arm's length away she looks back over her shoulder, still smiling, and takes hold of the material of her robe down beside her right thigh. Slowly she slides it up, gradually and sweetly uncurtaining her calf, her thigh, her right cheek. She bends forward then, offering that clear golden oval to him.

Leonard lifts his hand and smacks her hard.

The crack of hand on flesh is like a gunshot.

Josephine makes no sound. She stoops and kisses the palm of the hand that spanked her. Then moving slowly, thoughtfully, she collects the dildo and the oil and leaves the room, bearing the burning print of his hand on her bottom like a blessing. Leonard catches a glimpse of it blushing through the perforations of her robe as she goes out of the door. Briefly he strokes his declining penis, then tucks it back into his clothes and zips himself up.

He returns his attention to the papers.

|3|

The Arizona sun beats down on the Bluewater Lodge, glaring off the concrete, softening the tarmac. A radio plays softly from one of the cabins, giving news of the temperature, which is in the nineties, the probability of precipitation, which is zero per cent, the traffic on 66, which is backed up to Valentine because of a multi-vehicle pile-up. No one is listening to the radio. No one seems to be around. The only cars under the shade trees belong to Louie, the manager, and the maid. Everyone who stayed at the Bluewater Lodge last night has either checked out or driven off to Lake Mead and the Hoover Dam, or over to Lake Mohave. Or more likely they're off in Kingman selling solar panels to homeowners or delivering accessories to sport stores. It's singles that stay at the Bluewater Lodge, singles or couples. It's not so much a vacation motel, not what you'd call a family motel.

There's not a lot of water either, blue or any other colour, in the immediate vicinity of the Bluewater Lodge, only the air conditioners dripping softly on the scrubby ground. In the distance Mount Tipton lords it over the foothills, looking dark today against the deep blue sky. A local homemaker phones the radio station, answers three questions about Frank Sinatra, wins a hundred dollars. A semi growls past along the road. A sparrow pecks something in the bleached grass under the window of cabin five. Then it flies away.

Inside cabin five, Cadence Szathkowicz is working. Actually, she's goofing off, but really she's working, this is just a break she's taking, a cigarette break, you could call it, though in fact she's not smoking a cigarette, Louie says she's not to smoke in the cabins. What she's doing is looking at the pictures in a glossy magazine.

Cadence has already done the bathroom, pretty much, put the old towels in the bag for the laundry pickup, folded the new towels neatly

23

over the rail, wiped out the tub with tub cleaner, wiped the mirror with a cloth. She hasn't wiped the john yet, she hates that, she never in her life had to wipe a john. Cadence always leaves the john till last. Meanwhile she's taking a break, looking at this magazine.

Bondage Torment.

It isn't her magazine, it belongs to the couple staying in cabin five. Cadence just found it, she's just looking at it, then she'll put it back where it was, under the bed. It's kind of an interesting magazine.

It's a magazine with pictures of women and men in all kinds of weird positions. Tying each other up with straps and rope. It's called *Bondage Torment* . On the cover is a colour picture of a woman wearing just black stockings and a garterbelt, lying on her belly on the grass. Someone has tied her legs together at the ankles with a great hank of shiny white rope, and her hands are tied behind her back. The rope goes between her legs and her hands, so she's pulled up into the shape of a bow, with her feet in the air and her head off the ground. Her tits are quite big, they're touching the ground so you can't quite see her nipples. On her face is a pleading expression, like she's trying to persuade the person taking the photograph to untie her. There's a black gag in her mouth.

Bondage Torment. Cadence wonders how that would feel, to be trussed up like a turkey. You'd have to like it, or you wouldn't let them do it to you. Cadence remembers when she was a kid, playing cowboys and indians with her friends from kindergarten. Maisie was always getting tied up and carried around, she was always the prisoner. Maisie liked playing like that. They didn't play it at kindergarten, the teacher wouldn't let them. Cadence turns the pages of *Bondage Torment* again, looking to see what happens to the woman on the cover.

There is a full-page picture of this other woman sitting on a couch. She's not pleading, she looks kind of sulky. She's got some other kind of gag that looks like a rubber tube, like the bit you put in a horse's mouth. Her arms are tied behind her back with lots of cord, and she's wearing some kind of girdle round her middle made of metal and black leather, it pushes her tits up. Her tits are bare. Her tits aren't as big as the woman's on the front of the magazine, but they're nice tits. Her legs are tied up too, in what looks like a black sack, with straps and ropes and pulleys that tie her knees to her girdle.

Pulleys?

Cadence wonders about the couple who are staying in cabin five.

24

She hasn't seen them, only the nightdress and pajamas she already folded up and put square on the pillows. She pulls abstractedly at the covers to straighten them, still looking at the magazine lying open on top of them. It makes her legs shiver to look at it. She wonders if the couple are into this stuff, or if they just like looking at the pictures. Or maybe the magazine belongs to the husband and his wife doesn't even know about it.

Cadence looks at her watch, but by the time she puts her hand down she's already forgotten what time it said. She sighs. She lights a cigarette, and sits down on the floor for a minute, sticks her legs out. There's seven other cabins to do yet, god damn. Two days she's been her at the Bluewater Lodge, it feels like forever already, she doesn't know how she's going to make it through to the end of the week. And some women do this every day of their lives, all their lives. Maybe Cadence will have to now. No, no, she'll go back to L.A., where she should have gone in the first place if the book hadn't said no. Get her money out of Kelly and Scott, make some more movies.

Right now Cadence feels like she never wants to see another camcorder as long as she lives.

There's this other picture, right, where the woman, not one of the first two women, this other woman, with real small tits and short dark hair, is standinng up being stretched inside this weird wooden machine by two guys. One of them is wearing just regular clothes, shirt and jeans. His haircut is terrible. He's pulling on the cord that runs up to the top of the machine, pulling the woman's arms up in the air; and with his other hand he's pulling a long lever that's strapped to the woman's thigh, making her bend her leg. The other guy is wearing a shiny black leather catsuit, or maybe it's black rubber, and long black boots. He even has a black leather hood over his head, with just holes for his eyes and nose and mouth. The woman is naked, but for a pair of panties, which they've pulled down to the tops of her legs. The man in the black leather catsuit is doing something to her tits, you can't see what because of the camera angle. But you can see the way her arms and legs are stretching, her back is arched, her head thrown back. They've tied a white bandana around her eyes, her mouth is open in pain or maybe it's pleasure. Quickly Cadence looks over the page to see what happens, the pictures are all out of order, what happens next, she has to know.

Just then the door of cabin five opens and the couple walk in.

Everybody looks surprised.

There are the couple: in their early forties, maybe, white, the guy heavyset, broad shoulders, very short dark hair with streaks of iron grey under the strap of a beat-up visor and a plaid sport shirt and a pair of cutoffs, socks and sandals; behind him his wife, shorter, dyed blonde hair in long waves down on her shoulders like a country singer, white tennis shirt and shorts, big hips, strong-looking legs like a horserider, a pink flush on her face from the sun.

There is Cadence, a cigarette burning in her hand, kneeling on the floor in her blue nylon overall dress with the buttons all the way down the front, with *Bondage Torment* lying open on their half-made bed.

The man is in front. He is the first to recover. His dark brown eyes take in the scene, the maid, the magazine. A smile spreads across his face and he rubs his jaw. 'Well, 'scuse us,' he says, in a deep, deep voice.

'I'm just the maid,' says Cadence. 'Just the maid, that's all. I was just making the bed. I didn't mean anything.' She is scrambling to her feet, closing *Bondage Treatment*, looking round where to put it.

The man stretches out his hand. It is big, tanned and hairy. 'Don't get up, honey,' he says. 'You look real cute down there.' He turns to his wife, coming into the cabin behind him. 'Don't she, Fern?'

'She does, George,' says Fern, as Cadence sinks down on her knees again on the motel carpet. Fern looks down at Cadence with a little twisted smile on her face, like she feels real sorry for her but anyway she thinks she looks cute, on her knees.

Cadence looks at George, at Fern, at the cigarette in her hand. 'I'm not really meant to be smoking in here,' she says, with a little apologetic laugh, and she reaches to put the cigarette out in the ashtray on the bedside shelf.

She sits on her heels and straightens the front of her overall dress. She puts *Bondage Torment* down on the bed, picks it up, puts it down. 'I'm sorry,' she says again. 'I guess I'll be going now, come back later for the bed, to make the bed, I mean. I'm sorry about the magazine.'

George is easy. He turns his head slowly to speak to his wife. 'Look at that Fern. She's got a magazine.'

'Well so she has, George,' says Fern. They're westerners, country folks, come up through Tucson and Phoenix, going to have a look at the Hoover Dam on the way to waste their children's inheritance in Vegas. Is George pretending to his wife he never saw the *Bondage*

26

Cadence finds herself pawing the magazine again, unable to leave it alone.

'You like that magazine, Miss Maid?' George asks her, in a friendly voice.

Cadence looks at him, at his wife. They're both waiting for her to speak. She licks her lips.

'I'm just curious, I guess,' she says. 'I'm a Virgo.'

George smiles his broad smile again. 'You don't say,' he says, in a voice brown and slow and sweet as cola syrup.

'I have to go now,' says Cadence .

George stands with his hands on his hips, his feet comfortably apart in his yellow cowboy boots. 'But we ha'n't been properly introduced, Miss Virgo. Whyn't you lock the door, honey,' he says, turning to his wife without waiting for Cadence's reply, 'and let's all get ourselves comfortable here. Get to know each other little bit.'

Fern locks the door with Cadence's passkey. She puts the key on the top of the chest, next to the TV. She says, 'What's your name, honey?'

'Cadence,' says Cadence, not thinking too fast, not thinking much of anything. Her heart is beating fast though, now.

'Well isn't that a real pretty name, George,' says Fern. She flaps a hand in his direction, but she doesn't look at him while she's speaking.

'Oh, I like Fern,' says Cadence. 'I've always thought Fern is such a pretty name.' She tries to smile, frowns, bites her lip. She looks down at the magazine. There is a picture of a woman with an expression on her face just like hers.

'Can I go now?' she asks the couple. 'Please? I wasn't going to take anything, I promise.'

George hunkers down to look into her face. 'Well, Cadence,'he says, slowly, like a bear, 'we don't know that, do we? And anyhow, you were smoking a cigarette and reading this very sinful magazine right here in our cabin. I think we're going to have to get the manager in here.'

'Oh no, no!' says Cadence. 'Don't tell the manager, really, you don't have to do that, really.'

George looks as if he's chewing something, he rubs his chin again. 'Well, we could go straight to the law,' he says, like it's a problem, like it's something he really doesn't want to have to do. 'What do you think we should do here, Fern?'

'Maybe you better go to the law, George,' says Fern.

'No,' says Cadence. 'Uh-uh. That's not a good idea. You don't want to get the law.' She's working illegally here at the Bluewater Lodge, and she doesn't want anyone to know where she is, not her father, not anyone. 'Please don't,' she says.

'Then I guess we're gonna have to deal with you ourselves, sweetheart,' says George, as if he feels sorry for her, as if she's forced him into an awkward decision.

He spreads his hands on his belt buckle. It's made of pewter, as big across as a saucer.

'All right,' says Cadence. 'All right.' Her heart is really thudding now. Her stomach is just a big hole, like the hole in the doughnut that's all Louie lets her have for breakfast. She looks apprehensively at the couple in cabin five. She reaches for the magazine, pulls back her hand.

Bondage Torment.

'What do you want me to do?' says Cadence.

'Whyn't we all make ourselves comfortable here?' George says again. He runs his eyes over Cadence's body, over her blue nylon overall dress. 'I guess you must be pretty hot in that there dress.' He nods at the overall dress, not waiting for Cadence to say anything. 'Honey,' he says to Fern, 'whyn't you help her out of that thing?'

He sits on the bed, leans back, taking his weight on his hands.

Cadence looks helplessly up at Fern, who comes and squats down in front of her. Cadence's hands are hovering at the button between her breasts. Fern smacks them lightly, fussily, patting them out of the way. She unfastens the buttons of Cadence's blue nylon overall dress, all the way down the front, then steps behind her to help her out of it. She pulls it back off her shoulders and down her arms.

Cadence folds her arms across her chest, then drops them to her sides. She sits back on her heels.

Under the blue nylon overall dress Cadence Szathkowicz is wearing nothing but a pair of red cotton panties.

Fern and George make noises of pleasure and delight. Cadence can feel their eyetracks. She closes her own eyes, shakes her head, touches her hair.

When she opens her eyes she sees Fern squatting in front of her again. Fern reaches for Cadence's breasts, cups them in her hands, running her thumbs over her little brown nipples. 'Oh honey,' she says, reprovingly, and looks deep in Cadence's eyes. Her own eyes are hazel, she flutters her long false eyelashes. Her breath smells sweet and fresh. Her dry, tough hands make Cadence shiver.

'What a bad girl you are, Cadence,' says Fern.

Meanwhile George is unbuttoning his shirt. He takes it off slowly, not taking his eyes from Cadence's breasts. A scent of Old Spice and fresh sweat wafts down over her. Cadence in turn looks at George's chest.

George's chest is a regular forest of brown hair, going winter grey. There is a picture of a truck moulded on his belt buckle. He opens the buckle, and the zipper beneath. He slips his cutoffs out from under, pushes them to the floor. He is wearing Y-fronts, blue with a deep red stripe. The hair on his chest runs on down his belly into the waistband of his Y-fronts. He slips the Y-fronts down too.

George's prick is not long, but thick, like a horny red thumb, thinks Cadence. She feels her breasts rise, her loins stir.

George pauses, sitting on the edge of the bed, still gazing at Cadence's tits. He hasn't touched her. He lifts his right hand to his mouth and bites a piece of skin off the side of his thumbnail. With his left hand he lifts his prick, as if offering it to Cadence.

She reaches out, uncertainly, to take it.

'Uh-uh,' says George at once. 'Honey.' He catches Fern's eye over the top of Cadence's head. Cadence hears Fern open a zipper on a bag, something clinks, something metal.

Firmly Fern pulls Cadence's hand behind her back. She puts cool metal around her wrists. Handcuffs.

Like the women in *Bondage Torment*.

Cadence kneels up straight. She is thunderstruck. She feels totally helpless already, even with just her hands cuffed behind her. She explores the handcuffs with the thumbs and fingers of the opposite hands. She is breathing quick and shallow. Sweat trickles down between her breasts. She stares at George's penis like a rabbit at a rattlesnake.

Have they got rope? Masks? All that stuff?

George spreads his legs, beckons her with one hand, like someone signalling to the driver of a car.

Cadence kneels up between his legs.

His naked thighs are warm against her arms.

They are so quiet in the cabin she can hear Louie's radio in the office, playing something with a steel guitar. She wonders what Fern

29

is doing, out of sight behind her. Preparing something else, she expects. She is rigid with fear, hot as the weather.

'Open wide there, Virgo.'

The rabbit opens her mouth and takes the rattlesnake inside.

He tastes of tobacco and piss, male flavours. She starts to melt inside. He stirs on her tongue, thickening.

Through her panties Cadence feels Fern's hands on her butt, gentle, fingers spread. She leans forward on her knees, slipping her tongue down the shaft of George's cock. He grunts.

George works his way backwards onto the bed and Cadence follows, nuzzling, then slowly sucking. Fern's hands urge her onto the bed. Doesn't she mind another woman, a total stranger, sucking her husband's dick this way? Maybe it's good for her too.

Cadence hears the sound of the glossy magazine sliding off the bed as the covers ruck and shift and she lies along George's legs and Fern's weight comes up onto her from behind. They have her imprisoned between them. She lifts her head for a mouthful of air. It's hard to move without your hands. The fear is like a wave, hot and glassy, she's surfing. Raising George's surf. She works her tongue around George's quivering cock, bathing it in her saliva. His thighs tremble. He reaches beneath her for her tits, grabs them tight. It takes her breath away. His dick touches the back of her throat and she gags a moment, losing it.

She feels Fern take a handful of her hair and lift it. Fern is kissing the back of her neck.

Jesus.

Fern is gone then for a while.

Cadence wants to look around and see, but George growls, presses her head down with the flat of his hand.

'No rest breaks, Miss Virgo,' he says. 'Get back to work there.'

She nips the shaft of his cock lightly with her teeth, drawing them up its length and worrying it under the glans, shaking her head. She hears him snort and shout out loud. He presses her breasts cruelly between his thighs. Her hands are starting to get uncomfortable behind her back. She sucks for her life, and thinks dimly of the seven other cabins waiting for her. Maybe if this is all she can get to them soon. She sucks harder, washing the glans of his cock hard with her tongue.

While she sucks, she can hear the rustle of clothing in the room. Then Fern rejoins them on the bed.

30

Cadence feels the warm, naked body up against her back, the breasts pressing into her shoulder blades. Fern pulls on her hips and Cadence lifts her ass, trying not to lose hold of George's cock.

Fern pulls down Cadence's panties.

She pulls them down over the curve of her bottom and leaves them there, stretched between her thighs.

Like the woman in the machine in *Bondage Torment*.

Cadence gasps, breathing a gust of warm air over George's cock, when Fern slips her hand between her legs from behind. Fern's fingers are stiff and sure. They flex unerringly into Cadence's groove, Cadence creams hot and wet and sticky.

'Oh baby,' Fern murmurs over her shoulder. Fern clasps Cadence in her arms, rubs her tits, nibbles her ear. She squashes Cadence's arms with her body. 'What a wicked baby.'

Now Cadence lets George slip through her lips, twists around hard in Fern's grasp, trying to kiss her on her lipsticked mouth.

'Cadence,' rumbles George, reaching for her. He snaps his fingers in the air, points to his stiff red wet dick.

Cadence turns around between his thighs, her back to him, and takes him in the grip Doug taught her, with the thumb bent. 'Well I declare!' says Fern, kneeling naked face to face with Cadence.

Cadence hears George hiss through his teeth. All right then. All the while she is still kissing Fern's face, playing with her mouth. She grinds her pelvis into Fern's groin, feels her pubes like soft wire press into her skin.

Fern strokes Cadence's back with the flat of both hands, then grabs hold of her legs. Cadence laughs.

'She's laughing, George,' observes Fern, over Cadence's shoulder.

George puts his hand over Cadence's where it grips his cock, grips her hand. 'I thought this was supposed to be a punishment, Fern.'

'Well, that's right, George.'

'Mm,' says Cadence.

She's never had this kind of punishment before.

George comes up off the bed and kisses the nape of her neck. He rubs his mouth hard in her hair and lets go her hand. Still kissing him, she looks down over her shoulder. She changes her grip so the chain of the cuffs rubs against the underside of his cock and begins to pull on him harder and faster.

'Whoa there,' he murmurs.

Fern pulls her legs and Cadence slides down onto George's body. She loses his dick immediately, rubs her cheek in the fur of his chest.

Fern takes Cadence's panties off. Cadence feels them go, lifts her legs in a surge like a wave. Her arms are hurting, so she rolls over on her face. She rubs her bare breasts across George's crotch.

Ferns slips Cadence's panties around her neck from behind, stretches the elastic across her throat, pulls the ends in together.

She says, 'You like our magazine, Cadence?'

Without thinking, Cadence lifts her head from George's belly, looks for the magazine. She sees it lying open on the floor. She can see a picture of a man with his elbows chained together, wearing a steel and leather chastity belt.

Cadence reaches up above her, locates Fern's crotch. Her fingers slip slickly between Fern's taut-muscled thighs. Fern is wet and steaming. Fern is ready.

Should she give him to her first? Cadence masturbates George while she thinks about it. George stretches his neck reaching to chew on her tits. His hands feel enormous on her flanks.

'George, Fern,' says Cadence, sitting up again, ducking out of Fern's soft garotte, straddling George's legs. 'You don't know how sorry I am I looked at your fuck mag.'

But it's not a fuck mag, she thinks. No one was fucking in there, they were just tied up or tying someone else up. TERRI'S TUESDAY TORTURE, said the headlines on the front cover. AGONY FOR ANDY. It all looked pretty terrifying, nipple clamps and stuff.

Jesus Christ, her insides are tight as tight rubber, she is *hot*, hot as a chilli dog.

Confused, Cadence rears up, letting her arms swing like a dead weight slung between her shoulders, thrusting her breasts into the warm and odorous air.

She hotches forward on her knees and poises her hips directly over George's straining dick. He parts her soft lips with his huge fingers, hurting her. She squats, pushing him up into her, crying out with the old familiar shock.

No two men the same, she thinks, as she often does at this moment.

'Jesus fucking Christ,' moans the man between her thighs.

'Jesus, oh,' echoes Cadence.

Fern gags Cadence with her own panties.

She puts something in the elastic to hold them in place and comes round to kneel by George's head.

Cadence is amazed, stunned, drugged by her own smell. She falters, sways above George. 'Oh man, oh God, oh Christ,' expostulates George, succinctly.

'Honey pie!' says Fern in the voice of a disconcerted Sunday School teacher.

Cadence sways. She lilts. She fuzzes up inside. She is a tube of fizzing desire like a firecracker, restrained by a band top and bottom, the gag and the handcuffs. She imagines the woman who was sitting on the couch with her legs in a sack. In another picture you could see her back, they had her gag and her wrists joined on to a metal pole that ran down her spine.

Cadence imagines she was strapped to one.

Cadence bounces on George, Fern sits on George's face, kisses Cadence on the mouth.

There is a knock at the door of cabin five.

Fern frees her mouth, clasps Cadence's shoulders, stopping her motion. She shouts, 'Yeah, what?'

A man's voice calls out, 'You got the maid in there?'

It is the manager of the Bluewater Lodge. It's Louie.

Fern looks at Cadence. Cadence is shaking her head no, no.

Fern looks down at her husband, trapped beneath her butt. She lifts one muscular ham.

'We got her,' shouts George, moistly.

Cadence is frantic, scrambling off him, thrusting her hands at Fern to have the cuffs off. Maybe she can hide, maybe in the bathroom.

'Phone for you Cadence,' calls Louie the manager.

|4|

Phone? I: can't be, no one knows she's here.

'It can't be,' she says into the gag.

'Maybe you have an admirer, sweetheart,' says George. Cadence is more freaked out than he is. Maybe because he has another option. Cadence shakes her cuffs at Fern, cranes over her shoulder.

'Mmff!'

Fern smacks her hard on the bottom.

'Bad girl,' she says softly.

She unlocks the cuffs.

Cadence pulls her panties out of her mouth and puts them on where they should be, slides them up her long brown legs, puts on the overall dress, buttons it, it takes forever. She looks at the couple on the bed. Fern's breasts droop, she notices, she's pretty chubby. Not in shape. Fern is looking after George's erection. George has his fingers jammed firmly up between her bottom cheeks.

'I'm sorry,' says Cadence one more time. 'I have to go now.'

'Bye now, honey,' calls Fern, and they laugh.

Cadence goes and opens the door. Louie is standing there, scratching his fat neck. Louie reminds her of Barney Rubble, but she used to like Barney Rubble.

Louie raises his eyebrows. She brushes past him, she won't look at him. She wonders how much he could hear, stood out there.

The Bluewater Lodge doesn't have a mobile phone, she has to go to Louie's office to take the call. She's lucky he doesn't come too, he stays talking to George, who has pulled on his cutoffs and come to the door to scratch himself in the sun.

She knows who it is. Who it has to be.

Her daddy.

She closes the office door. The inner door is half-open, the one marked *Private*, that leads to Louie's own rooms. The trash basket is full of Schlitz cans. The radio on the shelf above the desk is playing the Everly Brothers, they sang beautiful miserable harmonies, off stage they wouldn't even speak to each other. '*Hello loneliness, I think I'm gonna cry —.*'

Cadence looks at the stained white handset lying on the desk at the end of its coiled cord. Nerves herself to pick it up.

Her hand reaches out. How he's found her she doesn't know. In Washington all things are possible.

In Washington, or somewhere else maybe, in Delaware, in Michigan, her daddy was at some stag party, some conference. Somewhere all the guys got together, guys together, all the wives left back home. Whisky, beer, cigars, blue movies.

One of the grunting men starting up out of his seat, 'Goddamn it, turn it off! Turn it off!'

'Sit down, shut up at the back there!'

'Turn it off, Charlie, damn it!'

'What's your problem, are you feeling jealous?'

Pointing his cigar accusingly at the mobile pink flesh spread across the king-size screen. '*That's my daughter up there!*'

Something like that, Cadence imagines. All she got was the message on the answering machine: '*I'll be there Thursday, Cadence. I want you to know I'm very angry about this.*' She read the I Ching, took the Toyota and fled. First thing she knew he'd cancelled all her cards. Cadence Szathkowicz, fleeing south, east, not a cent to her name.

She picks up the waiting phone, puts it to her cringing ear. Louie doesn't even have the phone santitized, yecch. 'Hello?' she says, full of dread.

'You're looking for Josephine Morrow,' says a voice she doesn't know. A man's voice, a young man.

Not her daddy, that's all Cadence can register right at this precise moment in time.

'Who is this? How did you know where I am?'

All the man says is, 'I have a message from her.'

Cadence can barely think of anything to say. 'Did the newspaper give you this number?' What is she talking about, the newspaper doesn't know where she is. 'Did my father tell you to call me? This is a trick, right?'

'Josephine Morrow has a domino mask tattooed between her breasts,' says the man calmly, like he wasn't listening to a word she said, like he was on tape. He has an accent, but it's not an English accent, she doesn't think so, anyway. 'At the Concord Reef Hotel on Dominica she put your fingers in her mouth, one by one.'

Nobody could know that. Nobody could. Unless Josephine had told them.

Josephine.

There is a pause.

Frightened, Cadence says, 'Is that the message? Hello? Hello, are you there?'

'Now you must prove who you are,' says the man. He isn't any older than she is, by his voice. Cadence thinks about him and Josephine, feels a sudden twist of jealousy like a cramp in her gut.

'Is she there? Let me talk to her.'

'Do you even know who you are, Cadence?' he asks.

'What are you talking about? What do you *want*?' She jigs up and down in Louie's office, agitated.

She hears the guy on the phone breathe in through his mouth, like he's sucking on a cigarette.

Sucking on something.

Josephine had sucked her fingers. That felt incredible, it went all the way down her spine.

'A photograph, for one thing.'

'Where are you?'

He's not American, definitely not, but he gives her a US postbox number; no name. A postbox in a city she's never heard of, in a state where she's never been.

'Send me a photograph,' he repeats.

Cadence brushes the hair back from her forehead. She's totally confused. 'What kind of photograph?' she asks him.

'A photograph of you,' he says, unhelpfully. 'Of all of you.'

For a second she thinks of Fern and George in cabin five, it's some kind of weird set-up, some blackmail thing. Then she realises what he means.

'Wait, wait,' she says. A nude photo, he means. God, he could have a whole movie.

'You get an adult channel down there?' she asks.

For the first time, she's confusing him now. 'I don't understand,' he says.

'Cable?' says Cadence.

'Cable?'

'Cable TV.'

'No.'

'You got video?'

'There is no television here at all.' He says it as if he's never seen one, as if he barely even knows the word.

'Okay, well —'

He's gone. Hung up.

Cadence shivers. She looks out of the window at the blazing sunshine.

The radio is playing Bon Jovi.

Cadence reaches up under her blue nylon overall dress, presses her hand to her crotch.

Her panties are wet, her mouth is dry, her heart is beating louder than Bon Jovi's drumkit.

Louie's not back yet. How is she going to get a nude photo? Fern and George are tourists, they must have a camera. Wait, wait.

Cadence goes to her car, gets a piece of paper out of her purse. Thank God she's so untidy, it's still there. Piece of paper with a phone number on. She goes back to the office, purposeful now. The radio is playing the Pretenders, she switches it off. Phones the number.

'*Hello, this is Kelly —*'

'*— and this is Scott.*'

'*We're not home right now —*'

'*— but we'd love to have a message from you —*'

'*— so please leave your name and number after the tone.*' Then in chorus: '*Thank you for calling!*' Cute. Almost as cute as getting bored rich kids to do their skin flicks, then not sending them their *money* .

'Hi, Kelly and Scott, this is, um —'

Does she dare give her name? Stupid, she has to.

'This is Cadence Szathkowicz, please would you do me a favour, send one of my tapes to this address.' She gives the postbox number, she's remembered it, zip and all, holy cow.

'No wait, that's no good.' Goddamn, the guy said he didn't even have a fucking video. 'Well, maybe if you could just print one frame, like, one really good frame of me, you know? Could you send it there, like I told you already, could you do that for me?' She pauses an instant,

37

as though she's expecting the machine to reply. 'I'd really appreciate it,' she says lamely. 'Well, so long.'

Even as she hangs up, Cadence is beginning to think this wasn't such a good idea. She was sure those guys never sent her check. Unless maybe it was waiting for her in Laguna Beach, she daren't go back there yet, her daddy might be home.

The screen door bangs and Louie comes in.

'You turn the radio off?' he says. He's always beefing about something, Louie.

She tries to smile at him. 'Oh, hi, Louie.'

'Who said you could turn the radio off?' He snaps on the switch in the middle of a commercial for a two-for-one special on Havoline.

'Hey, sorry, Louie, I was on the phone . . .'

'Didn't say you could make phone calls either,' he says. 'You want to make a call, you use the payphone.'

'Oh, c'mon Louie –'

He gives her a little grim smile. He must know something's been going on; maybe he can smell it on her. He comes towards her, she backs away, fetches up against the desk.

'Okay, hey, well, it was just a local call, anyway,' lies Cadence looking at him without blinking.

His little grim smile turns into a big grim smile. She tries to rush past him out of the door, but he blocks her.

'No go, Cadence. You fool with the radio –'

'I what?'

Louie overrides her, ticking off crimes on his stubby fingers. He's pretty pleased with himself, you can see that. ' – you make unauthorised phone calls; you smoke in the cabins; and you interfere with the personal property of the guests.'

Cadence's mouth falls open. 'Those bastards!'

Louie puts his head down, looks at her kind of sideways, like he's asking her does she really intend to get herself in more trouble than she already is?

Louie is wearing a lightweight printed cotton shirt with the sleeves rolled up. He reaches one thick hairy arm past Cadence's chest to push the door marked *Private*.

'I think you and me should go in and have a little talk, Cadence.'

Agitated, numb, Cadence follows him. She can't believe this. Just a couple of minutes ago she was having wild kinky sex with a pair of complete strangers. Now her crummy boss is steamrolling her into some kind of phoney confrontation.

Phone-y, she thinks, oh, yes, Cadence, very smart. Very funny.

'I didn't do anything wrong,' she says. She's stroking at her hair, trying to straighten it with her fingers. She looks around dazedly. Louie's steering her along now, one firm hand on each shoulder. He's steering her into the bedroom. He's closing the door.

Louie's bedroom smells of feet and booze. Cadence hasn't been in Louie's bedroom before, he doesn't use his own maid service. It doesn't look like anyone's serviced Louie's suite for a long time. The bed is a pit and there's a whole wall of pin-up pictures, girls in (and mostly half out of) fancy lingerie.

Louie's talking to her while she looks around. He's opening the closet, rummaging around in it while he's talking to her.

'Now the problem here is what you call a management-employee problem. What we have to do is re-establish proper manager-employee relations, right? Are you with me so far, Cadence?'

'What are you talking about, Louie?'

Louie looks out of the closet at her. 'You call me sir, Cadence, that's your proper manager-employee terminology there.'

'Yeah, well, you call me Ms Szathkowicz, then,' mutters Cadence, but not really loud enough for Louie to hear her with his head in the closet.

'Now,' he says, emerging again with something in his hand, something black and white and frilly and hanging on a Bluewater Lodge coathanger. 'I am the boss, okay? And you are the maid, right?'

Cadence has a funny feeling in the pit of her stomach. She looks round out of the window, which no one has cleaned for a long time, even longer than the time no one's made the bed or picked up the trash. 'Yeah, right, okay, sure,' she mumbles.

Louie sticks his face in her face, forcing her to look at him. '*Sir*,' he says.

'What is this anyway, the fucking U.S. Army?'

Louie only smiles again. Each time he smiles that smile it gets wider and wider and less and less pleasant. 'You're only making it worse for yourself, Cadence.'

Cadence is focusing on the thing on the hanger. 'What *is* that?' she asks.

'This —' He shakes it at her. 'This is a proper maid's uniform. Not that sexless blue crap the union makes you wear. Here,' he says, and throws the hanger at her. 'Put it on.'

'Here?' she says, suspiciously. There doesn't seem to be very much of this uniform, as far as she can see.

'Yup.'

'No.'

Louie's looking pleased, like he can't believe his ears, can't believe his luck. 'No? *No*? Oho, Cadence, you're making this very very bad for yourself.' He actually shakes his finger at her.

'Okay, okay, I'll put it on in the bathroom, okay?'

He smiles, gestures broadly in a pantomime of generosity. 'Sure, Cadence, you just hop along in there and change into this real uniform, why don't you?'

Cadence, even more suspicious, disappears through the connecting door.

Louie lies back on his bed in a state of great satisfaction. He rubs his chin. He unzips his fly and pulls out his pecker, rubs it till it gets hard. He can hear scuffling, slithering sounds from the bathroom as Cadence gets out of one uniform and into another. The sounds excite him. He rubs his prick some more, then makes himself put it away. He looks across the wall of pin-ups, eyes slithering around excitedly, unable to rest on any one woman. He's entertaining himself with imagining what's going on in the bathroom.

Then Cadence comes out again, transformed.

She's wearing a black dress so tiny it barely covers her butt in back. It's made with a kind of built-in stiff bra top that pushes her tits up and out in front; it doesn't cover her nipples at all. The front of the dress, if you can call it a dress, is covered with a little heart-shaped apron, all flounces and lace. That just about covers her crotch.

Under the dress she's wearing tiny black panties hardly thicker than a piece of thread, and a lacy, frilly, frothy garterbelt with long fishnet stockings on it. On her feet she has little dinky black slippers.

Of course everything's the wrong size. The stockings are loose and the bra top is too big, and the panties would fall down if she had to take more than another step in them. But by the glow in Louie's eyes and the bulge in his pants Cadence can see that he's looking at his ideal vision of a woman.

Jesus Christ Almighty on a sesame bun.

'Now that's a *real* maid's uniform,' purrs Louie, manager of the

40

Bluewater Lodge.

'This? This is a whore's costume,' says Cadence frankly.

Louie points a finger at her. 'Now that's your problem, Cadence. You're disrespectful. You talk back to your superiors. You don't show the proper manager-employee humility.'

'I'm wearing the fucking costume, Louie, okay?'

Pink spots appear in Louie's flabby cheeks.

'Every time you don't call me sir,' he says quietly, 'you get two more.'

'Two more what?' asks Cadence. 'Sir?' she adds, cautiously.

'Reach in the drawer behind you,' Louie orders her.

Cadence turns round. The drawer is low down near the floor. When she bends down, he gets an eyeful of her backside. She can hear how much he enjoys it.

In the drawer is a bunch of crap, packs of condoms and some videotapes with no labels, pens and pencils and tools. 'What am I looking for?' she asks; then she says, 'Oh.'

She's found it.

She takes it out and looks at it. She turns around to look at Louie. 'This.'

Louie nods his heavy head. 'That,' he agrees.

It looks like a cheeseboard: an oblong piece of ply, varnished and with the corners sanded off. It has a wooden handle on the end, with a stained towel grip. On one side of the board is stencilled a crude black cartoon drawing of a woman with her eyes wide and mouth in an O. They've drawn her holding up her skirt in both hands and sticking out her butt, which is bare, and on her bottom cheeks they've put two big round patches of bright red. Next to the picture, it says: 'FOR GETTING RIGHT TO THE "SEAT" OF THE PROBLEM!'

'Bring that over here,' says Louie.

Belatedly Cadence realises George has told him what they were doing in cabin five, and now he thinks he can have some. Well, shit.

She takes the paddle over to him.

And he takes it from her.

Sitting down, his eyes are just about level with her crotch. He's staring for all he's worth. He takes hold of her hand and swivels her round, gazes at her ass like a kid at a giant candy bar.

'Come here,' he says, and his voice has gone all husky. 'Come here, here, bend over here.'

He offers her his lap.

Cadence takes hold of the hem of her so-called skirt. She's about to lift it, just like the woman in the drawing.

Then she looks at Louie and she realises she doesn't like him. Not at *all* she doesn't.

He's got his hand on her arm, ready to pull her down over his lap. Cadence says coolly: 'I don't have to take this, you know.'

Louie looks a little irritated. 'It's this or your job, honeybuns,' he says.

Cadence hooks her hands in the bodice of the maid's dress and rips it down the front. She tears off the apron, it's crummy cheap stuff, rips easy. She rips it right off and throws it down on the floor of Louie's scuzzy bedroom. 'You can keep your stinking job,' she tells him.

Then she walks out of the room, and out of the cabin. The too-big panties with the cheap elastic roll down as she walks across the yard in her stockings and slippers, and she kicks them aside with an angry curse. She starts to run, the tatters of the dress flapping. She runs to her car, gets in and starts up, stalls, starts up again and drives angrily round to cabin five. Why did they have to tell Louie? Why do people have to be such jerks all the time?

Cabin five is locked, and there's no answer when she stands there with the torn dress hanging off her, pounding on the door. Fern and George have finished and gone. Cadence feels a pang of disappointment. She'd just been beginning to enjoy herself and they screwed it all up.

'Cadence! Cadence, hey wait!' It's Louie, running after her to make another proposition. 'It was just a game, Cadence, don't get mad —'

Cadence snarls at him, kicks the door of cabin five, gets back in her daddy's car and drives away.

As they reach the jetty, Josephine Morrow gets to her feet and jumps lightly ashore. She walks away without a backward glance, leaving Francis to moor the launch. Behind her, across the strait, a flock of white birds rises over the trees, flying up from the lagoon of Giens.

They have come south, the whole household, to the island the Greeks called *Proté*, first of the Iles d'Hyères. The light is better here. The house can be approached only by sea, the path down through the neglected vineyard having been allowed to become tangled and overgrown. Josephine is quite naked, apart from her Italian sunglasses and sandals and the tiny Scandinavian pouch of white kid that hangs on a string around her neck. The Danish call this a 'cat', but Josephine never uses the word, which signifies another device to her entirely. Delicious sweat runs from her bronze throat and trickles down between her large breasts, where the pouch bounces softly as she walks.

The ancient paving among the rocks up to the door is unsettled and broken. In a daze of heat, Josephine imagines the slaves that might be set to repair it: gleaming bodies chained together, muscles swivelling, naked men and women toiling in the pitiless sun. Josephine has just been visiting the Ile du Levant, strolling through the busy streets of the naturist village of Héliopolis, drinking a Pernod or two and flouting the ubiquitous *No Smoking* signs. Such a pretentious name! Such a vulgar place, it amuses her, when she is tired of playing with the novices, to have herself oiled all over and ride over to Héliopolis, to flaunt her magnificent body in public: her splendid breasts, the full swell of her bottom, the luxurious groves of her crotch. She has been sitting outside an *estaminet*, one foot on the ground, the other leg up on the bench, watching the passers-by trying to disguise their disconcertedness. The tourists are disturbed by her insouciance, the villagers by her beauty.

Naturists are the most repressed people in the world, Josephine believes. The only way they can mingle in such dull, banal congregations is by suppressing all imagination, all awareness of themselves and each other as sexual beings. It is almost comic. To maintain their obligatory state of purity they must co-exist without acknowledging one another's flesh; though their bodies are naked, their minds are more clothed than the clothed. They have a post office; they have *estate agents*, in the village of Héliopolis.

On the door of the beach-house, a knocker of dull, unpolished brass is decorated with an ivory double-six domino, inset. Not even glancing at the knocker, Josephine reaches a key from the pouch between her breasts and unlocks the door.

Despite her contempt for the denizens of Héliopolis, she feels their ethic has a certain piquancy. To live and go about naked while being denied ever to touch oneself, ever to entertain, much less express, a single impulse of desire — surely there are candidates for whom such a discipline would be appreciate. Once, too, while staying here on Porquerolles, Josephine sent the incorrigible Prudence to spend the day in Héliopolis bearing the six bright lines of a recent caning fresh and precise across her bottom. Anyone who showed interest was to be told the truth, or a portion of it, and invited back to the house.

No one did, of course.

The hallway is red-tiled, shuttered, cool. Silent in black suspender belt and stockings and a plain black collar, Yvette comes to greet her mistress. She wipes Josephine's skin with a sponge dipped in a bowl of cool water scented with frangipani, and pats her dry with a towel. The performance is quite without sensuality or even affection. The slave's hands are steady even as she attends to the most intimate areas of her mistress's body. Water beads wink like jewels in Josephine's pubic fleece.

On a word from her mistress, Yvette removes the bowl and returns with a salver on which lies another slim collar of black leather, this one set with alternating silver studs and winking, icy diamonds.

Removing her sunglasses, Josephine kisses her slave on the mouth. She notes with approval that without being told, Yvette has put a little blusher on her pale cheeks, a little more on her nipples and on the narrow lips beneath her sparse and springy pubic hair. Josephine fondles her there. Yvette opens her mouth in a silent gasp. She stands motionless, holding up the salver.

Josephine pats the white thigh where it emerges from the neatly turned stocking top. Then she takes off her pouch from around her neck and exchanges it and the sunglasses for the collar, which she fastens around her neck. She sniffs her fingers, relishing Yvette's scent. The girl stands now with her eyes modestly downcast, ready for whatever may happen.

Josephine dismisses her.

Yvette looks up then, involuntarily, breaking discipline in her disappointment. Josephine smiles chidingly and Yvette's eyes drop again at once. She has no tattoo, no liberty, no will. The slave does not know yet whether her mistress will be magnanimous enough to forgive her this slip, or whether it will be added to the never-lessening list of infringements that require, only and always, punishments of the most severe and exquisite kind.

She does not need to know.

She returns to her work, while Josephine goes to her dressing room.

She puts on black panties and a stern corset of black leather that constricts her waist and covers her breasts, forcing them into even more prominence than they have from the hand of Nature. To the

44

suspenders of the corset she clips seamed black stockings identical to Yvette's; then she pulls on a pair of mock-leather knee-boots in black PVC. She brushes her short blonde hair and makes up her eyes with mascara and a fierce purple eyeshadow, and her lips in a deep blood red. She considers a pair of elbow-length gloves in black satin; pulls one on and considers the effect in the mirror; pulls on the other.

Then she dons a domino mask of black velvet, lined with ultramarine silk, and adjusts it across her eyes.

It is time to attend to the novices.

They are very young, all of them, twenty or twenty-two, rescued from language schools or lives of intense dullness serving customers of bistros and airport concession stands. They were something of a surprise, delivered here to Le Lointain as soon as she and Leonard arrived. Leonard had arranged for them without telling her, knowing her skill at the exacting tasks of preparation and training.

She goes to a bolted door at the back of the house and pauses there, listening, her hand on the bolt.

There is a movement inside, muffled voices, the rustling of bedding. A giggle, swiftly suppressed.

Josephine releases the bolt. Inside there is scuffling, sounds of hurried motion.

Josephine opens the door.

The room is a small plain dormitory, furnished with half a dozen iron beds. There is an iron ring set in the whitewashed wall at the head of each bed, but the three occupants have not yet been chained up. Josephine is introducing them bit by bit to the whole truth of their condition. She has been hoping for a moment such as this.

Three pairs of eyes regard her solemnly, frozen wide in apprehension. Each novice has dived back to his or her own bed; it is impossible to tell where they were at the moment their mistress arrived outside the door of the room.

It does not matter. Both Ahmed and Alexandra have been showing an interest in Peter, the quiet little Dutch boy. Josephine cultivated this development, pleased to see how the Arab's dark loins twitched at the removal of his confrère's travelling clothes; while the English miss, stripping for the first time in male company, blushed scarlet from head to toe and tried to look as if she wasn't looking, though secretly she ogled the frail, hairless youth at every chance she got.

In the bolted and shuttered confines of the dormitory, events have obviously moved on.

Josephine glares at the trio. They are all naked but for a slim black collar. None of them yet wears the domino tattoo, or has ever seen it, probably. Peter, the only one with a sheet over him, is white with fear; Ahmed expressionless as a statue poised in tense and improbable repose on the very edge of his mattress. Alexandra, as precarious on her own bed as Ahmed on his, is biting her lip, stifling nervous laughter. Her long brown hair is in disarray.

Josephine signals to her to strip the sheet from the recumbent Peter. In a clumsy paroxysm of agony and desire, she obeys.

There is nothing fearful or anaemic about Peter's impudent erection. It stands up from his crotch like a slim white bone.

Josephine stares coldly at it, but it does not wilt.

Shyly, Peter smiles.

Seeing that, Ahmed slowly moves his hip, turning his knee the degree or two that will reveal to their new mistress that he too is hard. He is mutely, deliberately, declaring his own complicity in Peter's shame.

This is how mutual nakedness should be, thinks Josephine: bold, yearning, helpless in the fact of its own desire. When it is aroused, then that desire must be channelled, trained; disciplined.

Her boot-heels sounding loudly on the bare boards, she crosses to the washstand and snatches up a hairbrush. It is long, with an oval back of hardwood and old-fashioned bristles that prickle and sting.

Josephine smacks it hard against the side of her boot, making the novices jump.

'Stand out, Alexandra,' she commands, in a voice of smouldering rage.

The boys glance at Alexandra. Even the wicked, macho Ahmed shows a trace of fear. Naked and pink, slightly plump and long-faced, Alexandra slips from her bed and stands in front of her mistress, her hands at her sides, her eyes on the floor.

'Turn around.'

The girl does so.

'Legs apart,' says Josephine, goosing her rudely with the hairbrush. Alexandra squirms, spreads her feet a few inches.

'Touch your toes.'

She obeys. Her soft young breasts tilt forwards, and her hair brushes the floor.

Transferring the brush to her left hand, Josephine thrusts her right between the girl's parted thighs. Alexandra gasps, 'Oh!' – a clear, high sound in the tense silence.

Josephine ignores her. She is young and untrained. Josephine examines her crotch by touch. She is still dry; unlike her companions, her arousal is still only nervous, not physiological.

Josephine fancies she will warm them all up with a good stiff brushing, then take them to the dining room. There are irons set in all four walls, more than enough to take three wayward novices spread-eagled, naked of course, their sore bottoms pressing against the rough whitewash. If what they witness before, during and after dinner doesn't have Alexandra's love-juices dripping down the wall and the boys ejaculating helplessly, Josephine vows to herself, then she is no queen.

She takes the hairbrush back in her right hand and plants the spread fingers of her left firmly in the middle of the bending girl's back.

The boys are watching. Ahmed is smirking to see his rival so discomfited, while Peter looks on in horrified fascination. They are already eager to witness one another's punishments. Next time Josephine will forbid them.

She raises the brush.

There is a knock at the door.

'Come,' she calls, pausing in her upswing, but not relaxing.

It is Yvette. Behind her, holding her on a trim red leather leash, comes Leonard, in a black singlet and tight leather shorts. The dust of the road is still on him. He comes in, appraising the scene at a glance. He steps up behind Josephine and runs his hands down her corseted flanks.

'How is she?' she asks, in a casual tone.

Leonard nods. 'On her way,' he says.

He pushes his silvered sunglasses up into the mass of his wild blond curls. He says, 'Please do carry on, my dear.'

|5|

Fred Campodoro pumps gas. He works at an Amoco station east of Gallup, right after where you turn if you missed the main turn for McKinley and you have to go the long way round. Fred is on duty there right now, and he is bored. Fred hasn't had a customer for three-quarters of an hour. He hasn't seen a car for ten, no, wait, eleven minutes. He's finished reading the only thing to read around here today, which is an issue of the *Incredible Hulk*. From the window he can see two-lane blacktop, red earth, blue sky. Fuck, Fred is *bored*.

Fred is all alone at the station, he thinks about jacking off. He wonders if other guys his age still jack off. He's sure they do, because what about all the stroke mags?

He wonders if maybe every man jacks off, every man in the world. Maybe, he thinks. He's pretty sure they do. Like, even if you were married, sometimes she'd be out, or she'd be mad, or on the rag, or something, and you'd just have to.

Fred wonders if his pop jacks off.

Man he is B. O. R. —

Cool it.

Fred gets up, wanders outside the booth. He goes and leans on the pump. He looks both ways, up and down the road. Nothing. He folds his arms and shuts his eyes against the sun.

Fred would rather be somewhere else than here not pumping gas. He would rather be *pumping* gas than not pumping gas. He would rather be taking speed and going downtown. He took some speed yesterday, and went downtown with Frankie and Sue. Drank some beers, played some pool, laughed a lot. He is feeling kind of spaced today. It must be the speed draining something from his system. That can make you feel like this.

Like shit, basically.

But Fred never knew it could give you hallucinations before.

And what just drove up to the pump has to be an hallucination.

Women like that don't exist outside of stroke magazines.

She is older than him, but not too much older. She's white, with short blonde hair that's brown at the roots. It looks like her hair's jumping off her head. She has a face like the Virgin Mary and a T-shirt with nothing on under it. Her breasts bounce and lift as she pulls on the parking brake. She turns her face to him, looks over the top of her shades, a long, approving look, and a smile that reaches all the way down into his shorts and fondles what it finds there.

It's when she gets out of the foxy little Toyota that she really makes him break into a sweat.

She is wearing a little black flared skirt like an ice-skater, only it's all torn around the waist. As she swings her long, neat brown legs out of the car the skirt rides up under her and Fred sees those are stockings, not pantyhose. He glimpses the strap of a garterbelt. He glimpses her panties, which are red, bright attention-getting red, like just in case you somehow failed to notice them.

The smile doesn't stop, or change, when the blonde sees him staring. But she straightens her skirt as she gets to her feet, and then she straightens her shades.

She sways as she walks, just the right amount in all the right places. She comes up to Fred and puts her hand on his arm, very, very lightly. She puts her head slightly to one side.

'You want to fill my tank?' she asks.

Her mouth is very beautiful when it moves, when it smiles, when she speaks. She has that perfect, untouchable health and beauty that spell CALIFORNIA the way those big white letters spell HOLLYWOOD.

And her incredible tits are almost touching his chest.

She's holding them there, deliberately. standing there and dangling those beautiful pumpkins for him to admire. Fred wouldn't mind if she touched him with them. With either one of them.

'Sure do, ma'am,' he says.

His voice comes out much higher and more shaky than usual. He's glad none of the guys are around to hear it and laugh at him. He's glad none of the guys are around period.

He turns and unhooks the hose from beside his elbow, but he doesn't move his feet.

The goddess brings her face closer to his. He winces, she doesn't smell of honey and peaches, the way she should. For some reason she smells of industrial-strength cleaning fluid.

It doesn't matter. It doesn't piss him off at all. All he can smell is gasolene anyway, mostly.

'Do you have — a bathroom?' she asks delicately, in a soft and flattering voice that makes it sound as if she's expecting too much, and that she will be forever indebted to Fred if he will only say they do.

'Yes, ma'am, right around the side,' he says. He points, awkwardly, getting his arm tangled in the hose. He's still leaning back against the pump, he must look pretty strange, he thinks desperately.

'Oh *thank* you,' says the vision, and away she sails across the cracked asphalt.

'Right around there,' Fred calls after her.

Still walking, she turns and looks at him, and makes a kind of move with her shoulder.

Fred goes hot and cold.

She's moving on, not pausing to see if he's seen.

She wants him. That was a sign she gave him. She gave him a come-on sign.

Fred jerks his eyes away from her succulent ass. His heart is beating like a speed rush.

Hot *damn*! he thinks, explosively.

He jams the nozzle in the gas tank of the Toyota, but he doesn't start the pump. He looks back over his shoulder again. She's found the door and gone in. Fred rearranges his shorts so his hard-on isn't hurting, and duck-walks fast and quiet over to the door.

She's not standing in the doorway, and he listens for a while.

Nothing.

Maybe she's waiting for him in there.

A guy she only just met and hardly looked at one second.

Maybe she's a robber. Maybe she's crazy, like she's waiting in there for him with a knife.

Or more like he made a mistake and if he goes in there she'll slap his face and call the cops and everyone and embarrass him in front of everyone.

Fred comes to a swift decision.

There's this one place where you can stand and look through a crack in to the ladies' room, if you move the rusty 7-Up sign that's propped

50

against the wall.

Fred moves it. He makes no sound, picking it up and putting it down again. He knows how heavy it is. He hunkers down and sets his eye to the crack.

He can't see her.

Then he hears her footsteps inside and he straightens up real fast and turns to face her as she steps out the door.

'There's a leak in your bathroom,' she says, in that breathless, heart-stopping voice. She makes it sound like the dam's out.

Fred licks his lips. He has the sun in his eyes, he can't see her face too well.

'You want me to come in and fix it?' he asks.

'Oh, I think you should,' she says.

And she turns and goes back in.

He follows her.

Inside the washroom she's standing against the wall, her fingers spread on the wall beside her. She has one knee raised a little, so he could maybe see up her skirt again if he ducked his head. The washroom is kind of small.

He looks around.

'Where's the leak, lady?' he asks.

She takes one step forward and seizes his hand.

'Here,' she says, and pressed his hand to her crotch.

Fred just has enough time to confirm with his fingers what all his other senses are telling him, that she's hot and wet as a Louisiana gumbo, when she snatches his hand out of there and holds it away from her.

'I don't have any money to pay for the gas,' she tells him.

Fred smiles. He slowly reaches up one hand and when she doesn't stop him, strokes her shining hair with the back of his hand. His palms are pretty oily. He says, 'That's okay, lady.'

He presses her neck gently with the back of his hand. Her lips are parted, reaching for his.

He kisses her.

' 'Cause I didn't put any gas in the tank,' he says.

She puts her hands in between them, pressing on his chest, but he's not letting her go.

'Afterwards,' she says, less seductively.

'That's right, señora,' he says. 'Afterwards,' he repeats, and kisses

51

her again softly, but lingeringly. 'Afterwards I put gas in the tank.'

She snatches off her shades and glares at him. 'Now, goddammit.'

Fred lets go of her. He stands there looking her over, smiling placidly. He puts his hands on his hips, backing away just far enough so he's almost still touching her breasts but not quite. Then he says, 'Okay.'

And he goes out.

Cadence leans against the wall. Why did men always have to screw you about before they screwed you?

Thinking that, she thinks she'd better go and make sure he is really putting gas in.

Fred sees the amazing, beautiful, scantily clad blonde woman come out of the washroom and stand watching him suspiciously.

She can see the numbers going round. When the tank is full he releases the trigger, takes out the nozzle, tilting it to catch the drips, and hangs it back in place on the pump. He puts the cap back on the gastank.

He turns and comes towards her.

Cadence hesitates, turns, goes back into the washroom. She catches sight of the wall where she was leaning. It is not very clean.

The guy comes back and presses her against it. He puts his knee between her thighs.

She pushes his shoulders. 'Wait a minute,' she says.

'No,' he says.

'Goddammit,' she says, offended, and she wriggles between him and the dirty wall. 'Don't you have a couch or somewhere?'

'No,' says Fred again. He puts his oily hand on her tee. Her breast feels warm and firm, and perky as a rabbit. It moves under his hand, smudging oil across her shirt and making him hard again.

'Wait,' Cadence says, dodging his mouth. 'Wait! In the car. We can go in the car.'

'You can't,' he says.

'Why not?'

'Because I have your keys, baby.'

Cadence gives a big sigh of exasperation and pulls away from him, presses herself against the wall. Then, for the second time that day she lifts the tiny little maid's dress and she tilts her pelvis at him.

'Come on, then. Come on!'

Fred laughs and reaches for her bright red panties. Her hand is with

52

his, tearing them down. Man, she is so hot and sticky she smells like a fish-fry.

Fred likes fish-fries.

He rubs her crotch with the heel of his hand. Cadence gasps at the shock, moans at the pressure. Fred kisses her, pressing her against the wall with his body and his hand, leaning the other hand up by her head. Cadence returns his kiss, energetically. She bumps her pelvis against his hand. The hair is soft and sticky under his palm, her secretions mingling with the oil on his fingers.

Her hand finds the outline of his prick inside his bluejeans. She traces it with the tips of her fingers, up and down, round and round, making it kick up against his fly, straining for release.

Fred goes to unzip his fly, but Cadence is there before him, tugging the zipper down with difficulty along the length of the swelling obstruction.

Fred pulls up her tee, exposing her breasts for the first time. No bikini marks, he notices. And not an ounce of fat on her, except in the places where God in his infinite wisdom ordained that women should have a little fat.

Fred lowers his mouth and chews on her nipple, first with his lips, then when she breathes hard, clasping his back, running her spread hands up inside his T-shirt, biting it lightly and repeatedly. The nipple feels thick and firm in his mouth. He spreads his hand across her breast, squeezing and stroking, while he sucks on her nipple. Then the other. Then the first one again.

Cadence has his prick out of his pants now, and she's running the palms of both hands up its underside, making it kick and kick. It's a large and painful erection, it came up too swift and sudden to lubricate properly, so it's still dry. She kicks off her panties, lifts her leg and wraps it around his back, resting it on his opposite hip. She pulls the head of his prick into her crotch, frigging herself with it. She's muttering, gasping, rolling her eyes up in her head. He's kissing her mouth, swinging his hips back and forth and back and forth, getting some action out of her self-gratification. Between them they are smearing her juice across her belly. And Fred is getting wet too.

He can't believe this is happening.

Cadence's skirt is getting pushed right up in front until it's like a strip of cloth, a sash, maybe, around her perfect waist. Fred puts his arm round her, bearing down on her, kneading her breast, searching for the root of her tongue with his own.

She growls in her throat like a cat.

Man she is a hot one.

Fred cannot believe this luck. God must be pleased with him.

Maybe she's one of those nympho-whatsits the guys talk about.
Maybe she travels the highways hunting for good-looking young men
to hump.

He slips his cock between her legs, so it's pressing upwards into her
crotch. 'Mmm,' she says approvingly, and slides back and forwards
along it, sashaying her hips from side to side. Fred says, 'A-aa-a-a-aah.'

'You like that?' asks Cadence softly.

He kisses her ear. She has oil from his hands on her tits and her T-
shirt. He cups her butt in his hands, squeezes her.

Cadence has a sudden vision of him spanking her, putting her right
across his knee, right there in the gas station washroom and spanking
her, the way Louie was fixing to. She didn't want Louie to do that, no
way. But this guy, she wouldn't mind, if that's what he wanted.

Fred senses her hesitation, something going through her mind.
'Whassappenimg?' he asks, his voice thick and slurred as he mouths
her tit.

'Nothing,' she says quickly. 'It's nothing.'

Boy. She is having some weird thoughts lately.

Fred lets her tit go and kisses her mouth. 'You want something to
happen?' he says, in an evil, horror-movie voice.

Cadence freezes, looks at him. 'What?' she asks, tightly.

'This,' says Fred, and slips it to her.

'Oh, oh, o-o-o-*oohh* . . .'

Her voice goes up at the end and breaks off in a little gasp that gets
him hornier and harder than ever. He clutches her ass and thrusts slow
and relentless up inside her. This is the stroke Fred always thinks of
as exploring the territory. How tight is she, how loose? How far can
he drive himself into her?

That far, huh?

He comes back and tries again.

Cadence bucks and pushes off the wall, engulfing his prick again
and again. Each time it slides smoother, each time she works on it with
her hips so that it's continually jostling her, nudging her, reminding
her of what a good thing this is to do. Every time Cadence screws, and
Cadence, basically, screws quite a lot, a lot more than some people,

it always seems to her like it's been ages, months, *forever*, since she last screwed and god, she's wondering why she ever stopped. To have a cock inside her is so nice. She humps the cock, drawing him up until he's falling over backwards from the hips, grinding her ass against the greasy gas station bathroom wall, shoving at her like a rodeo rider trying to keep his seat on a steer.

Mmmm. Cock. It's good.

And women are nice too.

Josephine, thinks Cadence suddenly. The picture.

'Do you —' she says, as they hump and thump, '— have — a — camera —?'

Fred is perplexed. What's she talking about? Is she collecting pictures of her humping, is that her kink? No, she'd have her own camera.

'Uh-uh,' he says.

'That's too bad,' says Cadence.

Fred starts wondering if her mind is really on this. Plus, it's hard trying to do it against a wall. He nuzzles her neck, her cheek, her ear. 'Let's get down on the floor,' he pants.

Cadence thinks the floor must be dirtier than the wall. 'Oh, I don't know —'

'C'mon,' and he lowers himself down to the linoleum, pulling her hand. 'It'll be fine.' He lies on his back, she sits on him, he says, 'Oh, *oh*!', loud but hoarse too. Cadence is sitting on him with her knees up, bouncing juicily up and down. He holds his head up from the floor, watching their joined crotches. Cadence's is framed by the crazy little skirt and the straps of the garterbelt straining at her black stocking-tops. Fred has never made love to a woman wearing black stockings before. Suddenly that's the sexiest thing he can think of. Just looking at that makes him want to come straight away.

Cadence senses this sudden surge in him. She's not in any great hurry, really, but this is a fuck with an ulterior motive, a fuck in trade, and it *is* on the bathroom floor of a New Mexico gas station, yuk, how sleazy can you *get*, Cadence Szathkowicz? And though the guy is fine, young and willing with kind of dark Spanish sulky good looks, he's not anyone she wants to spend the rest of her life with. He's not Josephine.

Cadence thinks of Josephine. She thinks of Josephine undressing in the shadowed light of her bedroom at the Concord Reef. She thinks of her warm, smooth, naked body and a jolt of liquid fire surges up

55

her spine. She's calling out and moaning, and pumping at the pump attendant's groin like an athlete, and he's shouting, 'Oh! Oh, Jesus, Maria, Jesus, Christ,' over and over again.

Cadence doesn't see what they have to do with it, so she stops.

Starts to stand up.

Holds the very tip of his cock just inside her.

Hovers over him, poised.

Pivots around on his cock in a circle one way, then the other.

Fred's eyes are popping out of his head.

Cadence Szathkowicz sits down, suddenly, hard.

Fred arcs up off the floor like an electrocuted alligator.

Faintly, distantly, deep within her, Cadence feels him pounding semen.

Her own orgasm has dissipated, broken up and wandered away. Josephine came in and took it, she thinks, abstractedly.

She leans over her man.

'The keys,' she says.

Fred has stopped thrashing, is lying there like a beached porpoise. He's panting, moaning every time he exhales. His mouth is hanging open. She can count his cavities.

Cadence withdraws him. She squats above him. His seed drools out of her on to his belly.

'Keys,' she says.

Fred's having trouble responding. Some kind of pre-emptive strike just took out his entire nervous system. He's stunned, like someone just goosed him with a cattle prod. Now he knows how quadriplegics feel. Jesus, maybe he'll never recover. Maybe she's damaged him for life. He tries to feel his own hand, tries to get it to grope towards his hip pocket.

Cadence grabs his hand, wriggles her own hand under him. Can feel the keys but can't get in the pocket. Rolls him over briskly on the floor.

'Come on, cowboy, I'm history,' she says.

She thrusts her hand in his pocket harder than he thrust his cock in her cunt. She grabs the keys, hauls them out with no consideration for this sensitive region of his person. Grabs a handful of paper towels from the dispenser and wipes her crotch, front to back, three times, firmly.

Fred is getting up, getting up onto one knee, groping for a handhold

56

to rise. He reaches for Cadence's hand.

Cadence shakes her head. 'You wanted to get down there,' she says. She's not sympathetic. She's found her discarded panties and is pulling them on, straightening her stockings, trying to pull her skirt far enough down to look like it's a skirt again, not a belt.

She throws up the keys and catches them. 'Have a nice day now,' she says. And she walks back out to her car.

Fred rises at last, swaying, tugs ineffectively at his pants. He finds he's all wet, swabs himself clumsily with paper towels, give up and drops them on the floor. Man, that took the top of his head off. That was so sudden and so powerful he lost track of it. Lost track of everything there, all systems red. He doesn't even know if he enjoyed it yet.

Man!

He hears her car start, screech out of the forecourt and burn away, up towards I-40. Whoever the hell she is, she drives as dangerously as she humps.

Fred goes outside, into the blasting hot sun. He still feels weak, he has to lean on the wall by the 7-Up sign.

He feels like she just mopped the bathroom floor with him.

Cadence didn't mean to be so rude, up and leaving him on the floor that way. For one thing, she was going to ask if she could use the phone. But with guys like him, it was always best to get out as soon as you could get ahead. How could she have known he'd fall apart so soon? Some guys, well, they were like that. Lot of mouth, not a lot of follow-through. Cadence blamed their parents.

Cadence, notice, takes no credit for her powers, which are remarkable, really. She doesn't consider that she completely blindsided Fred Campodoro riding in like that, and with the black stockings and all; not to mention her uncanny sense of technique. This is one of her major attractions: her innocence, you have to call it that, for all that she is thoroughly, unquestionably depraved and corrupt. These things happen to her all the time, how is she to know they don't happen to everybody that way?

Anyway, Cadence pulls in at a Jack in the Box, steals a tip, calls Scott and Kelly one more time, and what do you know, Kelly is actually there, she actually gets to speak to Kelly in person. She hits on them for her back pay, and they hadn't been planning to rip her off at all, they're just too laid back to have got it together yet. At least, that's what Kelly pretends. And maybe it's true, because they come through, when Cadence tells Kelly the crazy things that have been happening, about her dad and the stag night and all. Kelly and Scott have problem parents too.

Kelly says they got Cadence's message, but it's a lot of hassle for them to print a frame out of a tape. Cadence will have to find somebody with a camera. They send her some funds to Albuquerque, where she picks it up easy enough. Not a whole lot of funds. Not as much as Cadence was hoping. Not the whole cheque for the last movie, let alone before that. But funds. She can eat. And sleep. She heads for the border thinking that there is a God, she always knew there was, and He always comes through for her in the end, even though God is kind of laid back too. Cadence scored before she left Albuquerque, and she's feeling pretty mellow. Cadence looks at herself in the mirror. 'I am a message on God's ansaphone,' she says aloud.

She has to come off Route 66 at Santa Rosa. There is only one place to go in a desperate situation like this. She has been going there all along, even before she knew it. Unconsciously, her destiny was leading her to her, right, to her *destination*, wow, amazing. It's fated, it's in her genes. Or maybe she decided already and forgot.

She can pay for gas now, too, but there's nothing much but country music on the radio, and the grass gets her horny, so she tries her gas station trick again at some nowhere place on the Fort Sumner turnpike. Fat black guy in bib overalls. On his bib a tag says, Hi! My name is LONSDALE. Beautiful face like an old-time movie star.

Lonsdale takes some time getting in the door of the ladies' room. Seems a little slow, like he's having trouble understanding what the woman showing him her day-glo orange panties has in mind. Suddenly he blinks, looks shocked, then very, very dignified. 'Lady,' says Lonsdale, injured, 'I'm a faggot.'

'Well, that's okay,' says Cadence. 'I don't mind. I'm kind of both ways too.'

But Lonsdale says no, she has to pay for the gas, it's not his gas. If it was his gas, he'd give it to her gladly because she's a very pretty woman and he's flattered she should ask, but he doesn't have the authority to give away the company's gas. His job isn't that secure that he can take a risk like that, not even for a pretty lady like her. He keeps on like this until Cadence wishes she'd never tried. It would have been quicker to blow him. 'Can I use your phone?' she says, interrupting. 'Don't worry, I have change.'

There's no answer from the bar, they must be busy. So Cadence turns up there, two days later, unannounced.

The place is closed, she rings the bell. A woman twenty-eight-going-on-forty-five comes to the door, mouths through the glass, 'We're closed, sugar.'

Cadence bangs with the flat of her hand. 'It's me! Let me in!'

Woman frowns. She's wearing a black leather miniskirt and fishnets, trainers with the laces undone. Her legs are meaty, the way they like them out here, and her breasts too, under her oversize football sweater. 'Cadence?' she says. 'My Lord, honey, what are you *doing* here?'

'Hi mom,' says Cadence.

Crystal's Bar is empty, blinds drawn. Mother and daughter hug, awkwardly, then really. Cadence's mom smells strongly of bourbon. They sit at high stools at the bar, Cadence's mom pours a sizeable Jim Beam, refreshes her own.

'Let me tell you something, lover,' she says, 'I just knew you were coming. I had a dream about you.'

'Amazing, momma!'

'It's mental telepathy, sweetheart,' she says, hugging her again.

This is the woman who called Cadence Cadence. Her own name is Christine, though she called herself Starchild back then. Later at a sacred ceremony involving fifteen peyote buttons and a bottle of rye, she compromised on Crystal.

Cadence starts out to tell her how she comes to be there. She doesn't tell her about the Bluewater Lodge, or about Josephine or anything. She tells her about the movies, and the message from Daddy, how she knew she had to leave. 'And momma, I asked the I Ching.'

'Well, you did right, honey. I don't doubt it for a moment. I remember your father. Jesus, that asshole.' Cadence's ma lights another Pall Mall, looks sideways at her. 'Cock on him a mile long, did you know that?'

'Uh-huh.' Cadence devours another handful of olives.

Crystal looks worried. 'You *did*?'

'Mother, you told me. You told me a million times.'

'Well, it was remarkable,' says Crystal, asserting her right to speak with authority about a former lover's genitals. 'Is remarkable, I guess. I mean, even *I*'ve never seen one —'

'For Christ's sake, mom, will you shut up?'

Cadence's momma looks melancholy. 'You kids these days are so uptight. When I was your age we used to talk about that kind of thing. *We* used to too, you and me.'

Cadence sucks her teeth. 'Yeah, sure, mom, I mean, talk about all the cocks you want to. Just not his, okay? I mean, he happens to be my father, you know?'

'Sure.' Crystal knocks back Jim Beam. 'So what?'

'So what? So *what*?'

Cadence thinks about it. 'You're right,' she says. Crystal laughs, a terrible rusty wheezy laugh, but Cadence drinks and feels terribly sad. What a sad thing, to renounce your daddy, she thinks. Even if he is a total asshole. Even if he's revoked your own goddamn plastic and kicked you out of the house like your mother before you, or as good as. Maybe she should forgive him, like if it was a movie. Maybe they should be reconciled.

Christ, no. That bastard.

Just at this instant Cadence can't recall any specific harm her father ever did her. As a matter of fact she can't recall just at this instant, what he looks like.

Bastard.

But the spasm of hatred has already waned. It's boring, hating people. It's really fatiguing and anyway it's bad for you, it makes all kinds of poisons in your system. Bad karma. You shouldn't hate people, you should be cool and just give them space. Like, he could have all of Southern California. Om nama shivaya.

Cadence finishes her Jim Beam, takes some more. She finishes the olives. She says: 'What happened to that guy you had in Chicago?'

Her ma raises her eyebrows: 'Honey, *which* guy?'

'You know, that black guy, worked at the fast food place? Burgers, fried chicken, something like that? Mexican, maybe?'

'I don't know who you're talking about,' Crystal says dismissively, and turns on her stool to greet a couple of the other girls who've just arrived.

'Well, time to go to work,' she says, and downs the rest of her drink.

Then she takes off her football shirt.

Under it she's wearing a big nylon bra, laundromat-grey.

She takes that off too, balls it up with the shirt and chucks them behind the bar.

Her breasts are full, falling but firm. She looks younger with her shirt off. Cadence notices her underarms are shaved, which they never were before she bought this place.

The other girls are introduced. They smile, say hi, start stripping too. Cadence feels a little lonely. She says to her ma, 'You want some help?'

'Well, sure, honey. Whatever's right. Just don't let them hit on you is all.'

Cadence feels better with her T-shirt off, in a borrowed black leather skirt and hose. Also she needs the money, but the work is really no fun. Waiting tables kills your back and legs, and when things get busy later she finds she really doesn't have the memory; she has to keep apologising to these guys whose eyes waltz continually from her tits to her face and back again.

Two of the guys keep asking her questions, keep her hanging around their table. When her mother passes by, they call her over too.

'Sweetheart,' says this one guy, with a foxy grin, 'This beautiful young lady here has just been telling us she's your daughter. Now that can't be true, can it? She has to be lyin', don't she? Me and Al here, we have ourselves a bet. I say she's lyin'. I say you should take this lyin' child out and paddle her ass.'

Crystal lowers her false eyelashes (another innovation). 'No,' she says, 'she's my daughter.'

Across the table, Al laughs, coughs, spits. His pal turns to him. 'I say she's lyin' too,' he claims. 'I say they both ought to have their asses paddled. Maybe they should paddle each other!'

Waving his hand, Al speaks to Crystal in a deep voice, not even looking at Cadence now. 'You'll please excuse my friend Eugene, ma'am, he's had a couple of drinks. Ma'am, I have to say, looking at you, excuse me, it's goddamned incredible you could be this child's mother. Tell us poor wrinkled old fools: what's your secret?'

Cadence's ma looks at him. 'Silicone,' she says.

Mother and daughter walk away from the table.

The good people of Turkey Flat are most unhappy Crystal's bar is within spitting distance of their fine town. They would like to see it shut down. The trouble is, nobody can quite fix on whose responsibility that is. Every few months the *Turkey Call*'s editor calls upon the police chief to do it, and the police chief looks at the judge, while the judge quotes statutes and points to the mayor. Some of Crystal's best and

61

most regular clients sit firmly on their fat behinds, passing the buck around.

Meanwhile, the women are organized against them too. There's the Episcopalians, who don't signify, and the Sisterhood of the Glorious Spirit, but only those whose husbands can't keep them in line. Then there are the feminists. Crystal doesn't mind them. Feminists are right, she knows that, about men. They're right about power and politics and all that stuff. It's just they're so uptight.

Crystal never could see the need to stop people having a good time. Besides, she likes to think her bar is a kind of women's refuge. When she says so, the feminists grind their teeth and say she's a part of the problem; but she knows she's part of the solution. Dig. The sisters are safer here than they would be anywhere. This is the one place men can't touch them. And they are sisters, too, kind of. Don't they borrow each other's clothes and yell at each other all the time?

Well, thank Goddess, it's surely a refuge for her daughter, thinks Crystal to herself.

Then she goes in the stockroom and finds Cadence there, being groped by a customer.

Cadence gulps when she sees her mom. She pats the joe's hands away, turns to face her mom, looking ashamed of herself.

'Honey,' says Crystal wearily, 'what did I tell you?'

'I know ma,' pleads Cadence, 'he's doing something special for me.'

'Looks to me like something pretty ordinary.'

The joe is from out of town. He already has his pants down. He gets aggressive, shakes his fist. 'What is this?' he demands of Crystal. 'Get out of here!'

Cadence elbows him, not looking at him. 'You just shut up, okay?' she says. 'This is my mom.'

His mouth drops open. He looks from one to the other. He curses blackly and pushes past Crystal. He scuttles away, pulling up his pants as he hops down the corridor.

'Mom!' wails Cadence. 'He was going to take a picture of me! Come back!' she shouts.

Crystal is confused. 'What picture?'

'Oh, nothing,' says Cadence, straightening her skirt. It's too complicated to explain. Without thinking she pops a can of beer and drinks deep. 'Ma? Can I ask you something?'

'What, sugar?'

'What those guys were saying in the bar — did you ever spank me, when I was a kid?'

Crystal strokes her daughter's cheek. 'No, lover!'

'Daddy never spanked me, did he?'

'Daddy? Daddy was never home. No, baby, we loved and cherished you.' Her voice goes soft, ragged with nostalgia and too much smoke. 'We wouldn't ever have hurt you, you know that. 'Sides, you weren't home a lot either.'

'You ever let a man spank you?'

Crystal purses her lips. 'What have you been doing, honey?'

'Oh, nothing,' says Cadence again. 'I was only wondering.'

Then she laughs.

'What, hon?'

'I was just thinking what you told those two.' They both laugh. 'Silicone!' says Cadence.

Few are the men who can resist Cadence Szathkowicz when she propositions them. When he sees Crystal go back through the swing door towards the bar, the photographer sneaks back into the stockroom. A couple of days later Cadence drives down to the post office with a letter addressed to a P.O. box in another state. Inside it is a 5×8 picture of herself, naked, sitting on a pile of shrinkwrapped sixpacks like a model in a cheesy calendar. It's not a picture she likes at all, but she smiles to herself as she drops it in the mail.

Cadence has a plan.

|6|

They say you meet all kinds if you wash windows, deliver pizzas, have any kind of job where you have to go visit people in their homes. Door-to-door salesmen. People used to make jokes about the Fuller Brush Man, the Fuller Brush Man always used to get the pick of it: crazy widows, bored young housewives. There were even these little cartoons you could buy, or trade in the schoolyard anyhow, little comicbooks, the Fuller Brush Man on the job. Every time he rang a doorbell there was another horny lady ready to check out what the Fuller Brush Man had in his box for her today.

Ted Tagar will tell you he meets all kinds just sitting on his butt behind the post office counter.

Ted Tagar is pushing fifty. He's got bad ankles, a big belly he keeps lovingly stuffed with T-bones and prime ribs and Whoppers with extra fries. He's got a wife that spends all her time over at the meeting house and a no-good son he only sees when the cops bring him home at four a.m. in the morning. He's got a mother and a mother-in-law that have got their own husbands totally browbeat and hogtied, now they're working on him, this one from this side, that one from that side, like Attila the Hun and Genghis Khan every Sunday, weekdays too. Ted Tagar can use a little entertainment. He sits behind his counter and watches the dizzy redhead come tripping into the post office on her stack shoes, watches her tits move and her ass keep time. Ted doesn't move. Only his eyes move. Though maybe if you watched very close you'd see the corners of his mouth move just a little this time. This is the third time the dizzy redhead has come around today, and it's only ten-fifteen a.m. in the morning.

She's a redhead like out of a bottle; but Ted doesn't have anything against bottles. Some of the best things Ted knows come out of bottles. She's got freckles to match her red head, they go all the way down

64

between her tits to her tummy. This Ted can see because the redhead is wearing a tee that's low at the top and high at the bottom, and the way she walks on those stack shoes, she's giving everybody an eyeful of that pair of beauties.

She's got an ass on her too, boy has she, and the way she keeps it covered you'd think there was fabric rationing. Those shorts aren't so much running shorts as flying away out of there altogether. The elastic on them sits snug round her little brown belly that's so neat it looks like you could get one hand around her (and Ted would be very happy to try). What hangs down from the elastic is so scooped and tailored and trimmed it would scarce make a grown man a handkerchief. The way those itty-bitty cutaways cut away you can tell she's not wearing any too much under 'em neither.

The first time she came jouncing and bouncing into the post office Ted Tagar couldn't believe his eyes. The second time he couldn't believe his luck. The third time he couldn't remember when he'd had more to feast his eyes on without paying for it.

Ted Tagar sits motionless as a frog on a log with his fingers laced together on the counter. That dizzy redhead swivels so much he doesn't have to move to see every side of the question as she comes up to the counter, up to *his* position this time, smiling like your long-lost sweetheart and fluttering those phoney eyelashes.

She leans on the counter. Leans. On the counter. His counter. If she leaned any further he'd be able to check out her appendix scar. Ted thinks maybe they turned off the air conditioning in here and nobody told him.

Her voice is deeper than you'd think, husky like some country singer that smokes too many Marlboros, but with plenty of honey and cinnamon and maple walnut ice cream in there too. Two scoops of maple walnut ice cream. Big sc —

'Thirty-cent stamp, please,' she says.

It's the most erotic request Ted Tagar has heard since Mae West. So it was last time, and the time before. It's even more erotic now she's requesting it of him.

'You sending a postcard, lady?' says Ted Tagar, slowly searching through the stamp sheets for the thirty cents, which are right on top, but better check the whole pile for her, just to make sure.

'Oh — yes,' she admits, winsomely. Ted Tagar didn't know he knew the word 'winsome', didn't even know what it meant, but that's the way she says it all right. She says it like he's the world number one class A genius for knowing where she's going to stick her thirty-cent stamp, even though it's her third thirty-cent stamp in thirty minutes.

'You sure send a lot of postcards,' says Ted Tagar.

If there's one thing prettier than a dizzy redhead in a tiny tee leaning over your counter, it's a dizzy redhead in a tiny tee leaning over your counter and blushing.

'I do, don't I?' she says.

She gives him a dollar.

Now usually Ted Tagar would be a mite ticked off at that, because last time the dizzy redhead came in she gave Gladys Johnson a dollar for her thirty-cent stamp, and the time before she gave Mike Wesselman one, so she must have a whole stack of change rolling around in her little purse there. She could give him the exact thirty cents if she wanted. Some customers are just plain born awkward.

The awkwardness of this one customer Ted doesn't mind at all.

He takes hold of her dollar and slides it gently and slowly out of her magical brown fingers, and he works out the change on his little calculator there on the counter, holding it up in front of him because it's easier that way, easier to keep looking at those freckles over and around the calculator display that is. Then he gets seventy cents out of his change rack and he checks it, holding it up in front of him, seventy cents, he takes her hand and counts it out into her warm, soft palm, coin by coin, and in his mind he starts to say goodbye to her, because their beautiful relationship is now surely over, and he's thanking the Good Lord for all the wonderful things they've shared together.

The dizzy redhead clears her throat.

With anatomy like hers, this is an operation you can actually watch.

She leans even lower over the counter.

'Uh — I have a problem,' she confides.

Ted Tagar looks into her eyes, which are green, and as beautiful as the summer his wife went off to prayer camp and took her mother with her.

'I'm sorry to hear that,' he lies.

The redhead is digging around in her purse, pulling out a little scrap of paper with something written on it.

'You see, my, ah, uncle lives right around here some place and I'm so stupid —' She gives a little giggle, which is like the throat-clearing but with music. 'I lost the address,' she confesses.

'Right around here, you say?' says Ted Tagar, the gallant knight, and he reaches for the big yellow street directory. 'Well, lady, here's the deal. You just tell me your uncle's name, and I'll tell you where he lives.' He smiles at her. 'And we won't even charge for the service.'

'I forgot,' she says.

'You forgot your uncle's name?'

The dizzy redhead looks so dizzy her eyes almost cross. She shrugs, which again is something that's quite all right by Ted Tagar.

'We're not real close.'

Ted Tagar thinks about it. 'Lady,' he says, 'if you don't know his name *or* his address —'

'I got his P.O. box,' she says quickly.

She shows him the piece of paper.

'P.O. Box 3616, that's right here, right?'

'Well, that's right, lady,' says Ted Tagar slowly, wondering what the hell kind of scam she's into anyway. He clears *his* throat now, and nods over her shoulder. 'It's one of them boxes right over there.'

'Oh!'

The dizzy redhead turns and looks happily at the wall of shiny metal doors with numbers on, just as if she'd never noticed it before, as if she hadn't been hanging around staring at it and at the people coming in and opening the shiny metal doors and taking their mail out, and looking all the time at her little piece of paper, the first time she came in, before she even bought her first thirty-cent stamp.

She turns back to him. 'Well then,' she says triumphantly, 'I guess if you check in your file you can tell me my cousin's name *and* his address!'

'I thought he was your uncle,' says Ted Tagar.

The redhead furrows her pretty brow. 'What did I say?'

'You said cousin.'

'Oh. Well, my cousin lives there too. He's my uncle's son, you know,' she says, seriously.

'And what's his name?' Ted Tagar asks.

'I forget. Isn't that the craziest thing, I forget both their names! I'm so stupid, I guess! So can you just look then up for me anyways, please, huh, hm, can you do that? I'd certainly *appreciate* it . . .'

Regretfully, Ted Tagar shakes his heavy head: 'I'm sorry, lady,' he says, 'but that's against the federal law. I can't do that.'

She looks as dismayed as if he'd told her her uncle and her cousin had both just been killed in a freeway smash. 'You *can't*?'

'I can't do that,' repeats Ted Tagar. Really, he's thinking about all the things he *could* do for her, and all the things he'd *like* to do for her; but he wants to keep his job, and besides it's broad daylight. 'Tell you what you can do,' he says. 'You can write a note to your uncle and your cousin both, and tell them you're in town, and you can slip it right in that Box 3616 with your own fair hand.'

'I can?' she says, unhappily.

Ted Tagar nods judiciously. 'You can,' he says. 'The U.S. Mail will even make you the loan of a pencil and a piece of paper to do it.'

The redhead looks really miserable and pissed at this kind offer. She hangs her head, which isn't nearly as attractive as shrugging or giggling or clearing her throat. And because he's a kind and considerate man, and he hates to see a lady looking so unhappy, and especially because when the dizzy redhead hangs her head all that red, red hair gets in the way of him looking down her tee-shirt, Ted Tagar says, 'Or if you don't want to do that, what you could do is ask that kid who's just opened Box 3616 and collected all the mail from out of it.'

She jerks her head up as fast as if the next person in line had just taken a grab of her shorts. She stares at Ted Tagar with her startled big green eyes; then she swings around and stares at the kid in the Bon Jovi shirt and torn jeans who's slamming the door of Box 3616 and walking out of the door of the post office, stuffing a couple of brightly coloured flyers in his hip pocket.

Without a word of thanks or farewell in honour of their beautiful relationship, the redhead grabs her purse and heads out of there faster than a turkey come Thanksgiving.

A turkey with stack shoes on. Ted Tagar watches her beautiful tail every inch of the way. He laces his fingers in front of him on the counter.

'You oughta be ashamed of yourself, Ted Tagar,' says Gladys Johnson.

As she hobbles out of the post office on her stack shoes, Cadence Szathkowicz is pleased with herself. It was a smart move coming here. Guys who ask you for a naked picture and don't even tell you their own name are guys you can't trust, not at all. Even if he does know

Josephine. Maybe he doesn't even know where she is and he only said that to get the picture. Or maybe he's a blackmailer or something, a kidnapper with Josephine locked up in his basement. This way she can check him out without him knowing. She can follow the little kid who picked up the letters.

Glory, maybe the little kid *is* the guy who phoned her! Nah, he's too young.

The mall is not too busy. People move kind of slow and easy here anyways, not like in California. She hopes no one sees her following the kid, they might think she's a child abductor or something.

Then she sees she's not going to be able to follow the kid because the kid is getting on a bike.

Cadence doesn't have a car. She doesn't have any money. The money from working her momma's bar ran out, then the money her momma lent her. The next thing that ran out was the gasoline, miles from anywhere on I-35. She had to abandon the car and hitch, because her daddy cancelled her AAA card too, goddamn him. Seeing it was his car anyhow, she didn't wait around for the highway patrol to cruise by and see her at the side of the road. She hitched out of there faster than a fly off a firecracker. Cadence never did understand when guys at the college complained about how hard it was to hitchhike these days. *She* never has any trouble getting a ride.

She jams her shades onto her nose and calls and waves. 'Hey! Hey, kid!'

The kid stops, puts one foot to the ground, looks back. Looks her over. His face says, Me? Women like Cadence Szathkowicz don't customarily call after kids like him. Women like Cadence Szathkowicz don't even *exist*. Customarily.

She goes up the mall towards him. There's a park beyond the mall, with trees and bushes and paths every which way. If he takes it into his head to ride off she'll lose him in a second. She breaks into a run.

He watches her run. He is a little Ted Tagar in the making.

Cadence stops beside him, chest heaving from her run.

He watches it heave.

'You pick up Box 3616?' Cadence asks.

'Uh-huh.'

He's a real little kid, his voice not broken yet.

She smiles at him suggestively. 'Oh, I was wondering: who's it for?'

He stares at her boldly. 'Who wants to know?'

69

'I'm a U.S. Mail inspector,' says Cadence Szathkowicz.

He looks at her tiny tee, her tiny shorts. 'Bullshit,' he says levelly.

'Well, okay,' says Cadence, 'Really the guy who lives there is a friend of mine, see, and I'm in town and I want to surprise him.'

The kid is tough. 'What's his name?'

'Oh, I know his *name*,' says Cadence, stretching her arms up so her tits rise softly in her T-shirt.

'You just don't know where he lives,' says the kid stolidly.

'That's right,' agrees Cadence. 'That's my whole problem right there in a nutshell. Boy, you're a real smart kid, you know that?'

'Don't patronize me, lady,' says the kid. He turns up his nose and scuffs his sneaker toecap on the roadway. 'You're full of shit, you know that? I have to go,' he says witheringly.

'Wait. Wait! Look, it's real important, only I can't explain it to you, you just have to tell me the address, okay? I'll find it myself. Is the guy your dad or something? He'll be really pleased to see me, I promise you.'

'Yeah?'

'Yeah.'

The kid considers. He starts to ride his bike into the park, standing up on the pedals. Cadence jogs alongside. 'Old friend, right?' he says, not looking at her.

'Right,' she gasps.

'Then what's his name?'

'John,' says Cadence.

'John,' repeats the kid, disgusted at the feebleness of her invention. 'Bullshit.'

'No, wait, that's what we used to call him. Old John. Good old John. Maybe he has another name he didn't tell us. Or maybe I forgot. Show me the mail, I'll tell you if it's the right name?'

'Fuck off, lady,' says the kid.

Cadence is losing her temper. 'You know, you have a real bad mouth, you know that? Anyone ever tell you that?'

The kid stops the bike, suddenly. He sits up on the saddle, pulls his feet up, balancing. He scratches his ass. 'Lady,' he says wearily, 'what is your problem?'

'No problem,' says Cadence. It's hot in the park and she's sweating. She wants a soda but she's running out of money. Man, now she knows how private detectives feel, she wouldn't want to do that job. 'No problem,' she says, 'really.' She points at his T-shirt. 'Hey, you like Bon Jovi? I do too. That's my number one favourite band,' she says.

While she's speaking she suddenly reaches out and grabs the handlebars of the bike. She says, 'Just tell me the name and address and I'll let you go.'

The kid sticks his feet back on the pedals and pushes the bike forwards. Cadence loses hold and almost falls over. She clutches at the rear wheel as the bike rolls forwards and hurts her hand on the spinning tyre. She doesn't have a whole lot to bargain with here, she realises.

The kid seems to think differently, however. He stops a yard or two ahead.

'Show me your tits and I'll tell you,' he says.

'What?'

'You heard me.'

'Jesus Christ,' says Cadence.

She looks around. They can go aside under the trees, no one will see them there.

'How old are you anyway?' she says.

'Twelve.'

'Ten,' she says.

They stare at one another for a moment, expressionless like masked Mexican wrestlers. Cadence jerks her head. 'Over there,' she says.

They go into the shade of the trees. There are condoms and cigarette butts on the ground, but no one's around.

'Name and address first,' she says.

'After,' he says.

Cadence considers. 'Address first, name after,' she says. She'd like to know his name, but it doesn't matter.

'Uh-uh,' says the kid. He goes to pedal away.

'Okay, okay!' says Cadence. She gets hold of the hem of her tee. 'Name first, address after,' she says.

He looks at the sky through the trees.

He sniffs.

'Mr Domino,' he says.

Cadence drops hold of her shirt. 'Bullshit,' she says.

The kid grimaces, pulls out the junk mail he just collected. He lets her have a flash of the mailing label on a catalogue. It says 'Mr Domino, Box 3616.'

This makes Cadence more determined than ever. That weird little tattoo Josephine wears, she called that a domino. Something's going on here. She has to find out where the guy lives.

She whips up her T-shirt, gives the kid an eyeful, whips it down again.

He doesn't look impressed, particularly. How many pairs of tits has a ten-year old seen, anyhow? A lot, maybe, if he hangs out with this Mr Domino.

'Now your snatch,' says the kid.

Cadence mouth falls open. 'I just showed you my tits!'

'You wanna know where this guy lives or dontcha?'

Cadence sets her teeth. 'Address first,' she says again.

The kid thinks about it. 'Chestnut Park,' he says.

'*And* the house number.'

'They're condos.'

'The number!'

He sniffs again, looks at the crotch of her shorts.

'After,' says Cadence.

'Now,' says the kid.

Snarling, Cadence whips down her runnings shorts, whips them back up again.

The kid says only: 'I knew you weren't a real redhead.'

She grabs at him, but he dodges, he's up on the pedals and riding away.

'*Come here you little bastard!*'

She lunges for him, wobbles on her stacks, falls over sprawling in the cigarette butts and the dogshit. The kid on the bike is scooting off out of the park, laughing at her over his shoulder.

Chestnut Park is a condo development fifteen blocks down from the mall. Cadence counts them. They are long blocks, and the sidewalks hurt your feet, especially in these stupid shoes. Cadence is sweaty and tired, and she hates it. Drivers look at her curiously as they cruise by, some of them calling suggestions out of their windows. Cadence ignores them all. She staggers on.

When she reaches the door, the kid is long gone. She presses a button at random.

The entryphone buzzes, spits.

'Pizza for Mr Jackson,' she says.

The entryphone crackles. '*Whuh*?' it says.

Cadence holds her nose. 'Pizza for Mr Jetson,' she says.

The door buzzes and she goes in.

Cadence looks down the hallway and she's in luck, she can see the coloured papers sticking out from under one of the doors. She takes off her shoes and tiptoes along to check. It's the right stuff, Mr Domino, Box 3616. The kid must have shoved it under the door instead of putting it in the mailbox. But no one has taken it in, so maybe Mr Domino isn't home. Cadence listens at the door, but there's no sound from inside.

She wishes she had her I Ching.

No, come on, Cadence, you can make it. Make a decision. Well, you may as well be bold, right?

She puts on her shoes and rings the doorbell.

There's no answer.

Cadence rings again, knocks.

Nothing.

She goes back down in the lobby and phones her ma.

'I found him, ma. In a condo in a place called, ah, Chestnut something. What do I do now?'

'Stick with him, lover,' says Crystal on the phone. 'Stand by your man. A woman's place,' she proposes, 'is by her man.'

Cadence sighs. Her ma is smashed again. She is just a total lush, actually. Cadence likes a drink. She likes a lot of drinks. She likes them a lot. But it's basically pretty pointless, being drunk. And Crystal is drunk all the time, practically.

'Ma, I need to borrow some money.'

'I can't keep lending you money, Cadence.'

'Well, mail me a credit card then.' Crystal's Bar is into a scam in Turkey Flat and environs, whereby credit card applications can be approved with almost no credentials. In an emergency, Crystal could pull down some seventy thousand dollars of free money and just blow.

'You? You'll have the pigs on us. You'll fuck the whole thing up, Cadence, I know you.'

Mother and daughter relations are some of the toughest, Cadence thinks. But she gets her card, with the name she made up on it. She throws all her old clothes in a dumpster. She rents a room over from the condos. The rent is crazy, they want to take her card as a deposit, but she sweet-talks the clerk and he gives in. Later from her window she sees a young blond guy drive up to the condos, blue jeans, leather jacket, very sexy. Gets out, stands there a piece, looking round, like he hasn't been living there long. She is sure it's him. Mr D.

She watches him go in. Stays by the window. Later he comes out. Cadence stays in, watches TV, jerks off the Chinese delivery boy in return for a free King Prawn Special and egg rice. She doesn't see the guy come back. Maybe it wasn't him. In the morning she goes and stands outside his door for an hour, almost, before she decides he's already up and gone. She rang his bell once already. She doesn't feel like doing that again. She wants to see him without him necessarily seeing her.

She is turning to go when his door opens suddenly and he comes out. Looks at her hard.

'Excuse me,' she says.

He shuts his door behind him, locks it. 'May I help you?' he asks.

'Okay,' says Cadence suggestively. She put her hands on her hips, turns back towards him.

He's waiting. 'What's the problem?' he asks, neutrally.

Cadence's mind goes blank. He really is pretty groovy. Not a hunk like all the guys back west, but a real golden boy. 'Oh nothing!' she says brightly.

'Good morning, then,' he says, going on his way. Shit, no.

'I wonder if you can tell me the time,' says Cadence loudly.

He stops. He turns back to look at her.

Cadence smiles and beckons him with her body.

'No I can't,' he says. And walks away.

Cadence can't believe it. Nobody walks away from her. Not even the faggots walk *away*. She's convinced it's him. But he doesn't recognise her! He's had her nude photo in his possession for just *ages*, and he doesn't even recognise her.

She is going to call him back, but it's already too late.

When he comes home, Cadence is waiting. She comes walking past his door in thongs, big sunglasses, her skating skirt, her low-cut Mexican blouse. She's carrying a sack of apples in front of her, cradling it upright in her arms, and she manages to tip the whole lot on the floor in front of him.

He stoops, picks up one that rolled against his foot and tosses it into her sack, an easy catch. Then he puts his key in the lock, opens the door, looks back. Cadence smiles encouragingly, leaning towards him

74

as she bends so he can see right down between her tits. She squats, legs splayed, picking up apples. Her skirt is far from adequate. She sees Mr Domino's eyes fasten on the crotch of her white panties. She stays that way for a while, turning round to pick up the damn apples.

Hears his door close.

Now Cadence is mad. Still he didn't recognise her! Maybe there really are people, she thinks, shaking her head, who don't recognise her with her clothes on. Then she touches her hair and remembers, also she's a redhead now. That photo was when she was blonde.

Well, okay. Whatever. No more hesitating. She decides to go all the way with this. It won't be so bad, exposing herself to a guy who looks like him. In fact she has no objection to the idea at all.

That evening she puts a piece of paper with her address on and 'Please come, it's urgent' under his door. Then she goes back to her room and takes all her clothes off. She feels cold in this city, she wishes she were back in L.A. She feels kind of stupid, actually, like she can't remember how she got into this. She thinks of Josephine and looks at herself in the mirror, running her hands down her sides, wishing they were Josephine's hands. She massages her breasts. So much of her life she seems to have to undress for.

What the hell, it's bound to work. It always does. All Cadence has ever had to do is take of her clothes, and men melt. Soon after, they get feisty and start chancing their luck; but first they melt.

And while they're melted, they'll do anything for you. Anything at all.

She watches TV until he knocks.

She switches the TV off, get up, brushes popcorn crumbs out of her pubic hair. She goes to the front door and reaches for the catch. She looks through the spyhole. It's him. It is. 'Who is it?' she calls, her heart racing.

'There was a message,' he says.

Cadence opens the door and stands back.

He doesn't stare. He comes straight in, just as through nothing was wrong. He is wearing Crusoe shades, a red polo shirt, tight white Wranglers.

Cadence shuts the door. They stand there looking at each other. 'What's the matter?' he says.

Cadence gestures, running the fingertips of her right hand lightly down between her breasts to just below her navel. Usually that drives

75

men crazy.

This one doesn't even twitch.

He's so young. Her own age, not a lot more. His thighs look strong through taut denim. He has a little gold ring in one ear. He looks like California and sounds like continental Europe, Sweden, Germany, who gives a shit?

Cadence crosses her arms, pumping up her breasts. 'Don't you recognise me?' she says.

He looks a moment, as though making sure. Then he shakes his head.

Cadence has run out of ideas.

'Mr Domino,' she says. 'Where is Josephine?'

'I don't know any Josephines,' he says, levelly.

'Mr Domino,' she says again.

But before she can say anything else, he says, 'My name isn't Domino.'

And he turns to go.

'Wait!' shouts Cadence frantically.

He swivels.

And waits.

At last Cadence puts her hands to her head. 'Don't you even want to fuck?' she says.

The dishy blond guy looks at his watch, like she's just asked him the time again.

'No,' he says.

Then he goes out, and shuts the door behind him.

Cadence stands there, stunned. She hears his receding footsteps on the stairs, and hears the street door bang closed.

Then she shouts '*Wait!*' and hurtles out onto the landing, just the way she is.

Only then does she understand she's failed. It hits her in a wave of frustration and tiredness, and she slumps against the wall of the stairwell, slides to the nasty floor.

She blew it. She's got the wrong man. 'Oh fuck,' she says. Her eyes brim with tears.

Then quick smart footsteps come tap-tapping round the corner.

They pause in front of her.

'Well, well,' says a bright, cheerful voice. 'And what have we here?'

7

'The duty of a slave,' recites Alexandra, her voice quiet but clear above the soft waves of the Mediterranean Sea, 'is to remain mindful at all times of her own humility and of the obedience she owes her master, or mistress . . .'

Alexandra's eyelids flutter, like the wings of the moths struggling to immolate themselves on the terrace lamps of La Lointain. This last phrase is a delicate addition of her own, which the Domino Queen does not disapprove of, though she is still uncertain what the girl means by it. Is she trying to improve her status by currying favour with the woman who is currently her sole master on the island? Does she hope, naively and in vain, to become a favourite and be treated with a light hand? Or is she, *au contraire*, signalling subtly that she already understand more of the inner mystery than those who are stuck in conventional interpretations of gender?

'A slave has no duty but obedience, no thought but obedience, no will but obedience.'

Alexandra stands motionless, her hands behind her back, her eyes on the paved floor of the terrace. She wears a narrow black collar; a full skirt made of several layers of gauzy tulle gathered in a belt, a red elastic belt with a silver metal S-clasp; white knee-socks; English sandals; nothing else. Her long brown hair hangs down her bare back, firmly plaited. She stands close beside her mistress, who reclines on a sun-lounger, sipping a long drink. In the blue twilight, Alexandra's young breasts offer themselves sweetly like soft white fruit.

'A slave makes herself available at all hours to her mistress, or to whomever her mistress chooses. Her name is nothing; her state is submission; her body —'

Beyond the table the door of the beach-house opens and Alexandra loses the thread of her catechism, distracted. Her brown eyes flick from the paving to the three figures coming onto the terrace.

'Her body —' she repeats.

Instantly, Josephine's hand flashes out and catches her a loud smack on her plump white thigh.

'Ow!' cried Alexandra, which is already an offence. She forgets herself far enough to bring her hand from behind her back and clap it to the place.

'Be still, slave!' shouts Josephine.

The women's eyes lock. The slave's demeanour is lost, her passivity disrupted. There is only one possible outcome, though Josephine, glaring, sees passion in her eyes, then fright, then desperate apprehension. At once Alexandra resumes her position, ignoring the newcomers.

They are Ahmed and Peter, barefoot and naked. A weighty chain, no more than three feet long, hangs between their collars; the end is in the hand of Yvette, who follows them.

Now that their after-dinner chores are finished, Yvette is bringing the boys out to the terrace, as she was instructed to. She wears a plain black frock with an apron over it, an approximation to an English housemaid, though her legs are bare and she wears Mediterranean sandals on her feet. She carries a small peeled switch, with which she lashes the boys swiftly across the back and buttocks, because they too have raised their eyes, to look at Alexandra.

The invisible black sea breaks on the rocky shore of evening with a sound like a deep, moist cough, eternally repeated. Insects zip and hover. The lamp casts its glow across a picnic table of raw, gnarled olive wood, sanded and smoothed by years of use and exposure, here on the coast of the Ile de Porquerolles. Earlier this evening, it did service as the company's dinner table. Soon, Josephine has decided, it will be put to another use.

'Again, slave,' she says, very quietly.

Alexandra takes a deep breath. Her breasts rise. She moistens her lips with her sweet pink tongue.

'The condition of a slave,' she says, 'is a condition of quietness and tranquillity. The bondage of a slave is threefold freedom.'

'What are the three freedoms?' asks Josephine, her voice hard as a whip across the stillness of the group.

Alexandra is ready now to answer. They have been over this and over it, the training punctuated with the necessary punishments and rewards.

'Freedom from motion,' says Alexandra; 'freedom from thought; and freedom from will. The duty of a slave is to remain mindful at all times of her own humility . . .'

As the recitation continues, Yvette covertly inspects her temporary charges. Ahmed, she notices with dismay, has something, food or dirt, matted in the wiry hair of his shin — probably a residue of the brief period of horseplay she allowed them in the kitchen between clearing away and washing up. She knows boys of old. It is better to let them take out their hysterical high spirits on each other than risk them turning sullen and rebellious on her. Now there is the possibility that Josephine may take Yvette to task for inadequate presentation. She may even deprive her of the privilege of helping with their training.

Yvette hopes she won't. But even that would be preferable to being sent away, sent home. To be denied the chance to serve Josephine: that would be unbearable.

Yvette keeps her eye on the chained boys. She hopes the trouble is out of them for tonight. Ahmed is frantic with love for Peter; with jealousy of Alexandra; with the urge to vie for Josephine's favour in the half-formed hope, the vain hope, that she might award the pale, slim Dutch boy to one of them, exclusively and finally. He blames the boy for refusing to take sides. So when, in the kitchen, he began to pelt Peter with leftovers, and Peter began to nudge and kick Ahmed more and more openly, Yvette let them continue, finally commanding them to wrestle on the kitchen floor before whipping them both back to their labours.

It was not an unpleasant duty. Nor was the final task she always has to perform before presenting them to the mistress: to ensure that Ahmed and Peter are both rigid and ready.

Ahmed, hot-blooded and full of coltish aggression, is no problem. He is almost continuously erect. He takes pride, such small pride as even a novice may be forgiven, in needing no one's hand, no persuasion or discipline, to rouse his horn of dark flesh. In any case, Ahmed is still young enough that the constant nearness of his beloved Peter, naked but forbidden, keeps his cock yearning always towards him.

Peter, on the other hand, is moody, introverted, shy. He often needs Yvette's attention to get him into a fit state for their mistress to see. Barely a minute ago, at the door, she slipped her hand beneath his slender buttocks and between his thighs, to fondle his cool balls and coax his soft cock upwards with crook of her finger.

At other times she has not been so kind.

Alexandra's recitation has at last, faultlessly, reached its end. Her hands behind her, her eyes on the ground, she stands in readiness for whatever may now be Josephine's pleasure.

'Lift your skirt, slave,' says Josephine casually.

Alexandra gathers the springy layers of her skirt in her two hands and raises it in front. It is short enough and full enough that Yvette, looking at her from behind, can see Alexandra's knickers.

Alexandra is wearing knickers: plain white cotton knickers. Yvette is not allowed to wear knickers, or rarely. Yvette, who has become intimate enough with the novices to know that Alexandra's monthly courses are still some days off, suspects that Josephine has permitted Alexandra this privilege tonight for one purpose only, which is to say to her, as she does now:

'Lower your knickers.'

Under cover of the darkness, Yvette permits herself a smile. She knows her mistress.

Alexandra is as obedient as her word. At once she slips her thumbs into the elastic waistband and draws her knickers down over her chubby buttocks until they rest around the top of her thighs.

'Lower, slave,' says Josephine.

Alexandra obeys. Her bottom flexes as she bends forward to push the knickers down almost to her knees. The lamplight casts a deep shadow in the cleft between her legs.

At Alexandra's movement, Yvette hears Peter catch his breath. Glancing at him, she sees that though he is not looking up, at least not detectably, his white cock is now trembling hard; and also sees Ahmed glaring sideways at him under cover of his bowed head. Brought by the chain that links them close enough to touch his body, if he were commanded to, Ahmed is aware of every smallest shift of his beloved's flesh. And he hates it when Peter pays attention to Alexandra, resents it every time Peter's cock twitches.

Yvette understands Alexandra's feelings perfectly at this instant. She knows all about the position the English girl now finds herself in: knows it forwards, backwards and sideways. From the very dejection described by the curve of of Alexandra's shoulders she can tell that Alexandra is expecting a spanking; that she considers she deserves nothing less, for failing her catechism and spoiling her posture.

Josephine seems to agree.

'Go to the end of the table and bend over,' she tells her slave; and then, when Alexandra moves obediently towards the rough-hewn picnic table: 'No — the far end.'

Corrected, seeking further correction, here she comes, around the table towards Yvette and her companion novices. She shuffles slightly, impeded by the pants hanging around her knees, but keeps her eyes most firmly on the ground.

Yvette smiles again, secretly. She has no idea what her beloved mistress is planning, but she can tell this is already torture for Peter. Josephine is exposing his darling Alexandra, not two metres in front of him; and he is forbidden even to look.

Alexandra faces the table, presses her hips against it. She goes up on her toes and lays her upper body on the planking, pressing her soft breasts to the tabletop. Unbidden and with some difficulty, she tucks her skirt up inside her belt at the back, then grasps the table edges with her hands, extending her legs behind her, still pressing her toes to the terrace floor.

The gleam of her bare bottom distracts a passing moth.

'Open your legs, Alexandra,' Josephine calls, softly but firmly. 'Display your folds. I want you in a state of complete readiness. *Est-ce qu'elle est prête*, Yvette?'

From here Yvette can see the sheen of moisture in the tuft of soft hair that protrudes below Alexandra's anus. The English girl is sometimes closed and cold when it is necessary to be open and inviting; and sometimes she is punished for it. But her loins have already learned what her heart, perhaps, is also now learning: that the approach of inevitable punishment occasions a sharp, trembling longing that overrides all glands and undermines all reason.

'*Presque*, madame,' Yvette replies.

'See to it,' Josephine commands.

Yvette is beginning to guess her plan. She lets go of the boys' chain and steps forward to the girl on the table. A sweet scent of fear and arousal, and very faintly of shit, rises from the helplessly spread buttocks. Yvette takes pleasure in slipping her hand, palm upwards, between the table and Alexandra's crotch, and lightly fingering her clitoris. Alexandra stifles a cry. Yvette knows the motions she likes best.

81

'Boys,' calls Josephine unexpectedly. 'Look up. Look at your fellow slave. Do you see her spread before you?'

'Permission to speak, madame,' says Peter, equally unexpectedly. Josephine nods, minimally. 'I want to take Alexandra's place. Please,' he adds. His English is good but not natural.

'What you want does not concern anyone, Peter,' says Josephine. 'But your suggestion is interesting. Tomorrow perhaps.'

Yvette rubs her thumb quickly, then slowly, in a circle on the prostrate girl's seeping vagina. It dilates for her and she tests how ready it is: a finger? A thumb? Two fingers?

She takes a little longer over this part of the testing than is strictly necessary. Alexandra is well on her way. At last Yvette calls, 'Ready, madame.'

Josephine rises from her chair, but comes only to her end of the table, where she spreads her hands and leans forward to address them all. Her heavy breasts, unconfined, swing forward under the loose bodice of her sundress.

Yvette can hear the boys breathing tensely behind her, like animals hiding in the bushes up behind the house.

'We shall now conduct a little test, Peter, Ahmed,' Josephine announces, 'of your energy and discipline; and Alexandra, of what you have learned of the arts of − exaction.'

Yvette does not know this word. She wonders if Alexandra does. Daring, she continues to fondle Alexandra's folds while the mistress continues. Alexandra is trying not to gasp, not to squirm; straining every muscle to concentrate on her instructions.

'Look at her, boys. Look at her well. Is she not what you have dreamed of, at home, in your lonely beds: a beautiful, fresh young woman, spread and wet and ready for your eager little pricks? Do you not yearn to have her?

'Well so you shall,' she declares, in a bizarre imitation of a pantomime fairy. She bats her eyelids at the chained boys. 'But who shall go first?'

Peter and Ahmed are too well-trained to fall into the trap of attempting to reply to that.

'Yvette,' commands Josephine. 'A coin.'

Yvette feels in the pocket of her apron, finds ten centimes. She tosses it in the air, catches it on her palm, covers it with her hand.

'Peter,' says Josephine. 'Call.'

Peter calls heads but the coin has come down tails. He stares tensely, miserably at the patch of darkness between Alexandra's thighs.

'Alexandra,' says Josephine. 'Ahmed and Peter will fuck you, turn and turn about. I shall call the changes. The first to spend his seed in you,' she explains, 'you will punish.' Then, to the boys, she says, 'The other of you will punish her for disappointing him. Ahmed will begin. Place him, Yvette.'

Smiling proudly, the Arab boy steps forward, deliberately dragging his rival after him on the chain. He stands between the legs of Alexandra, takes hold of her legs. Yvette reaches for his stiff prick and guides it into Alexandra's cunt.

Ahmed slides it straight in.

Alexandra gasps, 'Ha . . . haa . . . haaa-a-aah . . .'

Ahmed pulls most of the way out, bumping Peter with his bottom. He pushes straight in again. Out. In.

'O-o-oh . . . ' cries Alexandra.

Yvette expects the mistress to command her to silence, perhaps to gag her; but she has been less cruel since the master has been away. There is a music in the involuntary cries of the slave that she may well find enjoyable.

Out Ahmed slides, and in again without a pause. There is a wonderful smile on his face. Yvette wonders which pleasure is keener, the unexpected fuck or the faith he can outlast his rival at it.

'Change!' says Josephine.

Ahmed looks mutinous for an instant, then, screwing his eyes up tight, withdraws with a jerk. He takes a step backwards, making sure to rub his bottom against Peter's hip as much as possible in the process.

Peter, ready as he is, surprises Yvette. He doesn't push forward at once to insert himself into his darling's still-dilating quim. He looks sidelong at her; at Yvette.

Yvette is amused, piqued. She wipes her fingers on her apron. Avoiding his eye, she reaches between the boy and his goal and takes firm hold of him. The she inserts him no less precisely than she did his partner.

Secretly she is impressed by his insistence on her touch. There is mastery in him. But he is not single-minded, like Ahmed. It is clear in his suddenly candid blue eyes that Alexandra is not the only girl he cares about.

Yvette averts her face.

Peter slides in gently, drawing a soft coo from the spread girl. In the dim light the planes of her body seem to shift, melting lovingly in response to the boy between her legs.

He rests his right hand on Alexandra's bottom. He has not been instructed to caress her, but he is daring. He affects not to notice that his head is being dragged to the side by the chain that attaches him to the boy crowded in behind him between Alexandra's legs.

And Josephine calls, 'Change!'

Ahmed smothers a laugh, and Yvette gives him a cut of the switch.

If Peter is upset, he does not show it. He circles his hips as he withdraws and lets Ahmed in.

Stroking Peter's bottom 'accidentally', Ahmed struts in and slots himself into Alexandra. He thrusts and thrusts. Josephine calls, and Peter replaces him. He thrusts slow and exploringly, his right foot coming up on tiptoe. His little bottom flexes with cherubic grace. He means to make this last. He has no intention of letting Ahmed punish Alexandra.

'Change!'

Ahmed is quickly in. He makes a dozen short, non-committal strokes, stirring Alexandra but not seriously hastening his own climax. She, on the other hand, has ceased to writhe passively and started to enter into the spirit of things. Yvette can see how the untutored English girl is trying to get a grip on the young man inside her. She would squeeze him in her vagina, if she knew how, and make him come soon. She too, Yvette can tell, has no desire to end up being chastised by Ahmed rather than Peter.

'Change! Change! Change!'

Josephine has the boys hopping, treading on each other's toes, elbowing each other, pulling each other off-balance with the chain in their eagerness and frustration. The edge of the table glistens with their juices. Alexandra mews openly, pants in frustration at the constantly interrupted rhythm, hauls more urgently on each cock as it is inserted. Meanwhile Josephine sits down and summons Yvette to her. Unbuttoning her sundress, she gives the maid her heavy, sun-brown breast to suck.

'Change!' she calls, continually. 'Change! Change!'

Peter seems to be losing. He is tired, his movements growing increasingly incoherent and mechanical. His pixie face contorts with

84

anxiety and intensity. His neck is angry red from the chafing of the chain pulling at his collar, and there are marks at his waist from Alexandra's belt. Still Alexandra tries to chew the table while he is shafting her.

Ahmed goes at her like a horse. His eyes roll up in his head, his lips draw back from his teeth. His sweat shines in the lamplight. He squeezes Alexandra forcefully with his elegant hands. He forces himself up over her back, using the advantage of his extra height, dragging Peter off his feet. Alexandra's legs flail and kick in the most undignified abandon. Her discipline is gone.

Josephine strokes up the short hair on the back of Yvette's neck. 'The girl does better in restraint,' she murmurs, confirming Yvette's thoughts. She has closed her eyes, she is no longer watching the bout. 'Change,' she calls, at random.

Still watching intently, Yvette mouths Josephine's tit.

Alexandra raises her head from the table. Her hair is coming out of its plait. Her face is blotched pink with intense arousal. As Peter enters her she strains up off the table-top, arching her back. Her breasts flatten against her taut chest. Peter toils, buried in her groin, his head pulled back as Ahmed deliberately drags on the chain. Peter hasn't the strength to fight Ahmed, or Alexandra, or himself, any more.

'Change,' called Josephine.

Alexandra is almost sliding off the table. Ahmed grabs her, shoves her back into place, entering her with the same thrust. Alexandra squeezes him between her thighs.

Then he yelps.

It is not clear what's happening at that end of the table, in the dim light, but Peter seems to be squatting down behind the struggling Ahmed. Yvette suspects that he is buggering him.

Ahmed shouts something in his own tongue. It sounds like a prayer, a curse, an imprecation. What it means is anyone's guess; but what it signifies is obvious to everyone.

Josephine slips her breast out of Yvette's mouth. She strokes Yvette's head approvingly, kisses her, then buttons the bodice of her dress.

Ahmed has come.

He hangs his head over Alexandra's fleshy back. His whole demeanour has changed. He is spent, drained, already wilting.

Peter stands behind him, hands behind his back, looking as if

Ahmed's sudden collapse is none of his business. His own prick stands up wet and red from his groin.

Josephine sends Yvette back to unlock the defeated companion from his chain. Ahmed casts doleful eyes on Peter, reproaching him. He makes not even a token resistance as Yvette draws him by the arm back from the table. His prick flops, dribbling. His semen glints wetly in the lamplight.

Alexandra clambers backwards down from the table. Her breasts and belly are red from chafing. Belatedly, Yvette hopes there are no splinters.

Alexandra has not climaxed, she is in a state of ebbing lust. As she puts her weight on her feet, Ahmed's seed drips out of her, drooling from her thigh to the floor. Then her skirt slides down, concealing her in all but outline.

She sits on the bench, facing away from the table, and combs the loose hair behind her ears.

Yvette takes Ahmed to her. Alexandra reaches for him readily, receives him across her knee. She plants her left hand in the small of his lean back, lays her right, open, gently on his bare bottom.

Peter has withdrawn into himself. He stands with his head and his arms hanging down, like a lifeless blond doll.

Josephine says: 'Alexandra, this slave has violated you. How many spanks does he deserve?'

Alexandra thinks about it a moment. She looks at Josephine. 'Ten,' she says. Her voice is diffident, rather dreamy.

'Ten,' repeats Josephine. 'I think you would have found him less lenient.'

Alexandra gives a sexy little laugh. 'I mean twenty,' she says.

Josephine shifts in her chair, crosses her long legs. 'Have a care, Alexandra.'

Alexandra is silent.

'Ten it is,' says Josephine. 'You may begin.'

Alexandra lifts her hand and gives Ahmed a firm smack, high on his right buttock. She smacks him again, lower down, and again, lower.

The boy across her lap gives no visible reaction.

Alexandra smacks him harder, right in the underhang. That one lands with a loud wallop, startling a squawking bird out of the bushes.

Ahmed's tense body spasms slightly. Still he makes not a sound. His eyes are wide open.

Alexandra goes to the top of his left buttocks and does it again, three descending smacks and the eighth underneath, in the same place as the fourth.

Ahmed's teeth are clenched. In the lamplight his skin glistens with sweat.

Alexandra adjusts her grip. She wraps her arm around Ahmed's waist. She leans in to deliver the last two spanks, swinging her hand back round behind her.

The ninth smack is inaccurate, but the tenth is a surprise, landing squarely on the back of his right thigh. Ahmed stifles a grunt. He is quivering, taut as stretched wood.

Alexandra looks at her handprints. She is clearly wishing she had the extra ten now, to develop what she has barely started. She tosses back her plait, which has swung over her shoulder. She looks as though she does not know what to do with her hands. She is remembering what happens now.

She smiles uncertainly at Peter.

Peter looks glassy-eyed, almost frightened. Yvette sees nothing now in his face of the cocky young man whose prick she had handled.

She helps Ahmed off Alexandra's lap, sends him to face the wall, his hands on his head.

'Get up, Alexandra,' says Josephine, boredly.

Alexandra gets up and stands there, absurdly, with her hands spread on her bottom. She hovers over Peter as he slips into place. She looks at him with glad, loving idiocy.

Peter smiles, gruesomely. His face is as stiff as his prick; he must be churning away inside.

This doesn't look promising, Yvette thinks.

'Peter,' says Josephine, with all the emphasis of a British registrar, 'this slave has failed to please you. How many spanks does she deserve?'

Peter doesn't look at her. He is staring into Alexandra's face. 'Fifty,' he says, almost too soft to be heard above the waves.

Alexandra's eyes widen. The colour leaves her cheeks.

Josephine waves a permissive hand and Yvette conducts the girl across her fellow slave's lap.

As he takes her weight, Peter looks extremely distressed. He closes his eyes and gulps. For a moment, Yvette thinks he is going to be sick.

But no, it is obvious what is happening to Peter. He is ejaculating.

87

After all he has suffered in the last few hours, his anguish had him on a hair trigger. The merest pressure of Alexandra's fatty belly on the cherry-tip of his penis was too much for him. The tension drains from his closed face as his jism drops in gouts to the floor.

'Oh, for goodness' sake,' mutters Josephine, getting up impatiently. 'Come on, come on,' she says, herding them. With one hand she hauls Alexandra up off Peter's lap, grabs Peter's arm with the other. 'Over the table, both of you,' she commands wearily. 'Yvette,' she adds, as the pair clamber stickily into position, 'go and fetch me a belt. Yes, and Ahmed, let's have you up her too, come along.' Yvette goes indoors on her errand. Ahmed, eyes downcast, comes and lies down next to Peter. Josephine dresses the line with her hands. The row of upturned bottoms reminds her of the Château des Aiguilles, the grand debauch at her coronation. She wishes Leonard were there, and touches herself through her dress.

Yvette reappears, running. She curtseys, hands Josephine an old belt of black leather, broad and thick.

'Thank you, Yvette.' She bends and kisses her devotee's forehead. '*Et depuis, à ma chambre,*' she murmurs.

'*Oui,* madame,' whispers Yvette.

'*Viens vite, ma petite …*'

Josephine is so bored tonight. She wonders how late it is, and what the time is in Arkansas.

She holds the buckle in her right hand and winds a turn of the belt around her knuckles, drawing the rest out to its full length.

Before she sleeps tonight, she will telephone and see if Cadence is ready to be moved on to the next phase.

|8|

It is a nurse. She is all in uniform: starched white dress, white apron in front, white folded paper cap on top of her head. Black nylons and flat black shoes. She is young, in her twenties, and as slim as Cadence, with the same freckles, only her hair is long, red-gold, twisted up in a bun behind her head.

She is smiling. She looks friendly.

'Whatever is the matter?' asks the nurse, and she drops down on one knee on the landing, beside Cadence's limp body. 'Are you all right?'

'No,' says Cadence. 'I've had it with this.' She sniffs back the tears.

'Had you not better go inside and put some clothes on?' the nurse asks gently, putting her hand on Cadence's back. She isn't an American either, where are all these Europeans coming from suddenly?

'Sure,' says Cadence, defeated.

The nurse doesn't take her hand away. 'Can I help at all?' she says.

Cadence considers a moment. 'You in a hurry?' she asks.

'No,' the nurse says, still touching her.

She is real pretty, this nurse. She looks really sweet.

'Fetch me a Coke,' says Cadence.

'Sorry,' says the nurse, 'but I haven't got any.'

'Beer?' says Cadence hopefully.

The nurse shakes her head. Sunlight comes through the window, her hair glows. 'Tell you what I have got,' she says.

'What?'

'Gin,' says the nurse unexpectedly.

She looks so clean and starchy and everything Cadence is confused. 'This is medicinal gin?' she says.

The nurse laughs and shakes her head again. She is real lively, she

89

is full of life. 'No,' she says. 'Just Bombay Diamond.'

'Great,' says Cadence. 'All right.'

The nurse stands up. 'You'll have to come with me,' she says. 'I've brought a car.'

Cadence looks at her. 'You don't live here?'

'No.'

'Oh well, hey, excuse me, I'm sorry. I thought — Well, okay, say, thanks, um —'

Cadence gets to her feet, backs into her room.

'Goodbye,' she says.

'I'll wait,' says the nurse.

Cadence leans forward, puzzled. 'Really? You mean it? You're really going to take me home with you?'

'Surely.'

'Wow! Well, okay! Um, come on in.'

She holds the door wide.

'I'll wait in the car,' says the nurse.

'I should shower,' says Cadence.

'You can have a shower when we get there,' says the nurse. 'I'll be in the car.'

She smiles and trots away downstairs, her flat black shoes tapping on the treads.

Cadence pulls on clean panties, her shorts, her sandals. She finds a Dick Tracy T-shirt, pulls it on, even brushes her hair. She feels good. She's forgotten all about Josephine.

She wonders which way the nurse swings.

She wonders if the nurse has a name.

The car is an old green sports model, right-hand drive. 'You have a name?' Cadence asks, as she gets in, shoves her bag down under her feet.

'Several,' says the nurse.

She revs the car loudly and turns to Cadence, smiling as if she approves of what she sees.

'We look alike, you know,' she says, dreamily. 'We could be sisters.'

She lets in the clutch and they jolt suddenly backwards out of the bay.

'Call me Jackie,' she says.

It's evening as they drive out of town, through a low-rent district where folk are sitting out on the porch, popping beers and lazily batting gossip and good-natured insults back and forth from house to house. Then they're in the suburbs, where everything's tightly locked up, the car in the garage, dinner defrosting, TV on. Cadence Szathkowicz feels like all her life she's been skating and now she's dropped straight through the ice into a world of water where everything flows. All these people in their tight houses, they live on another planet, not knowing what strange currents are running past under the shade trees at the end of the yard, dark and deep and swift and very strong.

She shifts her bare thighs on the crazed upholstery and looks at the nurse, Jackie. 'You're British, right?' she says.

'Irish,' Jackie says.

'I have some Irish in me,' says Cadence. 'On my mom's side.'

'We get around,' says Jackie.

'What sign are you?'

'Leo,' says Jackie.

'That's great,' Cadence says. 'We're compatible.'

'That's as may be,' says Jackie tartly.

Cadence doesn't know what she means.

She wants to ask why Jackie was there, at Chestnut Park, but she changes her mind. Probably she was seeing some patient, though she doesn't have any nurse equipment with her or anything. She was there, that's all that matters. If something is, then it's meant to be, right? Cadence isn't even sure why Jackie is taking her home. If you ask too many questions, good things go away sometimes. Yeah, but sometimes good things go away anyway, the way Josephine went away. Or was stolen away. Abducted.

If Jackie is good to her Cadence believes she can cope a while longer with not having Josephine. Jackie's house is just a way station, a stop on her search, a place to eat and shower and rest up a while. If the guy who answered her ad wants to find her, he'll find her. He found her at the Bluewater Lodge, he can find her at Jackie's house.

Later, the moon comes up, wallowing grease-yellow and almost full in the arms of a line of oaks. It is pretty hot still, darkness seeping into the air like it was a thick, tarry mist coming up off the blacktop. Cadence wants to ask if Jackie can take the top down, but the phrase feels strange in her mouth, like an obscene suggestion, and there seems to be no unambiguous way to phrase it. She can't even find a way to say Jackie's name; for some reason she knows she would sound stupid and clumsy saying it, so she sits in silence, fingering the upholstery.

It's that time of day when your headlights only seem to make things darker. Jackie doesn't know where they are any more. The last highway they crossed had a sign one way to Tallulah, the other to Monroe. Cadence has no idea where these places are. All they made her think of was movie stars. She figures vaguely they've crossed a state line somewhere. She's given up caring. Cast her fate to the winds. Not that there is any. Wind, that is. Motionless, the trees crowd round and hang their shaggy crowns into the road. Beyond them, slick silver tracts of marshland glimmer in the light of the moon. Gas stations and roadside bars show missing shingles, peeling paint. Chalkboards advertise BAIT – GAS – AMMO.

Jackie makes a left and drives through a little town. The house stands just beyond, back from the road a piece, screened from the world by uncombed thickets of scrub and live oak. For an instant, as the little green car roars up the unmade driveway, Cadence has an irrational feeling it isn't Jackie's house at all, it's someone else's house, and she's being taken to be presented to them, totally unprepared. She doesn't feel like meeting anyone. She wants to hide away for a spell. It certainly looks like a hideaway.

It's an old place, a real ramshackle collection of buildings propping each other up. There's a dog barking. Cadence sees it in silhouette, bounding stiff-legged at the end of a chain. Jackie snaps the lights off, gets out of the car and makes a fuss of it. Cadence gets out more slowly, holding her drawstring bag. She's stiff, she wonders how late it is, how long they've been riding. The air smells dank and earthy. There are tiny flies swarming everywhere, invisible. She tries to swat them away with her arms.

'Get along inside with you,' says Jackie, still crouching down petting the mutt. 'Bathroom's down the hallway on the right.'

More by touch than sight, Cadence finds the door, pulls the squealing screen door open, tries the huge corroded brass handle. It turns and she goes inside, groping for a lightswitch.

Two soft lights come on in big round bowls of heavy glass, like waterlilies stuck against the ceiling. The hallway is all wood panelling, thick crimson carpet, a big ugly green urn full of umbrellas and fishing gear, piles of big old books and magazines. Cadence walks further into the house, still expecting a man's voice to sing out at any moment, a deep, elderly voice, some huge, grizzled poet, planter, army veteran, with a chipped enamel pot of steaming coffee in one hand and a bottle of rye in the other.

No one stirs. The only sound is an old clock whirring, and the dog barking again outside.

Cadence finds the bathroom. It's old, all the fixtures huge, the way they used to make them, like for a vanished race of giants. There's a tub, a commode with a big tank up by the ceiling, a handbasin with a big mirror all patchy and worn behind it — and a shower stall in the far corner, open, without a door to it. The shower head is dripping. Cadence leans in, turns it on. It gurgles, chokes, then flings a torrent of water at the floor. She feels it: tepid, then soon very hot. There is a rail, piled thick with towels, nine or ten of them, within reach.

Cadence turns the shower off, goes to lock the bathroom door. It has a lock, but no key she can find. The hell with it. She strips off, takes a leak, then steps right in the shower.

There's no ventilation, the window's closed, junk all over the sill showing no one ever opens it. The room fills up with steam.

Cadence soaps herself all over, rinses. Does it again for the pure pleasure of it. Suddenly she wants to be very very clean, everywhere.

Through the fog she sees the door open and Jackie come in. She's still in her uniform. She smiles at Cadence in the shower, crosses over to use the john. In full view of Cadence she hitches up her skirt and pulls down a pair of green candystripe panties. Then she hunkers down on the great white china throne. Cadence feels a jolt of something, not desire, exactly, but a blast of intimacy with this pretty, secretive nurse she never met before, who hardly said a dozen words to her all the way up here. Cadence turns off the shower, which stops abruptly. She can hear the tinkle of Jackie peeing. Jackie sits there quite unworried, leaning forward on the john with her chin on her hands. She's wearing stockings and a garterbelt, not pantyhose, Cadence notices as she emerges from the open stall, rubbing her head with a cheap old towel.

Jackie finishes, wipes herself. She sits there watching Cadence dry herself. 'You don't have to get dressed,' she says, her voice low and warm, 'if you don't want to.'

But Cadence wants to. She pulls her panties back on, even puts on a bra, and a soft, long-sleeved McCormack shirt over it. Jackie lends her a pair of stone-washed jeans, they're pretty tight, Cadence is chunkier than Jackie after all.

93

Jackie helps her into them, helps her pull them up, squats down on the bedroom floor to button them for her. Her neat, antiseptic fingers brush the mound of Cadence's pubis through the thin fabric of her panties. 'I should let you do this part yourself, I suppose,' says Jackie.

'You're doing fine,' says Cadence.

Jackie raises her eyebrows.

She goes off to change and comes back in a casual skirt, bare legs, sneakers without socks. Cadence is very aware of the peaks of Jackie's breasts, bare beneath a skintight sleeveless top. She has the sleeves of a red cardigan knotted loosely around her neck.

The women sit at the huge, scarred kitchen table and drink gin and tonic. 'Is this your place?' Cadence asks.

'Sometimes,' says Jackie. She gets up, opens the enormous fridge, closes it again. 'I haven't been here for a while, that's why there's nothing to eat.' She sees Cadence looking at her breasts again. Smiling pointedly, but not saying anything, she pulls the cardigan on and buttons it up.

Cadence isn't hungry until they get to the restaurant. Then she's starving, eats two bowls of shrimp creole and a slice of pie. An old black couple start to play accordion and fiddle, singing heartily in an accent Cadence can't begin to understand. Jackie reaches across the table, covers Cadence's hand with her own. 'Shall we go?'

Cadence nods. Half in a dream, she puts the check on her suspect plastic, adds a tip, scarcely noticing what her hands are doing. She's tired, excited, bewildered but not caring. All the way back in the car she's conscious of Jackie's smooth, warm body moving neatly and efficiently in the seat beside her, inches away.

They fondle the dog and go into the house by moonlight. In Cadence's bedroom the bed is made up, the sheets already turned down. Jackie kisses her chastely on the cheek. Cadence reaches for her, but she steps away sideways. 'Sleep well, now,' she says, and slips from the darkened room like a ghost.

Cadence sleeps, dreams of waterlilies.

When she wakes, strong morning sunlight is shining through the trees. She lies, refreshed, remembering everything instantly. She feels poised, ready for something, a journey, a holiday, a new beginning. Twenty-four hours ago she was deep into her plan to confront Mr Domino, to trap him into telling her where he'd hidden Josephine. Today it all seems like a blind alley, a total mistake. She's convinced she screwed up, or the kid was lying. Maybe the real guy was paying him to lead her to the wrong place. Maybe —.

Ah, the hell with it. What does it matter now? She turns over, listening to the frogs, enjoying the feel of the crisp linen against her naked skin. It's good here.

Cadence doesn't find it strange that she's already thinking about moving in.

She supposes that means she'll have to find a job. She can't go on using the card for more than another day or two. She wonders where Jackie works, how much she earns. She's kind and sweet, but Cadence doesn't suppose she's kind and sweet enough to offer to look after her permanently.

Anyway, all Cadence's permanent arrangements break down.

Maybe if she is nice to Jackie she'll let her stay a while. Maybe if she makes a real effort to be sympathetic and together and easy to live with. She's never cracked that yet, people she tries to live with always get mad with her about something, or else they turn into just total assholes and say it is all her fault.

Cadence could get it together with Jackie, no problem. She is so laid back, she is real pretty too, much prettier than Cadence, whatever she says about sisters.

Think pretty, Cadence tells herself.

She gets out of bed and looks at herself in the full-length mirror. She lifts her breasts with her hands, turns this way and that.

Jackie said she didn't have to get dressed here. But Cadence puts last night's clothes on again, rolling up the sleeves of the shirt, and struggling to pull Jackie's jeans up over her hips. She doesn't like to be the only one to go around naked.

Maybe she should change her hair again.

Well, she's going to change everything, she thinks as she goes out into the hallway. There's a TV on in the house, she follows the muffled sound of the voices. She makes a vow to whatever kind goddess sent Jackie into her life yesterday that she is going to quit drinking and smoking as of *now*, she is going to get a handle on her life. Stop screwing around, for one thing.

She opens the drawing room door. On the TV screen, a guy with an ass like River Phoenix is slipping seven inches to a gasping blonde who is congratulating him rhapsodically. '*Give it to me, Frank!*' cries the woman on the TV screen. '*Let me have it all! Oh God! Oh my God!*'

The woman is Cadence Szathkowicz. The movie is *Dorothy Does*, her first movie, it must be on cable again.

Cadence goes in the room, staring at the screen, sits down hard next to Jackie on the couch. 'Oh my God,' she says hollowly. 'Oh my God.'

'Top of the morning to you, Cadence,' says Jackie, her eyes fixed on the screen, where Cadence's legs wave rhythmically either side of a pair of slender pumping buttocks.

'Oh my God.'

It's actually already afternoon, Cadence sees by the clock on the mantel, not that the information means anything to her just at present. Jackie is in a bathrobe.

'There's coffee and orange juice,' says Jackie, 'in the kitchen.'

The jock stands up, lifting Cadence with him by one hand under each buttock. The camera demonstrates that they are still united. '*Oh my Go-o-od!*' Cadence cries.

'Oh my God,' says Cadence.

Jackie pats her knee. 'Shh,' she says.

They watch the rest of the movie together in silence.

When it finishes. Jackie zaps it with the remote and turns to her guest.

'I suppose you'll be after some coffee?' she says.

There is a pool in the backyard, a sort of loggia on three sides and a sagging canopy of fine wire mesh overgrown with moss and splattered with birdshit. The water is not like the pools of California, more like a fishpond. It is dark, and weedy. Steps lead down into it, an inflatable ball floats at the far end. Lawn chairs stand around in various states of dereliction. Cadence sits huddled on one, nursing a mug of coffee, staring at the frogs jumping in and out of the pool.

Jackie comes out of the house and walks around the loggia towards Cadence. She has put on her nurse's uniform. She looks as clean and crisp in this heat as she did yesterday, only today her hair is in a ponytail, gathered high up on the top of her head. She puts down a folded towel at the top of the steps and comes to stand over Cadence. She is drenched in the gauzy sunlight that cascades through the wire net. She says, 'Is that what you do, then?'

'What,' says Cadence, 'that?'

She looks into the dark pool. Flies skim the surface.

'Yes,' she says. 'Sometimes. That's one of the things I do. I thought, you know —' She waves her hand. She lacks the energy to explain

96

herself. 'You know,' she says.

'Was it the money?' Jackie asks.

'Yes,' Cadence agrees readily. 'I needed the money. Well, I didn't really need it, I guess, not at the time. It's gone now,' she said.

'Are you not ashamed of yourself?' asked Jackie lightly.

Cadence looks up at her, shielding her eyes from the sun. She can't think what Jackie means. 'No,' she says. 'I had a good time. I know *he* had a good time.'

'But selling it,' says Jackie, objecting.

'People like it,' says Cadence. 'I mean, I guess you could give it away, the movie, I mean, but –' She wrinkles her nose. 'Somebody's got to pay for the tape. And the coke,' she concludes.

Cadence is not happy. She feels a funny crawling feeling in the pit of her stomach. She doesn't know why she's trying to justify herself. The uniform gives Jackie authority. Besides, she doesn't know this woman, she doesn't know how she feels. A lot of people are down on porno, she knows that.

They don't usually sit and watch the whole movie, though, those people. They're afraid of it. They're afraid of recognising things they don't want to recognise.

Recognising themselves, thinks Cadence. Like she just did.

Or recognising their daughters. Jesus.

Cadence looks at their combined reflection in the water. Jackie gleams whitely behind her.

'Are you going to work?' Cadence asks.

Jackie considers. 'You could say so,' she says.

She reaches down and pats the lawn chair.

'Sit up properly,' she says.

Cadence puts down her coffee cup, on the edge of the pool. She turns, lifting her legs onto the chair. She leans back.

Jackie goes and sits a little way off, just around the corner of the pool.

'What about him?' she asks. 'Was he nice?'

Cadence is getting depressed. Her resolution is a joke, she was going to turn over a new leaf and all there was on the other side was a xerox. 'Oh, well,' she says. 'He was okay, yeah. He was just this walking salami Kelly and Scott pulled out of the small ads.'

'Did you not like him at all?' asks Jackie sympathetically. 'You seemed to be very friendly with him.'

Cadence shrugs. 'You know,' she says. 'Men.'

Jackie asks, 'Are you not fond of men?'

'Oh, sure, some men,' says Cadence, thinking about Bob in L.A., Nick on the ranch, Jake and Richmond and Luis and all the others, countless others, she can't even remember their names. 'Some men drive you crazy. Actually, *all* men drive you crazy, the ones you want and the ones you don't.' She says this in complete faith that it will make sense to Jackie; and it seems that it does.

Jackie stands up. 'Do you prefer women?' she asks, as though it were a clinical question.

Cadence gazes across the water at the slender white figure. She thinks she knows what's coming next. But she doesn't believe it. She doesn't believe it's true.

'Some women,' she says.

'Get up,' says Jackie.

Cadence gets to her feet.

Barefoot, she is rather shorter than Jackie. She looks up into her face. The sun plays in the wisps of her hair.

Jackie puts her right hand above her left breast and turns up the watch that hangs on the bib of her apron. She looks at it, and then steadily into Cadence's eyes.

'It's time for your inspection,' she says. 'Will you take all your clothes off, please.'

She says it in a way that doesn't sound as though Cadence has any option.

Well, it was more or less what Cadence was expecting. Though this way it's also kind of scary, actually. The sun seems to disappear from her back, leaving her cold and goosepimply.

She unzips her jeans.

She pulls the plaid shirt out of them and leaves it hanging out all round her waist. She rolls the sleeves down and starts to unfasten the buttons.

'You know, I was just thinking yesterday how much time I seem to spend getting naked.'

'Be quiet,' says Jackie.

Cadence is nervous. She shuts up at once. Listens to her heartbeat. *Lump*-a. *lump*-a.

She slips off the shirt.

Her bra is just a chainstore brand, but it's pretty, lacy, with a design like daisies in a net. She unfastens it at the back, and slips it off her shoulders. Her knuckles brush her nipples, already erect, as she bares her breasts.

Then she hunches forward from the hips and wriggles herself loose from the borrowed jeans.

Her panties come off with them.

Cadence stands facing Jackie, nude, her hands at her sides.

Jackie's gaze is cold, dispassionate.

Cadence moves her feet an inch or two further apart.

'Into the water,' says Jackie. Cadence stares at her. 'Come on, now, quickly. Jump!'

Cadence jumps in the water.

It's not warm, despite the sun. She feels it overwhelm her. Furry fibres brush her naked body. She comes up, floats upright facing Jackie, blowing out water, pushing the hair back off her face.

Jackie kicks Cadence's coffee cup in the pond. Cadence sees it sink palely into the darkness. She frowns up at Jackie, confused.

'Fetch it, Cadence!'

Cadence dives, looks around under the water. It's seven or eight feet to the bottom, which is all covered in thick slimy fuzz. Little black blobby things swirl around down there. The water feels funny in her eyes.

Cadence surfaces, dives again head over heels. She's aware of flipping her crotch at Jackie as she dives. She hopes Jackie approves. She sees the coffee mug on the bottom, white in the murk. She grabs it by the handle and comes up with it, waving it in the air. She swims to the edge, holding it up for Jackie to take.

Jackie squats down on the edge, swivelling her knees round sideways. The updraught of her motion flaps her skirt, and from below Cadence gets a flash of pure white panties, black stocking-tops.

Jackie takes the mug with her left hand, takes Cadence's right hand with her right.

'Out now,' she says, and heaves.

Cadence emerges. Jackie points to the folded towel. 'Dry yourself,' she says. Cadence begins to rub herself.

Before she can get very far, Jackie says, 'Cadence Szathkowicz, you look abslutely delicious dripping wet, do you know that?'

Cadence is startled. How does Jackie know her surname? Has she looked in her purse? Last night, at the restaurant, she must have read the credit card; but no, that doesn't have her real name on.

'Time for your entrance examination,' says Jackie. 'Come inside, Cadence. Bring the towel.'

Jackie goes ahead, not looking back to see if she is obeyed. When Cadence comes into the room, Jackie is behind the TV, stooping, pressing the button on a VCR Cadence hadn't seen there.

Jackie comes out with a tape in her hand. Cadence recognises that tape.

So it wasn't cable.

Jackie has a copy of *Dorothy Does*.

Something very strange is going on.

Jackie fetches a wooden chair from the dining table. It has a velour seat and a carved back in a design of the flowers in a vase. She sets the chair in the middle of the floor and sits on it, her feet flat on the floor, some way apart. She holds out her hand for Cadence's towel.

Cadence hands it over.

It's a big bathsheet towel. Jackie puts one end of it on her lap, leaves the other end trailing on the floor beside her. 'Come here while I see to you,' she says.

Cadence steps forward. She stands on the towel.

'Come over my knee,' says Jackie.

Cadence bends over. She lies across Jackie's lap, bottom up.

Jackie pulls the towel up through Cadence's legs. She dries her bottom thoroughly with the towel, runs it in between her legs; drying her there. Cadence feels the firm, sure fingertips delving into the cleft of her bottom. Beneath the towel, Cadence is growing loose and warm. She starts to sigh. Her hair drips on the carpet.

Jackie pulls on Cadence's shoulder, bringing her left arm up, turning her face up. She bends and kisses Cadence bruisingly hard, invading her mouth with her tongue. Then she turns her face down again. She slips the fingers of her left hand into Cadence's mouth and Cadence sucks them.

Suddenly Jackie plunges her right thumb into Cadence's anus, and simultaneously rams a finger into her vagina.

No one has ever done that to her before. Cadence cries a broken cry, spasming on the pin of Jackie's cruel grip. She bucks across Jackie's knee. She can feel her eyes starting from her head, sweat bursting from her face.

Like Jackie said, she's examining her entrances.

100

Just as Cadence begins to feel the whisper of arousal curdling in her shocked loins, Jackie releases her. 'Stand up. Face me. Hands on your head.'

Panting, Cadence links her hands on her head. Jackie reaches in the pocket of her apron. She brings out a narrow strip of black leather with silver fittings. This she fastens around Cadence's neck, like a collar. She pats her bare thigh, sternly.

'Now then, slave,' she says, and something jolts hard in Cadence's womb. Jackie is still speaking. 'We're going to have a drink, and then I'm going to punish you.'

Alarmed, thrilled, Cadence blurts: 'Why?'

Jackie looks at her coolly. 'Double for speaking without permission.'

She clips a long leather leash to the collar and leads Cadence over to a hatch in the wall. Behind it is a cocktail cabinet. Cadence watches her mix two different kinds of rum, and add an apricot liqueur. She stirs it up with pineapple juice, squirts lime in and pours two glasses.

It is a zombie, like Josephine and Cadence drank a lot of in Dominica. Jackie knows Josephine. Cadence is sure of it now.

What have they done with Josephine?

Jackie holds out a glass. 'Kneel, slave,' she commands.

Dazed, Cadence kneels on the floor.

Jackie gives her the glass. 'You may thank me.'

'Thank you,' says Cadence.

'Call me mistress,' says Jackie.

Cadence starts to tremble.

'Drink up, slave,' says Jackie.

Facing each other, the women drink. The cocktail is powerful. Jackie empties hers quickly. She sets down the glass, straightens her white cuffs.

'Prepare yourself for a spanking,' she says, simply.

Cadence cries out inarticulately.

She finds herself standing up, trying not to shake. This is what she's been longing for, of course, but now it's here she's terrified. 'Mi-mistress?' she stammers.

'You may speak,' says Jackie, in a severe tone, sounding tired of interruptions.

'It won't hurt, will it?' she pleads.

'Of course it will hurt, you foolish girl. Come here, come,' says Jackie, and she takes Cadence over her knee.

She strokes and squeezes Cadence's bare bottom gently.

'It'll hurt more if you don't relax,' she says.

Cadence whimpers.

'Silence,' warns Jackie, and she smacks her.

Cadence grits her teeth, snuffles.

Jackie smacks her again, again.

It hurts. It hurts!

'Take it well, slave,' murmurs Jackie, nuzzling Cadence's ear with her warm mouth, 'you can have a treat later.'

Cadence does not take it well. It *hu-u-urts*. She tries to protect herself with her hand. Jackie rearranges her, pins her hands behind her back.

'I can see someone should have done this a long time ago,' observes Jackie. 'Open your legs, slave,' she says, and spanks her right there, in the crease.

Cadence can't believe how much it hurts. She mews in distress. She wriggles across Jackie's knee, flexing her buttocks, fighting Jackie's hands.

Jackie smacks her harder. 'Hold still,' she commands.

But Cadence can't. As the spanking continues she bucks, and jerks, and pants. She writhes on Jackie's lap like a captive animal. Her bottom is full of fire and her head is full of stars. She hears herself groan, hears the groan catch in her throat. Jackie is spanking her, she's bouncing up and down, she's —

Suddenly the whole world slides away in a silver fire and crying aloud —

She comes.

She lies there, gasping, across Jackie's knee. She comes lightly, sweetly, spiralling back into her body.

And hears Jackie shouting. She doesn't sound angry, just aggressive. 'Get up! Go and stand in the corner. Put your hands on your head.'

Her bottom burning, Cadence limps across the room, staggers into the corner. She wants to touch herself. She wants to stir her fire. Amazing as it was, amazed as she is at herself, she knows one thing, and that's that she's hardly started.

Jackie waits till she's calm. She makes her dress in garterbelt and stockings, black ankle boots with three-inch heels, no bra or panties, nothing else.

Except her slave collar.

Jackie approves. The mood has altered, as if they're slipping in and out of their roles. Jackie says, conversationally, 'I remember when Josephine wore that. Very good she looked too.'

Cadence knew it. She just knew it. She cries, 'Josephine was here?'

'Here? Oh no, not *here*. . .' Jackie's eyes are dreamy, wandering; then she suddenly pulls herself together. 'Now that's enough talk,' she says coolly. 'Come outside here and lie down.' Outside the dog is drowsing in the sun. It takes no notice while Cadence is chained by the collar to the handrail of the pool steps.

Cadence lies on her front to spare her tingling bottom. 'Jackie?' she says.

Jackie smacks her hard. 'Call me mistress,' she says, fiercely.

Cadence tries to think. Her brain is full of Josephine, and the strange fires building inside her. 'Permission to speak, mistress?' she begs.

'No. And if you speak again, it's the paddle for you.'

Cadence, astounded, falls silent. Jackie sits back in the chair at the corner of the pool. Cadence sees her pull up her skirt and push her hand inside her white panties. Jackie starts to masturbate, looking at Cadence.

Cadence longs to help her. After a while Cadence goes to touch herself. 'Uh-uh,' says Jackie, warningly.

Cadence is feeling scared again now. It reminds her of when she was a little girl, trying to get some guy and not really knowing if she could trust him but wet for him all night. Waves of lust flare off the swimming pool, dazzling her eyes. She stares at Jackie's busy fingers. She licks her lips.

'The paddle is hard, Cadence,' she hears Jackie say. 'Much harder than my hand.'

Jackie's hand wasn't hard, thinks Cadence. She only spanked her hard. Well, in fact she probably didn't. It isn't even hurting anymore, really, probably it wasn't that hard at all.

A paddle sounds like it would be hard.

'Can you do it, Cadence? Can you stand it?'

Cadence's mouth is dry. She stares at Jackie's circling stirring fingers, the way her hips rock, lazily, in the lawn chair.

Jackie's voice is gentle, rhythmic in the resonant southern air. 'You've never had the paddle, have you, Cadence? I think you're going to find it a bit of a surprise.'

Cadence says nothing.

Jackie sighs and sighs, but doesn't come. She get up suddenly, swings her legs off the chair and stands up, brushing at her skirt. She goes indoors.

At once Cadence's fingers creep to her crotch.

Jackie reappears. She is holding a pair of handcuffs, more like a cop than a nurse. She comes and stoops over Cadence, fastening her hands behind her back. She kisses her ear again, saying nothing.

She goes indoors.

Cadence doesn't last fifteen seconds. She calls out. 'Jackie! Mistress – please!'

Jackie comes outside again. She is carrying something. It must be the paddle.

Cadence begs. 'Not the paddle, mistress, no, just your hand, please –'

'On your hands and knees, slave,' says Jackie, ignoring her. 'Bottom well up.'

Cadence scrambles to obey.

Jackie walks around her, touching her hips, her thighs. 'Open your legs, slave,' she says. 'Dip your back.'

She squats down by Cadence's head, supporting herself with one hand on the chair. In the other hand Cadence can see the paddle. It is like a table-tennis paddle, only with a black leather cover over it.

The paddle smacks down on her bottom. Cadence kicks.

'Keep still,' Jackie orders. She pushes her legs back into position with the paddle, sits there resting it lightly against Cadence's agonized buttock.

'We'll teach you to keep still,' Jackie promises.

Then she finishes her paddling.

Cadence spends most of the day experiencing one discipline or another. She exercises at Jackie's command, bending and stretching. She carries things on her head. She plays with her breasts, and spreads her buttocks with her hands. She pisses and shits in a pot.

When she fails to do these things properly, which is to say readily, or neatly, or copiously, Jackie punishes her. Cadence learns the slap of the slipper, the crack of the hairbrush, the whisk of the cane. She shouts and cries a lot, and clings to Jackie's scented white front. Jackie torments her aching bottom with her nails. Cadence is forbidden to come again, even though she can hardly help herself.

104

She comes again and is punished for it.

At last Jackie strips her, dips her in the pool again and she screams at the shock of the cold water on her blazing bottom. After that it goes numb. Cadence is sure it is swollen. She walks with difficulty up the steps of the pool, into Jackie's enveloping towel.

They go into Jackie's bedroom. Cadence feels her bottom must be wounded and raw, half-expects a trail of blood on the carpet. She can't see anything. She has to stand in a corner now. She closes her eyes and rests her forehead against the cool wall.

Jackie goes downstairs again. Cadence can hear her moving around down there, singing.

Cadence tiptoes over and looks at herself in the mirror. She stands with her back to it, bends over uncomfortably and looks between her legs.

Her bottom and the backs of her thighs are fire-red, laced this way and that with cane marks. Everything throbs but there are no wounds.

It occurs to Cadence that she has fallen into the hands of an expert.

She goes back to stand in her corner. She presses her crotch against the wall and moans softly to herself.

She hears Jackie coming back into the room, drinking rum again.

Cadence is weeping, not from the pain but from the longing. How could she ever have known someone would do this to her?

Jackie fondles the back of her head, pulling her collar gently this way and that.

Cadence looks in the mirror, glimpses Jackie pulling back the bedcovers. Then Jackie unfastens her apron, lifts the skirt of her uniform dress, and pulls it up and off over her head. She stands there in old-fashioned lingerie, an uplift bra stiff with underwiring; full panties that stretch from above the waist to the top of the thigh; a broad, plain garterbelt and stockings. She looks hygenic and pure and Cadence has to look away.

Jackie sits on the bed. She calls her slave to her. Cadence hopes desperately she will fondle her and she does, cupping her thigh in one hand while she sips her drink with the other.

'It's very simple,' she says. 'You have to do everything I say.'

Cadence gives her an anguished look.

Jackie seems amused. 'You may speak,' she says gravely.

'Why, mistress?' croaks Cadence.

'Because you haven't got one of these,' says Jackie, and sticking out her chest she pulls down the elastic of her bra between her breasts, showing Cadence a small black design inked into the skin of her cleavage.

'Josephine has . . .' Cadence starts to say.

'That's right,' says Jackie.

Cadence sniffs. Her eyes prickle. 'Because I haven't got a little tattoo I'm nothing.'

'That's how we all start,' Jackie says.

'So I have to do everything you say.'

'That's right,' says Jackie.

She reaches behind her then and takes off her bra.

'Some of it won't be too bad,' she says, and she leans forward and kisses Cadence lightly on the lips.

'Some of it you're just going to love,' Jackie says, embracing her.

'Eventually,' says Jackie.

|9|

Today Cadence is wearing a suit, like a regular businesswoman: navy blue poplin with a white chalkstripe; padded shoulders, high waist, skirt-flared jacket with a short, tight skirt beneath. Beneath the jacket, a Girasole white viscose blouse with a scarlet ribbon bow in front; beneath the blouse, a white lycra bra, beneath the skirt, white lycra panties, garterbelt, black stockings, navy blue heels. Beneath the panties, a warm bottom, slightly tender from the spanking Jackie gave her after breakfast. ('We're off on a little trip today, Cadence, come here and take your travel medicine.') *Prophylactic*, Jackie called it. Cadence doesn't know what one of them is; but she knows her spankings now, the different feel you get when you have the paddle or the hairbrush or the strap, or Jackie's hand of course. She sits down carefully on the hard airport seat, swivelling her legs to keep her knees together, trying to keep her skirt neat, sitting down sideways it's so tight. She feels her bottom glow slightly underneath her, the faintest memory of Jackie's hand. The spankings fade so fast, it's surprising, though there's another one not too far ahead, usually.

She almost lifts her hand to her hair, then remembers not to. Her hair is up and back off her face now, sprayed till it's set like cotton candy, it doesn't move a whisker when she turns her head to look at the other women.

There are two other women going with her and Jackie to Chicago. One is called Rosemary, she's maybe a little younger than Cadence, very dark hair, short and curly, dark Italian looks: a round nose, arched eyebrows, deep lines beside the corners of her mouth. Which is a bright mauve pink, and she has a little powder blue eyeshadow. Big earrings like dishcovers. Rosemary seems nervous, can't stop looking all around.

The other one, Donna, is brown, older, very quiet. Her face is very pretty, clear golden-brown eyes with a kind of slant to them, she has a big jaw and her neck is thick, she carries her head high. Looks like a singer in a choir, waiting for the signal for her solo.

These two are also wearing suits, Rosemary's dark charcoal, kind of French, and Donna's a pale magnolia colour. With Jackie in plain black with her hair in a bun, you'd take them for a bunch of delegates going to a business conference. Cadence knows nothing about the other two. Jackie had the driver pick them up from a house near the airport, introduced everybody, then they all sat silent the rest of the way. The air in the limo smelt of feminine discretion.

Their plane is a regular commercial flight. Cadence is surprised, she had thought there might be a seven-seater Lear waiting for them. She sits next to Jackie, with the other two across the aisle. Jackie puts her hand on her knee, on the sheer black nylon just below the hem of her tight skirt. Cadence feels herself expanding, her nipples stiffening instantly as if her breasts are swelling in her brassière, her hips about to bust the zipper in her skirt. She looks at Jackie, wide-eyed. Jackie says: 'Would you like a pillow, Cadence?'

Cadence shakes her head, not trusting herself to reply. She glances across the aisle, sees Rosemary glancing nervously across at her. Their eyes meet, slide apart. Rosemary says something to Donna, and Donna replies, you can't hear what they say for the whine of the air conditioning.

'Who are those two?' Cadence murmurs.

Jackie pats her leg again, admonishing her. 'No questions now, Cadence.'

They fly over farmland, over trees, over a river. Clouds come along and blot out the land. It is as if the scenery is being changed down there, one place turned into another, when the clouds get rolled back they will be somewhere else. Everybody drinks airline coffee, and orange juice. Cadence leafs through the in-flight magazine, looking eagerly at the pictures of suave entertainers, young politicians, yachtswomen. The ads are for clothes, cosmetics, hotels, luggage. Cadence is very excited. She keeps thinking of Josephine. She looks in the magazine for clues to the existence of the world she lives in now, a secret world. She looks at Jackie, about to ask her a question, remembering only when she sees the cool smile on her lips.

Rosemary gets out of her seat and leans down to speak to Jackie.

'I have to go to the bathroom,' she says. She sounds ashamed, as if this is an admission of failure.

Jackie says, 'Take care, dear.' Warning her maybe to be careful in case there's turbulence. Or maybe something else.

There is another limo at O'Hare, another driver with a face like a Macy's dummy. Rosemary and Donna sit with their backs to him, Cadence sits facing Donna, Jackie next to her again. There is much arranging of skirts and nylon-sheathed legs.

They drive right through downtown. Cadence looks out of the smoked glass window, sees huge graffiti, grotesque versions of Garfield, Spiderman, sprayed up on the wall of an old warehouse. It's a hot day, but there are still trash fires under the El, bums and punks hanging around them. They yell things at the car as it slides past them smooth as a shark, but you can't hear what, you can't hear a thing from outside. They pass a theatre, on the marquee it says MUD WRESTLING 5.00 7.00 9.00.

'Rosemary,' Jackie says suddenly, very sweetly.

They all look at Jackie. She is leaning forward slightly, her hands folded on her knee, looking Rosemary in the face.

Jackie says, 'Did you play with yourself in the bathroom on the aeroplane?'

Now they all look at Rosemary. Cadence holds her breath. Rosemary is going pink. She can't speak.

Rosemary quivers. She opens her lips, moistens them with the tip of her tongue. Her eyes dart right and left, as if she's thinking of throwing herself from the moving car. They're on the freeway now, travelling at speed.

'Answer me, Rosemary dear,' says Jackie, pleasantly.

Rosemary answers. 'Yes,' she says. It sounds like the voice of a mouse in the car.

'Yes, mistress,' says Jackie, reminding her.

'Yes — mistress.'

'Pull up your skirt, Rosemary,' Jackie says, shifting forward in her seat.

The upholstery is leather. It smells of power and security. Rosemary leans forward from the waist, hooking the tips of her fingers under the hem of her skirt and sliding it upwards, up her thighs. She looks an instant at Donna, then at Cadence. Cadence understands that Rosemary is new too, though Donna maybe isn't.

109

Rosemary lifts her bottom an inch off the seat to slide her skirt up under herself. The skirt is very tight. It is dark in the car, with the windows up. Cadence sees a strip of glossy black material she thinks is a petticoat, then realises must be the lining of the skirt. Rosemary is not wearing a slip under her skirt. She is wearing a black garterbelt or maybe a corset, and black stockings. The elastic of the garter snaps bisects her tawny thighs.

She looks into Jackie's eyes, apprehensively.

'Undo your stocking,' Jackie says.

'Which stocking, mistress?' Rosemary breathes. She speaks reluctantly, as if she wishes she could remain completely silent.

'The left.'

Rosemary obeys. She unfastens the elastic above her thigh, then shifts over a little to reach the other one underneath.

'Roll it down.'

Rosemary rolls down the stocking top to just above her knee. Her thigh is bare now.

Jackie's hand is a flash of white in the dark interior of the car. It falls with a loud crack on the flesh of Rosemary's thigh.

Cadence and Donna look.

There is a red handprint there now.

Jackie has smacked Rosemary so hard she is biting her lip. her eyes glitter with a suspicion of tears. Cadence can see, anyhow she knows, Rosemary longs to shout out, to clap her hand to the place where Jackie slapped her, but she dare not.

The driver has not even looked in his mirror.

Jackie sits back calmly, satisfied. 'Dress yourself,' she says, and turns to watch as they pass three bikers on Harleys, riding in formation.

Cadence looks away from Rosemary. Her eye catches Donna's. Donna is looking right at her. Cadence would like to speak to her, but it wouldn't be allowed. The two women look at each other, neither of them giving away one single thing.

The house is big, stands back off the street behind a line of lime trees and a hedge. It looks pretty old, grey brick and tile, bay windows and a stubby six-sided turret thing in one corner. The limo parks, Jackie gets out and ushers the three of them into line. They walk up the steps in single file. Jackie first, then Cadence, then Donna, Rosemary on the end. A maid in a black dress and thick stockings, white apron and little white cap like a nurse's cap, opens the door and lets them into a hall. There's a big clock on the wall, big and round enough for a town clock, Cadence thinks. Its deep slow bass tick is the only sound in the hall. The floor is marble tile, white and black and blue triangles like a mosaic. There are several doors, each of them with an oval glass window at eye-level and a skinny rectangular window of glass down near the floor. The glass is ribbed so you can't see anything through it but light. 'I'll tell Madam Suriko you've arrived,' says the maid, and she goes through one of the doors.

'Stand over against the wall,' Jackie orders, and they do: in a line, up against the wall. They hold their hands at their sides, they don't look at each other.

The place smells of spray polish and orange blossom.

The maid comes back, says something quietly to Jackie, and the two of them go out together.

The women wait alone in the hall.

They stand with their backs against the wall, staring into space. No one speaks.

Cadence is next to Donna, who is taller than her. She can hear Donna breathing, kind of fast, like she's recently given up smoking.

The clock ticks.

They wait a long time there in the hall.

Suddenly the door Jackie and the maid disappeared through opens, the maid comes out, alone.

'Donna,' she says, looking right at her.

And Donna goes out with her. There is the sound of feet going up stairs.

That leaves Rosemary and Cadence.

Cadence can hear Rosemary's breathing now. It sounds kind of ragged and excited, like something's going to happen any minute, any minute now she's going to say something. She won't be able to stop herself.

Cadence closes her eyes and prays that Rosemary won't say anything.

She can't hear anything in the hall but the clock and Rosemary's damn breathing.

And her own heart, which is pretty fast too.

She glances to the side, catches sight of Rosemary's profile.

Rosemary is biting her lip, over and over again, pulling her bottom

111

lip through her teeth.

Cadence puts her hands behind her back.

She hears Rosemary catch her breath. Unwillingly she sneaks another look. She looks sideways at her, up to her face. Rosemary's eyes are closed, her lip is in between her teeth.

Swiftly Cadence looks down; and away.

Rosemary is touching herself. Right there in the hall of the house, Rosemary is touching herself through her skirt. Cadence can't believe it. She looks stiffly in the opposite direction.

The clock ticks.

The door squeaks open again suddenly, and the maid appears.

'Rosemary,' she says.

That just leaves Cadence.

The suit is pretty uncomfortable, the tight skirt, the heels and all. She wishes she could take it off.

Cadence is pretty hot now, thinking of what Rosemary was just doing, thinking what might be happening to her and Donna up there. With Jackie and whoever the hell's house this is.

She thinks of Rosemary's thigh, luminous and bare in the gloom of the limousine. Jackie may be skinny, she doesn't look strong, but she can certainly smack. She's good in bed too, though Cadence remembers she's not to say anything about that here, that's a no-no.

Until she gets her tattoo.

From Josephine.

The clock ticks.

Cadence wants to touch herself.

She tries to name all the states, then all the state capitals.

The clock ticks.

She wonders if it would be okay if she did just touch herself, or if there's a camera somewhere.

The clock ticks.

She doesn't think there is a camera.

The door squeaks.

'Cadence,' says the maid.

Cadence follows her through the swinging door, up wooden stairs with oilcloth on them, along a carpeted hallway, to a white door with no windows in it, just a line of Chinese characters in red paint up over the door handle. The maid knocks. Someone says to come in. She opens the handle, ushers Cadence in, shuts the door behind her.

Cadence is standing in a big warm white room with panels of moulded plaster all the way around the walls, to shoulder height. There are five tall windows, open slat blinds lowered over them. There is a breeze in the room. The smell of orange blossom is stronger in there.

Ten yards away is a big solid upright chair, like from a medieval banquet hall. It is made of polished wood, with a red leather seat and back, and brass studs all the way around the leather. The studs are polished and gleam softly in the diffuse light. No one is sitting in the chair. There is no sign of Rosemary, or Donna.

Jackie is sitting across the room on a big sofa, her arms stretched out along the back. On a yellow wooden folding table at her knee is a tray holding a Chinese teapot, squash-shaped with a bamboo handle, and two little Chinese teacups with no handles at all. On the sanded floor between Jackie and Cadence is spread an oriental rug, beautiful plum reds and old gold yellows. In the centre of the rug there is a low, heavy, round table with a big glass vase of dried grasses on it. Standing by the table is a Japanese woman.

She is in her thirties, her hair in a pageboy cut. She has a high forehead, little round glasses in wire frames on her little nose. She is frowning. She is wearing a burgundy silk top with a mandarin collar, buttoned up to the throat, and black leather trousers. She is not very tall. Her hands are on her hips. there is a big lacquer bangle on her left wrist.

What the hell, thinks Cadence, and she bows to her.

When she looks up, Jackie is smiling.

'Madam Suriko,' she says, her voice rather quiet and lost in the airy room, 'this is Cadence.'

Madam Suriko looks like she might have smiled too, when Cadence bowed to her, but she looks like the kind of woman you'd never see smiling even when she was.

'Cadence,' says Madam Suriko, formally. She doesn't sound Japanese.

'Mistress,' says Cadence.

'Come here.'

Cadence approaches her, stands a couple of feet in front of her, her arms at her sides.

She is aware of a sharp scent coming off the woman, as if she has been exerting herself recently. It is not unpleasant. She lowers her eyes to the leather trousers.

Suriko lifts Cadence's head with one hand under her chin. Her gaze is cool, inflexible.

'What are your attributes?' she asks her.

Cadence has no idea.

'I've worked in films,' she says. 'Also I'm in college, only I'm taking a vacation right now, a little Me Time, I guess you could say . . .'

Suriko's eyes are like hard jewels, unmoving. She lets go of Cadence dismissively and turns to the table. Irritably she lights a cigarette.

Cadence looks at the rug. It's a pretty rug.

'What are her attributes?' Suriko is asking Jackie, over her head.

'Josephine chose her,' Jackie says.

Cadence looks round. 'Is Josephine here?' she asks.

Jackie cries, 'Cadence!'

Suriko takes the cigarette from her mouth and throws it into a marble ashtray. She lifts her hand and slaps Cadence across the face.

Cadence buckles at the knee, clapping her hand to her cheek.

'Kneel!' cries Suriko. White marks have appeared in the skin either side of her nose.

Cadence kneels, stiffly in the tight executive skirt.

She bows her head.

Suriko steps across the room and back. Her boots rap on the yellow floor, rap, rap, rap. Forcefully she unties the ribbon bow from around Cadence's neck, opens the collar of her shirt, bares her neck. Cadence feels the familiar soft stroke of a slave collar, a narrow band of leather run around her neck and fastened with a buckle behind.

The buckle is cool against her skin.

'Josephine chose her,' says Suriko, sarcastically.

Jackie says nothing.

'I shall test you myself,' Suriko says to her. 'Take off your jacket.'

With nerveless fingers, Cadence unbuttons her jacket. Still kneeling, she slips her arms out of it, shrugs it off. She kneels there on the oriental rug, holding the jacket crushed in her hands. She looks up questioningly at Suriko.

With a snort, Suriko takes the jacket from her and hurls it across the room.

Cadence hears the clatter of its buttons as it skids across the polished floor.

'Stand up.'

114

She stands, with difficulty, in the high-heeled shoes.

'Lift your skirt,' says Suriko.

With even more difficulty, Cadence peels the tight blue skirt with the white chalkstripe up her thighs. She leans forward to work it up over the swell of her bottom. The hem catches one of the straps of her garterbelt and flips it open. Quickly she pulls her sagging stocking-top up into it and snaps it shut again.

She stands upright, holding her skirt up to her waist, displaying her underwear.

Suriko goes to sit in the empty chair.

She folds her hands in her lap. She looks at Cadence's display.

'Take down your panties,' she says.

Cadence glances at Jackie, sitting on the couch. The collar seems to tighten around her throat.

She skins down her panties.

The crotch is already sticky. An unmistakable thread of silvery mucilage stretches down from Cadence's moist vulva into the gusset of her panties.

She bares her crotch to Jackie and Madam Suriko.

And her bottom.

'Come here and bend over my knee,' orders Madam Suriko.

Madam Suriko does not fondle her first, squeezing the cheeks of her bottom and probing the deep cleft between, the way Jackie likes to.

She simply spanks her.

It takes only a moment or two of punishment before Cadence realises it is only her hand Madam Suriko is using, not some wooden paddle or the sole of her shoe. Her hand is hard and stiff as wood. She plants three hard smacks on Cadence's right cheek, then three on the left. Then she moves to the side, smacks her hips, rolling her efficiently back and forth on her lap as she strikes home, now this side, now that. She lifts her knee, tipping Cadence forward so she thinks she's going to slide off onto the floor. She smacks under Cadence's bottom, the fleshiest part just above each thigh. Cadence cries out. Her feet wave helplessly in the air, jerking at each smack.

'This habit will be unlearned,' she hears Suriko say, sharply as she continues to spank her. The sharp scent of her perspiration is now a tang in Cadence's nostrils. 'There is a great deal of work to do here,' Suriko comments, speaking to Jackie. 'You have not brought her a moment too soon.' And Jackie replies something in her soft voice that

Cadence can't hear.

When her spanking is over, Cadence is sent to stand in the corner with her hands on her head. The maid brings Madam Suriko and Jackie a fresh pot of tea. They sit conversing quietly, in a low murmur. Jackie comes and removes Cadence's skirt and panties. 'You won't need these,' she tells her. The fingers of her hand linger an instant on Cadence's neck, near her collar.

Cadence hasn't forgotten Josephine, but she thinks she is in love with Jackie a little bit. She can't stand it that she's been handed over to Suriko, who is a tiger. Cadence does not love Suriko. Her bottom burns.

They take her upstairs, into a big loft with bare white walls and apparatus. Donna and Rosemary are already there. They are both wearing collars like Cadence's, but neither of them is wearing her suit anymore.

Donna is wearing a black leather corset that pinches her waist in small and thrusts her tits up out in front. Her arms are strapped together behind her, around the wrists and around the forearms and around the elbows and around the biceps. Her shoulder blades are nearly touching. She's got black stockings and little short slave boots on, and her feet are locked wide apart in two staples in the floor of the loft, and she's on a chain that runs up from the ring on her collar to a staple in the ceiling. Her mouth is open. It looks very wet and very red. Her thighs are trembling. Cadence sees her pubic hair has been shaved. She wonders whether they've just done that to her now or whether she likes to do it for herself. A young man with long white hair is standing in front of Donna. He has a black domino mask on. His prick is sticking up out of his pants, Cadence sees he has five silver rings round it. The maid stands by him with a big silver platter. It has two things on it, a black riding crop and a white feather.

Rosemary is lying face down on an adjustable bed. The bed is tilted so her head is low, her feet high. She has a black corset on too, maybe they were both wearing them all along, Cadence thinks; but no stockings, nothing else except she still has her earrings. Her wrists and ankles are clamped to the corners of the bed. When she jerks her head up Cadence can see her neck is chained to the end of the bed by a collar. Her bottom is about shoulder height, it is richly scored with the strokes of thin canes. Two young women in domino masks and short black skirts and thick black tights are working on her. One of them is nude to the waist, her tits are minute, almost nothing there at all. When Rosemary cries out, Cadence cannot tell whether her cries are pain or pleasure.

Madam Suriko inspects her charges. She confers briefly with the two women, who address her respectfully. She speaks to the maid, who curtseys. Saying nothing to Jackie or Cadence, Madam Suriko goes back out of the room.

In the middle of the room, between two narrow round pillars, is a long wooden bar about waist height with a small dip in the middle. There are two other bars down close to the floor, four metal staples in each. The white loft smells of polish and desire, the air is thick with pheromones. They confuse Cadence, they make her dizzy. She turns to Jackie, she asks. 'Is this a brothel?' Jackie is shocked by the suggestion, she hides a smile.

'You nust be quiet now, Cadence,' Jackie says softly, urgently.

'But I hurt . . .' Cadence complains. It's okay really, she is just wanting Jackie's attention, thinking of the cool touch of Jackie's pale hands when they peel down her panties. She looks around. No one is watching them. She presses her hip against Jackie's. 'Stroke me, nurse, please . . .' Jackie's green eyes are luminous, wary. Cadence seeks her mouth, stealing a kiss.

'Jacqueline!'

It is Madam Suriko. She has come back. She is standing in the doorway of the loft holding something small wrapped in a steaming towel. She gestures, the maid comes, curtseys, takes the bundle from her.

Madam Suriko comes stalking across the room. She is taking something from the pocket of her black leather trousers. She gives it to Jackie, who accepts it meekly, without a look.

Cadence looks. It is a domino. A white one, with black spots.

Suriko snaps her fingers. One of the women, the one still wearing all her clothes, leaves off punishing Rosemary and comes over. She produces a pair of handcuffs and fastens Cadence's hands behind her back.

Donna is sobbing. There is a loud, thin crack, and she wails sweet and high.

Madam Suriko directs Jackie to the bar. 'This is not the first time I've had to do this,' she says to her sternly.

Jackie says nothing. She strips off her suit jacket and hangs it on

117

the end of the bar. Beneath her white blouse her breasts swell clean and fresh. Cadence knows those breasts, the mysterious black mark inked between them, like there is between Josephine's. Jackie hikes up her tight black skirt.

Cadence hears Rosemary shriek. She's the only one who looks over there. The maid has unwrapped Madam Suriko's steaming package. It is a long, curved brass device. She and the half-nude woman are inserting it into Rosemary. From here Cadence can't see whether it's her ass or her cunt they're putting it in. Maybe it doesn't matter.

Jackie's panties are black too, plain cotton, very brief. When she sets her toes, feet apart, beneath the lower bar and bends across the upper one, the black triangle of the panties tightens between the stretching muscles of her bottom. She unfastens her stockings and tucks the elastic up out of the way.

She reaches down to grasp the other low bar, the one for her hands.

She looks very beautiful like that, her offered flesh gleaming whitely in the soft light that pours through the high windows. Cadence wishes Jackie would unfasten her hair and let it trail on the floor.

The young woman in the mask has fetched straps and padlocks. She squats to fasten Jackie's ankles and wrists to the staples. No one is taking any notice of Cadence.

'Wait!' says Cadence urgently.

Suriko and the squatting woman look at her.

Cadence sighs.

'It wasn't her fault,' she admits. 'It was mine.'

She goes to stand at the bar, presses her bare crotch to the wood next to Jackie. She looks sideways at Suriko. 'I'm the one you have to punish,' she tells her.

Jackie doesn't straighten up. Cadence sees her looking up between her legs, looking at Suriko. There's a little triumphant smile between them then, so fast it's gone before Cadence can be sure she saw it.

Cadence thinks Suriko will be angry again, but she isn't, which is strange. She doesn't do anything right away. It's like she wants to give Cadence a chance.

'You will both be punished,' says Suriko. 'Jackie's punishment will be no less if you share it.'

Cadence lifts her foot and runs her toe along the foot bar, back and forth. She's been spanked twice today already, but this is no spanking.

She shrugs. 'Okay,' she says.

There is a flicker of motion in the air and a slicing, blazing pain slams Cadence's hips against the bar. As she shouts, Madam Suriko grabs a handful of her hair, brings her face very close.

'Kneel, slave, and beg!'

Cadence drops to her knees on the hard floor. She is sweating, her mouth is dry. Her bottom is burning horribly, her wrists hurt where she tugged involuntarily against the steel cuffs. She sees tropical trees in her mind, through the haze of pain; a beloved face: Josephine's.

'Punish me, mistress!' pleads Cadence, the slave.

They bend Cadence across the bar beside Jackie and lock them both in place. The staples are too far apart to let Cadence touch her.

Cadence hears Rosemary whimpering, the unmistakable sound of a woman coming to climax.

Through the black nylon arch of her legs Cadence sees Madam Suriko step back as the young woman in the mask raises her cane.

|10|

Cadence Szathkowicz has never been so horny. Cadence knows that, compared with some people, she is pretty horny. She knows what she likes, and she tends to get it. But in between the getting is always the wanting. And she's never wanted anything like she wants something now, through the long days and nights at Madam Suriko's.

She wants Josephine, basically. She keeps thinking about her. Even when she is being punished, when they are hurting her, she thinks of Josephine. Somehow, Cadence imagines, it is Josephine behind it, Josephine whom she loves and trusts. That makes it bearable.

But she knows she's fooling herself. Josephine is their prisoner too. They've taken her away and locked her up somewhere. They are hiding her from her. Josephine is suffering too.

Cadence likes to imagine that while they are hurting her, they are not hurting Josephine. She is doing it for Josephine. She likes to take that. Up to a point.

'Ouch!'

The maids smack her hard to remind her to keep still.

It's pretty bad, Cadence thinks, when even the maids are allowed to hit you. Like, they're servants, right? Cadence has never had servants working for her, unless you count people that work for her daddy, but she's eaten in restaurants, she's stayed in hotels, she's commanded whole armies of people with a single credit card.

Nobody else here gets spanked by the maids.

They haven't spanked her today, yet. They've bathed and dried and scented her. Before that they waxed her legs and shaved her armpits. Smacked her a few times, like that, but not truly spanked her.

Being spanked by hired help is about as low as you can go, Cadence supposes. It's like going into Wendy's for a quarter-pounder and fries and being spanked by the servers. Wow. Cadence imagines herself having to bend over the counter, being held down by clerks while the guys come out of the kitchen, rolling their sleeves up. They are carrying kitchen implements. Dough paddles. They are carrying the things you use to turn over a fried egg. Cadence doesn't know what they're carrying, she only knows what they're going to do with it.

When the busgirl pulls down Cadence's panties, she hears everyone in the restaurant stop chewing and turn to watch.

Cadence hisses.

Too tight the other side now.

In her chair in the corner, Jackie looks up from her clipboard. Her green eyes glitter. Her mouth doesn't move.

Disturbing Jackie. Cadence knows she is in trouble now.

The maids fasten the harness around her waist, pull the strap up between her naked breasts, buckle up the collar. There are two maids, one black, one white. Cadence thinks they're pretty cute. She wishes one of them would kneel down and lick her, the way they do for everyone else.

She tried to get the white one, Lucy, to do it, when they were alone in the bathroom earlier, but Lucy said sharply, 'You haven't got a tattoo, mistress.'

Lucy is British. When she says anything it reminds Cadence of Josephine.

The straps of the harness are thin. They burn Cadence's skin. She's never been so conscious of anything she was wearing as she is of what they make her wear here at Madam Suriko's.

The maids fasten the last strap and then they leave. Furtively Dawn, the black one, pinches Cadence's bare butt as she goes, trying to make her shout. Cadence grimaces, determines to return the favour some day.

The pinch throbs as she stands, waiting. She knows she ought to be looking around the room, she know this is like, classic Americana, all these drapes and plaster friezes and maple eye and stuff. It's just that she can't concentrate on anything except the possibility of finding Josephine, and the possibility of any of these bastards ever letting her come.

Two equally unlikely prospects, if she's going to be realistic about it. She hasn't had an orgasm since they came up from the south. No one fucks her, they chain her up at night so she can't touch herself.

121

They're watching her all the time. Even in the john, they watch her.

'Face the wall,' says Jackie, not looking up from her pad. 'You know what to do by now.'

'Yes, nurse,' says Cadence.

'And I don't remember doctor saying you could speak, Cadence,' says Jackie chidingly.

Cadence turns and looks at the wall. Her bottom is sore already. It pleases them to keep it that way here. But she knows better now than to put her hands on it. She keeps her hands on top of her head. She stares at the wall.

She thinks of Josephine's face.

It's like a meditation, she thinks. Like what she used to do with Nick at the ranch. What you do is, you trace each thought back to the place where it came from. Or maybe it's like, trace it back to the time it came from. Or maybe that's the same thing. Like, time is space, wow. Anyhow, what it does is really empty your mind, it makes your thoughts completely still.

Except you keep thinking of Josephine, combing the hair back from her face when she kisses you. You keep thinking of rubbing your cheek against the inside of Josephine's thigh. You keep giving a little shudder and feeling wet seep and trickle down from your crotch, and wishing you could just take someone, the way the rest of them seem to do in this place. You stand there wishing it wasn't impurity and attachment to the body and wishing the goddam white light of infinity would show up.

Yep. Just the same way it was with Nick.

'Turn around now, Cadence,' says Jackie, after an entire ice age, practically. 'Take two steps forward.'

There are no kisses from Jackie now, not even a hug. Only spankings.

'Bend over and touch your toes.'

The strap around Cadence's waist tightens as she bends. Her breasts bob forward either side of the strap that runs down her front, from neck to cincture. The legbands grip the top of each thigh.

She feels Jackie's hand on her butt. 'Six, Cadence, and no flinching.'

Muffled through the thick walls, Cadence hears the great front doorbell clanging. Josephine, she thinks automatically. If she can just take this, that will be someone bringing Josephine.

She hears Jackie go over to the closet and open it.

122

Cadence closes her eyes. Not the cane, she prays, oh god, not the cane.

For Josephine she'll even take the cane.

Jackie comes back. She touches Cadence's bottom again. Her fingertips are cool, her touch professional.

'Legs perfectly straight, now, Cadence.'

At least Jackie still calls her Cadence. The rest just call her Slave.

A slender wooden ferule is laid across the crown of Cadence's cheeks. Jackie lifts it, lays it back there, softly, measuring her swing. She lifts it again.

There is a scurry of feet in the hallway and an urgent knocking on the dressing room door.

Jackie, not moving, calls, 'Come.'

Oh god, thinks Cadence, I wish.

She turns her head a tad, peeking. It's Dawn again. She stands in the doorway, not coming in, her hands clasped in front of her apron. 'The Supreme Master has arrived, mistress,' she recites.

Cadence feels Jackie pull away from her. It feels like Jackie's all of a sudden very tense above her, like a spring has triggered inside her.

'He wishes to inspect the slave,' says the maid.

'Stand up, slave,' says Jackie at once.

The Supreme Master, Cadence thinks, straightening. Who the fuck is he?

Whoever he is, he's saved her from a caning. She can't help giving Jackie a smile, not thinking. She receives a cold glare in return, but the cane stays down. Cadence looks at the floor, the way a slave has to.

She wonders if Supreme Masters like to screw new slaves.

They walk her quickly, naked in her harness, down the hall, the maid leading, the nurse following.

Going downstairs Cadence wonders, can the Supreme Master be a woman? Is Suriko one?

The Supreme Master is a man. It's the guy from the condo, Mr Domino. Now he looks completely amazing. He's standing in the foyer with two younger men on leashes. The maids are taking a purple cape off his shoulders. Under it he is wearing a black leather singlet. His hair is long and soft and blow-dried. He has long black boots on over back jeans and he looks like a rock star just dropped in from Hollywood.

In the scoop of his singlet Cadence can already see the little smudge of the tattoo on a chest bald as a little boy's.

Suriko is there to receive him. She looks as if she's suppressing powerful excitement. She looks as if she's going to orgasm just looking at this guy. She's wearing her burgundy top with the Japanese embroidery and the mandarin collar, and the tight black leather pants. They are tightest across her bottom, which is tilted up by the four-inch heels on her shiny black boots. She's got elaborate brass bracelets on, bands of chased and sculpted metal that go halfway up her elbows. Her lipstick is the colour of plums.

Cadence isn't crazy about Madam Suriko, mostly, but she has a great body. Actually she wouldn't mind going to bed with her. She looks at those tight, muscular buttocks and imagines them naked, pressed hard down on her face. Cadence wonders what she has to do to get summoned to Madam Suriko's bed, the way the other slaves do. She imagines Suriko naked, her sallow breasts flattened across her chest. She imagines Suriko in a basque, lying on her back on a bed, lifting her feet up into the air. Jackie in her starched white uniform pushing on Suriko's legs, bringing her bottom right up off the bed. Lifting her cane. Josephine in a black corset and a domino mask caressing Cadence while they watch.

Suriko stares through her little round glasses at Cadence coming downstairs. The master is looking at her too and Cadence realises she's forgetting to look down again, she's always forgetting that. There's so many weird and amazing things happening here, and so much else they're hiding from her. They must be feeding her peyote or something too, the weird things she's seeing can't all really be happening. Still, Cadence's relationship with reality has always been a bit, like, casual. It doesn't really matter, who knows what's real anyhow? Not even philosophers can agree on that one. Cadence is convinced if she looks up at the right moment she'll see something so sexy she'll come right there on her feet. But she's not allowed to look up.

Cadence comes to the bottom of the stairs. She's looking at the floor now. She starts trying to focus on individual triangles. The air smells of leather. Cadence thinks of the blond master's two slaves, musky and potent, a few yards away from her.

'Is she under your control, nurse?' asks the master. Cadence remembers hearing his voice on the phone at the motel, its edge of impatience. Her daddy talks like that on the phone to people, always telling people what to do like he thinks they shouldn't need to be told.

124

But her daddy doesn't wear black leather and riding boots. Or maybe he does, wow.

'Yes, doctor,' says Jackie apologetically. 'She needs a firm hand.'

'I can see *that*, thank you, nurse,' says the master, 'you've no need to tell me.'

Jackie says nothing. Cadence can tell she is looking at the floor now too. She listens to the deep slow tick of the clock.

'I hope you are as efficient as you are presumptuous, nurse,' says the master.

'Yes, doctor,' says Jackie. 'I mean, no, doctor. I don't know, doctor.'

The master sighs. The clock ticks. Cadence hears Suriko and the master confer in an undertone. 'All right, nurse,' says the master. 'Let us have a look.'

Cadence doesn't know what he means, but even while she keeps her eyes on the tiles, it's obvious Jackie does. Cadence hears a rustle of starchy cotton, a fragrance of young flesh and laundry soap as Jackie pulls up her skirt.

There's a pause.

'Turn,' says the master. Suriko is still saying nothing.

Cadence hears Jackie turning around. She is showing the visitor her panties. Cadence wonders if she is wearing plain hospital white, or something lacy, or the ones with the green candystripe. She wonders if the crotch of Jackie's panties is as hot and moist as her own crotch is. Just thinking of it makes her hotter and moister.

'I imagine we'll fit her in,' says the master to Suriko, dismissing a problem. Cadence is expecting one of them to tell Jackie to take down her panties now, but they don't. The master tells her to straighten her dress. He hands the leashes of his two slaves to her.

Then he comes to inspect Cadence.

He places his hands on her breasts, making her catch her breath. She does not attempt to look up. He hefts her breasts, weighing them in the palms of his hands. He presses them tight against her ribcage until it hurts, but she doesn't make any sound.

The master turns Cadence around where she stands. He runs a finger around her collar, making her swallow tightly. He examines her harness. Then he takes hold of her right buttock, squeezing it, testing her muscle tone. He's like a masseur, like a butcher, like one of the studs in Scott and Kelly's movies: a man handling meat. He rubs the ball of his thumb hard down diagonally across Cadence's buttock and

125

delves his fingers between her thighs from behind. She knows he can feel now how hot she is, how much she wants him, hates him, resents him for interrupting Jackie's hateful punishment. She can feel her pelvis grind against his intruding fingers, automatically, as if her will had nothing to do with it.

The master returns his right hand to her left breast. He squeezes her hard while kissing her harder, thrusting his tongue between her teeth. Now Cadence knows she must be supposed to keep her own mouth completely still and passive unless he tells her he wants her to kiss him back. But her body seems to be independent, it must be the drugs, she's giving him as good as she gets and to hell with the consequences. Maybe if she kisses him hard he'll want to go further.

He does. But not in the way she was hoping. She can just see his hands when he lets go of her. He's pulling on a white rubber glove, oh gross.

'Bend down,' he says.

The slender harness creaks as Cadence touches her toes again.

'Legs apart,' he says.

She's sure his slaves are sniggering.

Her buttocks quiver as the cold shiny finger probes into her soft and dripping vagina.

'When was her last discipline, nurse?' asks the master.

'I was about to give her a caning, doctor,' says Jackie.

'I think we can save it for tonight,' he says. He pulls out his finger with a rude jerk. Cadence pants. The burning in her loins is not diminished. She feels the man turning to Madam Suriko. 'Have her wait on us at dinner,' he says.

At dinner, Cadence serves alongside the maids. The blond master's pet slaves stand behind his chair, either side. Their erect cocks stick out of the unlaced flies of their toreador pants. Any time one of them looks like wilting, the master does something cruel with his fork or a lighted cigarette. Cadence avoids touching them, drawing in her bottom cheeks and sidling past when she goes round pouring wine.

She wishes she could have some.

She's wearing an apron, garterbelt and stockings, like the maids. Only without the dress or any underwear. Her breasts stick out either side of the apron bib, so the master can fondle them any time he feels like it. He dabs wine on her nipples with the corner of his napkin, then commands one of his slaves to lick it off. The slave's name is Russell.

His tongue is soft and very lingering. Cadence struggles to control herself, keeping her eyes turned down, staring at the top of Russell's head, trying not to quiver. The master laughs joyfully and slaps the back of her leg.

Jackie is there, still in her nurse's uniform. She eats neatly, quietly, not acknowledging Cadence's presence. But Madam Suriko is cross, crosser than ever, as though Cadence has somehow embarrassed or dishonoured her. First there is too little wine in her glass, then too much. Nothing Cadence can do seems to be right. Madam Suriko thrusts out a hand and grips Cadence's crotch, painfully, through the fabric of her apron. She pulls Cadence to her, makes her pick up the jug from the table right in front of her and pour her another glass of ice water. She too slaps her spitefully as she steps away, making her stumble.

Cadence tries to catch Russell's eye but there is no action there at all. Russell and Ricky are already in heaven, standing here with their arms folded on their chests and their cocks on display at full salute. Russell is gaunt, in a sexy way, lazy eyes, long neck. Ricky looks like a football player or a ballet dancer, slim hips, powerful shoulders. Cadence wonders what kind of meat they like best.

The dessert is finished. With a glance at their visitor, Madam Suriko signals the maids to clear away. Cadence fetches the coffee. She hopes they'll let her eat soon, though in fact she's not too hungry. More horny. Full of anticipation.

At Madam Suriko's, the slaves give entertainments after dinner. Last night Rosemary and a fat girl brought each other off three times, first with only their tongues, then with only their fingers, then with a marzipan dildo. The dildo did not survive the event.

Cadence carries the coffee into the drawing room. Madam Suriko and Jackie are sitting down. The Supreme Master is standing beside his chair, speaking to the steward and the maids, who are all lined up to receive their instructions. The master is giving the steward a black iron key, telling her to lock up the slaves. 'This one will do perfectly well,' he announces, looking lazily at Cadence in her harness. Then he gives all the servants the evening off.

Madam Suriko objects. 'But our entertainments!'

The master smiles. Cadence brings him his coffee and a glass of cognac. His hair is like straw spun from gold, he has a small gold earring in his left ear. His two body slaves stand behind his chair.

'Tonight we shall make our own entertainment,' he says, to everyone in general. He fondles Cadence's bottom. 'Madam Suriko?'

Suriko shifts in her chair, straightening her back. 'Yes,' she says, as though it was her idea all along. She signs to one of the slaves, Ricky. He comes over, stands behind her and slightly to one side, and begins to massage her shoulders, rolling them in his powerful hands. She reaches round to toy with his cock. 'Jackie shall cane Cadence,' says Madam Suriko.

The master is not impressed with her suggestion.

'But that will be merely a postponed punishment,' he says. 'Where is the entertainment in that?'

'Then they shall cane each other,' says Suriko. Her voice sounds clipped, hard, as though she is on the point of shouting. 'And afterwards soothe each other's hurt, here on the floor, for our enjoyment.' She points to the soft blue rug with the toe of her boot.

The Supreme Master speaks softly, rapidly. 'Madam, you astonish me. You would put a cane into the hands of an untattooed slave of a bare week's experience?'

He gives Cadence a last lingering pat, dismissing her. Cadence takes Suriko her coffee and a glass of malt whisky. Suriko ignores her as she sets them on a side table. Cadence pretends to be concentrating on the glass and the cup and saucer, but she's really sneaking a close look at the cock of the slave, Ricky. It looks tough as leather, with veins like purple wire. Suriko caresses it.

The master is still speaking. He says: 'I think this pretty woman has turned your head, Madam Suriko. Stand out.'

Cadence takes Jackie her coffee and a glass of Cointreau. Jackie thanks her softly, smiling gravely into her eyes. Cadence comes to a stop beside her chair. She bows her head. She is very aware of the fragrance of Jackie sitting neatly beside her, holding her coffee cup on her snow-white lap. Still with her head bowed, she snatches a look at the others.

Ricky has stopped his massage. He stands behind Suriko's chair as motionless as Russell behind the master's. Suriko has let go of his cock. She is getting to her feet.

Madam Suriko is doing what she's told.

'Slave,' calls the master, in a voice like a preacher.

Cadence looks up, accidentally looking him in the face. She looks down again, walks forward.

'Kneel, slave,' he says.

He sips his coffee.

Cadence kneels, bows her head.

'Prepare your mistress for punishment,' he tells her.

His voice is soft as a bird now, but his accent is strong.

Cadence gets up again. All this kneeling down, getting up, she thinks: what a waste of time. But really she's excited.

Madam Suriko is going to be punished.

The mistress of the household stands upright and still in the soft, comfortable glow of the drawing room lamps. She makes no protest. She is completely in the power of this arrogant young man who has walked into her house and taken over.

Cadence remembers the look on Madam Suriko's face as she stood welcoming the master in the hall.

Cadence keeps her eyes down as she lifts the front of Madam Suriko's shirt and takes hold of the waistband of her tight black leather pants.

She wonders what the master has in mind for her instructrix.

She remembers the pictures in *Bondage Torment*, the magazine Fern and George had at the Bluewater Lodge motel. That seems ages ago, *ages*. Upstairs there might be a rack like that, where Madam Suriko can be strapped, with leather bracelets and chains of steel. Her hands could be drawn up over her head until they strain from their sockets. Her legs could be locked into steel fetters and drawn relentlessly apart. Cadence thinks of Madam Suriko's pearly yellow toes, quivering; the sinews standing out behind her knees. A broad belt might be pulled tight around her waist, squeezing her stomach and breasts hard against the body of the machine. Then Jackie could bring a fat silver flask, and unscrewing it, take out a thick curved device plated with chrome, dripping with disinfectant. While Ricky and Russell force open the pinioned woman's buttocks, Jackie would drive the thick rounded tip of the device up into the vagina, and crouch down to fasten it with strong clasps to the trembling labia. Because even Suriko would begin to gasp and cry out at this treatment, Jackie would next insert a gag in her mouth, positioning the leather flap delicately between her teeth, studded side downwards to dissuade her tongue from moving. Then, completing her restraint, a black rubber hood would be brought and pulled over her head, shutting her eyes and ears. Only then would the master rise, reaching for his whip.

Cadence unfastens the waistband of Madam Suriko's pants. Slowly she opens the zipper. She keeps her eyes lowered. She squats down to ease the tight leather over the swell of her mistress's hips. Her nose is mere inches from Madam Suriko's scented crotch. She smells leather, hyacinth, the salt sweat of desire.

The pants are difficult to remove. Madam Suriko stands stock still, with her feet apart. Her panties are black, cut full, with little panels of lace at the side. They look like panties she was expecting to have to show. The clinging pants drag at the panties as Cadence forces them down. She separates them, leaving her mistress's modesty still intact as first one marble-smooth thigh emerges, then the other. She pushes the thick fabric of the pants down to Suriko's ankles, where the boots stop it. She gets up and goes round behind her mistress to remove her boots.

Madam Suriko lifts her feet, one and then the other, for Cadence to pull off the spiky boots and the leather pants. Squatting on her heels in her harness, with her thighs parted for balance, Cadence is aware of the eyes of the young master gazing steadily at her crotch.

She tries to keep her own eyes down.

Madam Suriko's legs are bare now. She is ready to have her panties removed.

Cadence stands up and does it. She slips her thumbs in the elastic just above the lacy panels each side, and pulls the panties out, down over the strong, meaty buttocks of Madam Suriko, and down to the floor. She helps Madam Suriko step out of them.

She wonders if she should continue undressing Madam Suriko, baring her breasts and back.

But no. The master gestures Cadence back to her place beside Jackie. No elaborate punishment of straps and engines lies in wait for Madam Suriko. No concessions are to be made to her status. The Supreme Master is according Madam Suriko the deep humiliation of being punished like a child, across his knee.

She goes barefoot to him, and with supreme dignity and elegance, bends over.

Cadence forces herself to stare at the floor again.

She hears the first smack land, open-handed, loud in the silent intensity of the drawing room. She wants to look but she forces herself not to. The hard, deliberate, regular sound of the spanking continues. Under the hand of her young tormentor, Madam Suriko is absolutely silent.

Cadence feels her heart racing. Soon it will be her turn.

She jumps. A hand is stealing up between her legs, up the back of her thighs, stroking smoothly upwards past the legbands of her harness to the cleft of her buttocks. Cadence steals a glance at the woman in the chair at her side. Secretly, not looking at her, Jackie is caressing Cadence as she has not done since they got here.

Cadence shifts her weight, letting her legs open slightly, letting Jackie feel how wet she is. She sighs silently, staring at the floor, hands clasped behind her back.

Madam Suriko's spanking finishes with six hard smacks, deliberate and slow. Still she has not made a sound.

Jackie's touch melts away, and Cadence steals another look. Madam Suriko's bottom is blazing red. She is getting up, stiffly, slowly, suppressing the pain with her will. She is magnificent under punishment, more impressive than any of her slaves. Cadence drops her eyes again as Madam Suriko is sent to stand in the corner, just like a naughty child, with her hands on her head.

'Nurse,' says the master, in exactly the same tone as when he called Cadence from Jackie's side.

Gracefully, Jackie sets aside her coffee cup and gets to her feet. Cadence hears her footfalls, soft on the blue rug in her flat black shoes. She had been hoping the master would command her to prepare Jackie too, but he says nothing. Cadence hears again the rustle of Jackie's linen. She longs to watch as Jackie follows Madam Suriko across the young man's knee. She screws up her eyes and thinks of Josephine. Josephine naked, in chains, the marks of a fierce switching red across her smooth brown back.

Jackie does not take it as well as her mistress. From the first, she permits herself little gasps and tiny, stifled cries of anguish as the master's hand punishes her bottom. Cadence thinks of cuddling Josephine, they are naked in bed, the birds are singing outside, there are no marks on her beloved's perfect body. Josephine kisses her.

The flat crack of the master's hand, an undisciplined squeal from the woman across his knee.

Cadence jerks upright, unable to bear it any more. She gazes at the scene in front of her. There is the young blond master, looking kind of flushed now from the drink and the exertion. His feet are flat on the floor, a foot apart. Across his lap he holds the slim body of Jackie, face down, her white uniform skirt rucked up to her waist, her candy-striped knickers down around the tops of her candle-white thighs. Her black stockings are still hooked up to her garterbelt, her folded white cap perched properly on the top of her pinned-up hair, though fine golden strands of that hair are beginning to escape and fall around her face, which is hidden. Her bottom is a mess of scarlet blots and daubs, whole handprints visible, fingerprints like pink blossom spraying all across both cheeks. The master smacks her again and she cries 'Oh', very clearly and sharply, as if she has been offended rather than injured.

In the corner, Madam Suriko stands still as a decorative statue, her hands linked on her flat black hair. The lamplight catches her ornamental bracelets, and plays on the crimson glow of her buttocks and upper thighs.

The master lifts his head from his task, and sees Cadence watching. His eyes are amused, ironic. He says nothing, merely continuing Jackie's punishment; and Cadence continues to watch, defiantly, even though the master has seen her, she knows her punishment will be worse now. Behind him, Cadence sees Ricky holding Russell's cock, Russell with his hand behind Ricky's bottom, she can't see what he's doing there, but she can imagine.

The slaves stare at her, grinning openly.

Any minute now, thinks Cadence, he will finish with Jackie. He's saving me till last.

Her knees feel weak. She presses the palms of her hands to her bottom in anticipation, in sympathy for Jackie. She winces as the last slow smacks land, counts them, four, five, six.

Jackie is crying. She rises without dignity, clutching her well-punished bottom. The master smacks the front of her thigh and she squeals. Reluctantly she lifts her hands to the top of her head. The master fondles her crotch briefly, negligently. He is looking at Cadence. He sends Jackie to join Suriko in the corner.

'Slave,' he says again.

It is Cadence's turn. She is hoping desperately he will spank her, and not remember to send for the cane. She has not been spanked by a man yet. His eyes are strong and hungry for her as she crosses the room, as if dealing with the other two women has only stimulated his appetite; as if he has been saving the best till last.

She hopes he will spank her himself, and not humiliate her by

132

commanding Ricky or Russell to do it.

She crosses the room, the blue oriental rug soft and almost slippery beneath her bare feet. She stands at the master's knee. 'We call this the domino effect,' he says. 'Everyone goes over, one after the other. Bend over, slave,' he says.

Cadence shivers across his knee. She wants to be as poised and cool as Madam Suriko, but she feels as if she is going to slide forward and fall on her face. The master senses her insecurity and summons his slaves to hold her down. One presses her shoulders down, squashing her breasts against the master's thigh; the other holds her hands out in front of her, stopping her trying to use them to protect herself. Cadence hates them both, she refuses to look up and see which of them it is that's holding her hands, grinning at her discomfiture.

As the first smacks fall, Cadence imagines Josephine. She imagines a strange thing. She thinks it is Josephine spanking her. Man, how strange. Josephine was so gentle, she wouldn't ever do this — and this — and that. Josephine's image dissolves as quickly as it came.

Young as this guy is, he's an expert spanker. He doesn't seem to be tired or sore at all from the two spankings he's just handed out to Madam Suriko and Jackie. His firm hand rises and falls on Cadence's fleshy backside. She shouts and gasps. The pain takes her breath away. He lifts his knee under her, tipping her up and smacking her on the underhang of her bottom, right where she sits down. Madam Suriko likes to pay special attention to that area too, and Cadence understands she now has personal experience of just how keen that feels.

Cadence never imagined anyone could spank Madam Suriko, or that she would take it so meekly if they tried. Supreme Masters are something pretty special. She feels kind of honoured, in a weird way, that this one is working her over.

She saw the look in his eyes when she watched him spank Jackie.

He shifts his knee again and Cadence can feel the bulge of his cock through his pants, hard against her belly. He fondles her crotch, making her squirm. The slave's grip tightens on her wrists.

'You are learning, slave,' he murmurs. His fingertips probe her wet centre. Her bottom stings. She wants Jackie's cooling ointment. She wants Josephine to come and kiss it better.

'Josephine,' she moans.

She can feel he was just about to spank her again then, but stopped. He heard what she said.

'Let her go,' he says, and the pressure on her shoulders, the grip on her hands, are released. She tries not to touch herself but she hurts too much. She presses her hands to her bottom, exploring herself. The heat of her flesh is amazing. The pain is pulsating in her, making her pant. She remembers the first time Jackie spanked her, and made her come.

The master lets her fondle herself a moment longer, then prises her hand away firmly, but not roughly.

'We shall continue this upstairs,' he announces, 'across the bar.'

Cadence rises, shakily, in the grip of the slaves, one on either arm. Her head hangs down, her legs wobble under her. They support her out of the room, through the door into the tiled hallway. As she leaves, Cadence glimpses Jackie and Madam Suriko in the corner. They are no longer facing the wall, their hands are not on their heads but on each other's blazing bottom. Madam Suriko's head is thrown back, Jackie is kissing her throat. They sink to the floor together as the door closes on them.

Cadence is dismayed. She wants to stay in the drawing room and watch. She envies Jackie her chance to bring Madam Suriko's proud flesh to threshing, shouting abandon. She wants to be there when they come, to lick their juicy thighs, to spread ointment on their aching bottoms.

The slaves haul her upstairs, almost pulling her off her feet. The Supreme Master comes behind, herding her up to the big white loft. There is no one up there, it is silent and dark. Donna and Rosemary and the others are locked in their rooms. The sky is dark through the skylights.

The slaves hold her upright. The master stands in front of her and lifts her face in his hand. He looks with pleasure at her wet eyes, her flushed cheeks. He kisses her hard, sucking at her tongue.

He steps back. 'Stand, slave,' he tells her.

Russell and Ricky let go of her and step back behind her to either side.

Cadence Szathkowicz stands there in the dim room, panting in her harness and collar. She does not touch her bottom. She looks at the bare floorboards. She is a slave.

'Look at me, slave,' says the master.

She looks at him.

He has the face of a beautiful blond boy. He has put a domino mask on. His slaves are releasing his penis from the confines of his pants. They caress it. He slaps them lightly away.

'What did you say just now?' asks the master.

Cadence licks her lips. She wonders if her voice is working. 'Josephine,' she murmurs.

'Josephine is dead,' he tells her. 'Put her across the bar,' he commands.

Russell and Ricky grab hold of her elbows again and march her to the middle of the loft, to the bar. They spread her legs, setting her feet firmly under the lower bar, and bend her over the upper one. She hears the sound of padlocks. She smells sweat and the ghost of ancient semen. Tears drip freely from her eyes.

Through her legs she sees the masked master approaching with a broad leather belt, the buckle in his right hand. He presses himself against her sore bottom, making her cry out.

'Are you warm, slave? Are you prepared for your proper punishment?'

Too late Cadence realises everything that happened downstairs was a fake. Suriko and Jackie took their spankings to lull her into a false sense of security, to make her give herself away. If Josephine is dead, Cadence wants to die too. She hopes the belt will extinguish her. It slams into her bottom, making her scream. In a tempest of pain and noise she feels him work up one leg and down the other, then all the way back. The tip of the belt flicks cruelly between her straining thighs. Only when she has screamed herself hoarse does he mount her, pressing the slick head of his cock into the wet orifice of her anus. He ignores her womanhood, preferring to fuck her as if she were a boy, showing his contempt for her. She amuses him. Distantly she feels her own body begin to rouse; but it is too late, he is pumping hot seed into her ass and she will never come again, never. She begs him, hears herself beg him to bring her off, even to order his slaves to. But they grin, and leave her there, locked across the bar, in the blazing ruins of her own body. The master's wasted seed trickles out of her anus and drips glutinously on the floor.

It is completely dark by the time Jackie arrives, tiptoeing in stockinged feet.

'Poor Cadence,' she murmurs, trailing her fingertips across Cadence's abused backside.

Cadence does not reply. She doesn't wish to speak to Jackie. She only wants Josephine.

Jackie spreads healing ointment on Cadence's hurt. She pauses to fondle her vulva in a cool but not unfriendly way. It is too late for Cadence, too late for her to come. Jackie unlocks her and lifts her, supporting her with her hand on Cadence's left hip, Cadence's right arm across her shoulders.

'Be a good girl now, Cadence.'

Cadence wishes she was dead.

Together the women walk out of the loft and down the stairs.

Passing the doorway of a room she has never been summoned to enter, Cadence sees another of those scenes she can't believe, a hallucination. The Supreme Master is hanging naked from something she can't see, and Madam Suriko is whipping him with a snakeskin lash. They both wear domino masks, their faces contorted in an identical grimace of frenzy and pain.

Cadence wonders.

|11|

Not until the Supreme Master left did the house return to anything like normal. His departure was very sudden. A six-foot tall mute black woman with a bleached crewcut arrived one midnight in a black limousine, and took him away. It wasn't clear which was master and which servant. The woman was wearing a black PVC corset, fishnet stockings, high-topped black riding boots, a collar studded with industrial diamonds. In the back of the car were three identical blond youths in white surplices. In the front was an ocelot on a scarlet leash.

Cadence saw the departure from the corner of the hall, where she was being a coatstand. The master came striding downstairs, dressed in a black turtleneck and black leather trousers, and followed by one of his body slaves. He took his purple cape from Cadence's arms, pinched her right nipple hard in farewell and strode out of the building. Cadence glimpsed the chauffeuse through the open door; behind her was the limo, with the ocelot looking out of the window.

The master left his other slave behind. The man is still with them; he dresses as a woman and cleans the bathroom obsessively. Or perhaps it is a discipline.

Cadence dislikes being a piece of furniture. If they've beaten you first and they want to admire their handiwork, you have to face the wall; and then you can't see anything.

But if they stand you facing into the room you can see everything – everything you can see without moving, you're not allowed to move – and sometimes that's worse.

Today she can't see anything, except by squinching up against the window, and no one's been up to see her.

Cadence is in solitary confinement.

She wonders if the master will ever come back. When she saw the

137

car, earlier, she thought it was him returning. He has been gone several days now, two or three. Time moves strangely here. Time is measured by the interval between a master's orgasms, between two strokes of the whip. A long time? A short time? Eternity?

He told her Josephine was dead.

The morning after the master left, Madam Suriko ordered a nude parade and inspection. No orifice was allowed to pass unexamined. Madam Suriko went like a tight, angry whirlwind through the house, whisking from room to room. Slaps and cries rang through the walls. After that she called everyone together and commanded a general scourging. It seemed to be more to do with purification of her household than because they had displeased the master in some way.

After that, the old routine returned at once, as whole and exact as daylight after a dream. Sometimes Cadence wonders whether the man ever existed, or whether he was someone she only saw in a movie, or on TV, and made up a dream about. It's hard to be sure what's true and what's not, especially when nobody tells you what's going on.

Cadence has been locked here for more than a day now, she's sure of that. It was morning when they marched her up the turret stairs in her collar and high-heeled boots, gave her a meal and a spanking, then left her. 'We'll be up with the handcuffs later,' one of them said to her; but night arrived, and the next morning too, and no one has come at all.

Early this morning, waking from a dream about her mother selling hot dogs in a museum, Cadence heard voices in the street. She looked down through the window. It was the car again, or one like it. She didn't see anyone get out, but while she was looking Madam Suriko came out of the front door, followed by the whole household. Everyone except Jackie got into the limo. Jackie stood at the door, upright and composed as they drove away.

The house has been very quiet ever since.

Cadence wonders if Jackie has left too, and they have all abandoned her to die here. She falls into a confused dream of running after the limo with a green canvas purse, pulling out fistfuls of credit cards and trying to give them to everybody. She wakes to hear her name being called up the stairs. 'Cadence? Cadence? Are you up there?'

It's Jackie. Cadence's heart leaps.

'I'm in here!' she shouts.

She hears Jackie's hard-soled uniform shoes rapping quickly up the stairs. Then the key turns in the lock, and Jackie herself comes in.

Cadence is sitting on the end of the bedstead. She gets up as soon as she sees it's Jackie. She has a crazy impulse to rush over and throw her arms round her. She restrains herself, but only to blurting out, 'I thought you'd gone! I thought you'd all gone!'

'Hush, now,' says Jackie, walking up to her. Her voice is soft and firm, very reassuring. 'Let's have you on your knees now, Cadence, shall we?'

Cadence kneels down, then sits back on her heels. She hollows her back, sticks her bottom out a way, she knows Jackie likes that. She looks down, staring at a knot in one of the floorboards.

'Good girl,' says Jackie, and pats her shaggy head. Cadence's hair is black now. She quite likes it. Not that it's any concern of hers what colour they choose her hair to be. Jackie dyed it for her. Jackie's uniform smells of starch and primroses. After a moment, Cadence timidly lifts her face and touches Jackie's apron with her nose.

Not for the first time, Jackie lets her nuzzle her through the layers of her uniform. For a moment Cadence thinks she is even going to pull up her apron and skirt and press the crotch of her panties into Cadence's face, the way she did once back at the start. But she doesn't. She squeezes Cadence's bare shoulder and says, 'Kneel up straight now, Cadence.'

Cadence obeys. Jackie goes to the window and looks out at the city. 'Are you hungry?' she asks.

Cadence shakes her head, then realises that Jackie is not looking her way. 'No, mistress,' she murmurs.

Jackie eyes her speculatively, as if measuring her for something. 'Do you want to go for a swim?'

She leads Cadence downstairs. There is no sound from anywhere in the house except the great clock ticking in the hall. They pass through the lounge, through the dining room, past the kitchen. Cadence tries to keep her eyes on the ground, but even so she is aware no one is in any of these rooms. The house feels entirely deserted. She follows the swishing of Jackie's crisp skirt against her nylon-sheathed calves.

In the back yard they cross the lawn and go through a small iron gate in a hedged enclosure. Inside lies the pool, violently blue, its surface ablaze with sunlight.

Jackie conducts Cadence to the poolside. 'In you go,' she says simply.

Cadence steps out of her boots, reaches down to unfasten the strap of her garterbelt.

Jackie lays her hand on Cadence's bottom. 'In,' she repeats.

Cadence straightens up. She takes a breath, steps off the side and plunges into the water.

She bobs, water streaming from her. Jackie is watching.

Cadence swims slowly away, across the pool. After the stuffy attic, the water feels great. It soothes and invigorates her.

She swims back to Jackie, still standing on the side.

She swims across again.

Floating, she watches, willing Jackie to come in and join her, but knowing it is not for her to speak.

Life is so much easier now, than in the old days when she used to talk so much, when she was surrounded every minute by talk and music, TV, movies. Cadence knows now there is nothing she needs to say that will not eventually happen to her; or if it doesn't, what was the point in thinking about it anyway, much less talking about it.

And Josephine is dead.

Jackie is removing her apron.

She folds it and places it on the picnic table. She unfastens her dress, slips it off her shoulders, steps neatly out of it, puts it with the apron.

Cadence's heart is singing.

Jackie is wearing one of her old white bras, the pointed 50's kind with all the reinforcement.

She takes it off.

Jackie is wearing shiny black panties, quite thick but very snug.

She strips them off.

She strips to her stockings, garterbelt, shoes and cap. She squats and unlaces her shoes, then stands and steps out of them.

Her body is like a streak of bare heaven in the sun. When she was squatting, Cadence could look from the surface of the water straight up into her crotch. She felt her nipples harden.

Just as she is, Jackie sits on the edge of the pool and lowers herself gently into the water. She swims across to Cadence, keeping her chin high, swimming slowly and carefully, keeping her cap dry. She approaches Cadence with pride. 'There!'

Her nude body hangs in the blue water inches away from Cadence's own. Cadence aches. She says, 'Permission to speak, mistress.'

140

'What?' says Jackie. There are tiny beads of water on her eyelashes.

'This slave begs pardon.'

'What for?'

'Wishing to kiss the nurse.'

Jackie treads water. Her breasts bob, growing and collapsing as the water refracts their light. There are red pressure marks under them from the severe brassière.

'Is that a request, slave?' she asks, lightly.

Cadence nods. 'Yes, madam.'

'It will cost you.'

How much? Cadence asks with her eyes. She has no right to ask. Jackie tells her. 'A spanking,' she says.

Cadence swims a stroke towards her, spreads her arms either side of Jackie's head. Their breasts bump as she pushes herself forward. Her lips find Jackie's. She kisses her messily, avidly.

The women swim a little, petting underwater. Cadence kisses Jackie again and again. She can't get enough of her mouth, her breath, her tongue.

Soon enough Jackie orders Cadence out of the pool. Jackie sits on the edge, her feet in the water, and pats the textured concrete at her side. 'You can bend over here,' she says.

Cadence puts her hand up and launches her naked body out of the water. She lies down on her face on the cool concrete, her hips on the edge, her feet dangling. Her legs feel strange in the wet stockings, almost slimy. She looks sideways up at Jackie, screwing her eyes up in the brightness.

Jackie washes Cadence's bottom with a few handfuls of water, splashing it over her cheeks and wiping her cleft and the pouch of her snatch with wet fingers. She rests her palm on Cadence's right bottom cheek. 'It hurts more, wet,' she says, conversationally.

Cadence knows.

Jackie lifts her hand and starts to spank her, from the side. She spanks her slowly and casually, but not with any particular leniency.

It stings like hell.

Afterwards, Jackie allows Cadence to slip back into the water to cool her stinging bottom. Cadence floats in the water between Jackie's calves. Uninvited, she caresses Jackie's feet. Then she grasps one calf lightly in each hand, begging a favour.

'Permission to speak,' she says.

141

Jackie makes no attempt to free her legs. 'What is it now?' she says.

'The slave begs pardon,' says Cadence again.

'What for?'

Cadence looks up between Jackie's soft and tender thighs. 'Wishing to kiss the nurse's snatch.'

'Glory!' exclaims Jackie softly. 'And is that a request?'

Cadence nods, dipping her chin in the pool. 'Yes, madam,' she says.

Jackie toys with her pubic hair, twisting a damp curl around her fingertip.

'It will cost you,' she says again.

Cadence tears her gaze from Jackie's crotch, looks steadily up into her eyes. How much? she doesn't ask.

'A strapping.'

Cadence pushes herself forward, hanging on to Jackie's ankles. She stretches her neck and purses her lips.

Jackie shifts her bottom forward on the concrete and allows Cadence to caress her labia with the moist inner surfaces of her lips.

Then – too soon! – she pulls back. She beckons. 'Out again,' she says.

Cadence gets out of the water and stands dripping in the sun.

Jackie conducts her back to the house.

In the kitchen Jackie positions her bottom up over the back of a Shaker chair. Cadence shivers, water running down her taut thighs and stretched calves and dripping onto the oilcloth.

Jackie fetches a length of thick yellow leather, shaped into a handle at one end. She fondles Cadence a moment, letting her fingertips stray across the blotches left by the spanking.

Then she beats her with the strap.

The pain is immense, explosive. Cadence yelps and wails. She expects at any moment to be given a gag, but Jackie seems indifferent to these ill-disciplined outcries. Wet and naked herself, she swings the heavy leather with a will. Cadence shrieks and groans, her knuckles white where she grips the chair seat. The chair creaks under the stress.

Jackie likes to leave her strokes long, to take in more of the arc of Cadence's flanks, both sides. She pushes Cadence down on the table, her bare groin brushing Cadence's hip. The strap spanks down again, blazing a streak straight across the eye of Cadence's bottom.

After it finishes, Cadence lies a long while panting, mewing softly to herself in pain. It is some time before she manages to croak:

142

'Permission to — speak?'

Jackie leans down, pressing her right side, her right breast and stockinged thigh lightly against Cadence's aching body. She speaks quietly and precisely in Cadence's ear. 'And what might it be this time?' she says.

'Slave — begs — pardon,' Cadence manages to say.

Jackie doesn't move. 'What for?' she asks.

Cadence gathers her breath. 'Wishing the nurse would kiss her snatch,' she says.

Jackie levers herself upwards, remains hanging over Cadence's body. She trails her fingers along the angry rectangular blushes, making Cadence hiss and kick. 'And is that a request too, I suppose?'

Cadence's teeth are gritted. 'Yes,' she chokes out. 'Mistress.'

'It will cost you,' says Jackie again then.

Cadence throws caution to the winds. 'How much?' she asks.

Jackie pauses before answering. Then she says, simply, 'I'll let you decide.'

Then she takes her up to her room and binds her by the wrists and ankles to her bed, face up. And with a strange, fey smile, of sentiment, almost regret, she lowers her face to Cadence's tender crotch.

It is night before they leave, brownbagging the contents of Suriko's refrigerator into the trunk of Jackie's sports car. Their hair whips and flutters in the slipstream, two slender angels of the freeway.

Josephine is in transit too. Leonard has flown to Antwerp and she has gone to meet him there. At the baggage carousel she suddenly sees a former colleague of hers, a man called Anton; and he sees her. His eyes widen, his mouth drops open. He hurries towards her, holding out his hand in greeting.

'Josephine! Isn't it? Surely? Josephine Morrow!'

Josephine smiles pleasantly. 'Good afternoon,' she says.

She remembers him from the London office, years before. His hair is receding now, though his pale sandy eyes are as quizzically attractive as ever. He thinks she has forgotten him. 'Anton,' he says. 'Anton Frobisher.'

'How do you do?' says Josephine, and shakes his hand.

Behind the smile he looks doubtful. 'Don't you remember me?'

'Oh yes,' says Josephine. 'I remember you.' She had often been pleased to see him, enjoyed working with him, enjoyed his suave,

143

attentive manner, while knowing instinctively, from a million tiny signs, that he could never possibly satisfy her. 'How are you, Anton?'

He looks relieved, but still amazed with curiosity. 'I'm fine,' he says, cheerily, 'but how are you? What happened to you? Where have you been?'

She shrugs delicately, laying her fingertips gently on her bosom in a gesture of refined perplexity, as though he has asked her a question she can't possibly answer. 'Many places,' she says.

'But you disappeared! You walked out of a board meeting! You vanished in broad daylight. There was the most awful fuss, police and everything.'

Josephine smiles politely, as though he is telling her something that is of only very distant interest to her. 'Did I?' she replies, mildly.

Anton's smile is becoming a little strained. His eyes grow wary. Is he dealing with an amnesiac, a schizophrenic? 'Don't you remember?' he asks, gently.

'Oh yes,' she assures him. 'I remember. But that was someone else.'

'But you are Josephine?' he presses her, utterly confounded. 'Josephine Morrow?'

Josephine acknowledges it with a bow of her head. 'But I'm not the person you're talking about,' she says.

'But —'

Anton is growing tiresome. His imagination was never his strongest faculty, and now bewilderment has got the better of him. Any moment he will offer to buy her a drink, try to get her to share his taxi. It is all so unnecessary, thinks Josephine to herself. And with that thought she lifts her hand to Anton's cheek and reaches up to kiss him, slowly and softly, on the lips.

When she releases him, he looks as shocked as if she'd slipped a vibrator into his underpants. All the blood has drained from his face. He is beyond speech. He lifts his quivering hand, automatically, to his tingling mouth.

Josephine sees her bag coming around the carousel. With the merest wave of her hand, she steps quickly over, collects the bag, and walks directly into customs. She does not look back, and she does not see Anton Frobisher again.

Sinking into the upholstery of the air-conditioned Audi she allows herself an audible sigh.

'Tough trip, madam?' asks the driver, a bulky man with curly red hair and a single gold earring. Under his uniform jacket he is wearing a hideous green and white shirt.

'No thank you, Roy,' says Josephine.

He delivers her to the Hotel Medusa, where Leonard has taken a room. He is out. He has left a small padded envelope for her at reception. She opens it while she waits for the lift. Inside are a black silk scarf and a domino, the double blank. There is a card, signed simply 'L', as if anyone else could give her such a message. Josephine smiles.

In the room, bowls of pink chrysanthemums are already shedding their petals on the plush Kashmir. The air is stifling, the blinds are drawn. Josephine opens them, orders tea, the particularly good Caravan they keep here. She throws her leather jacket lightly on the bed, unzips her Gianni Versace skirt. She discards her slip, her stockings, her bra.

The tea arrives. Josephine stands drinking a cup at the window, looking across the park, feeling the northern sunlight cool after the Mediterranean. She showers, very hot and then very cold.

Meeting Roy makes her think of the first time she ever found a packet waiting for her at a hotel. The Green Man at Whittingtry. Her first encounter, blindfold. Her first spanking.

She hangs up her clothes and puts the envelope in a bin. She folds the scarf and lays it on one of the pillows, with the domino on top for a weight. Then she spreads the towel on the bed and lies down on it.

She touches herself lightly, stroking herself with two fingers length-ways. Her breasts rise and slide as her lungs fill. She wonders if Leonard has brought his slaves with him. She wishes one of them were here now. She could have done with him in the shower; and now to massage her, from head to toe, to bring her to the very brink of pleasure and sustain her there for a while. As an exercise. An appetiser.

Josephine sleeps. She dreams of meeting Cadence in a cellar bar, a dark, crowded place with a confusing number of rooms leading into one another. Cadence is very excited, she is trying to introduce a new boyfriend to Josephine. 'Josephine,' the man says. Josephine is surprised by him. She feels annoyed and betrayed. 'Josephine,' the voice keeps saying. 'Josephine . . .'

She wakes. The door is open, Leonard is coming in with an ocelot on a red lead. It is he speaking her name.

He looks gorgeous. The sun has lightened his hair and it is

beautifully cut, with an exaggeration of its natural curl. He is wearing a puffed, open-necked shirt of white linen, like Douglas Fairbanks in a pirate film. Over it he is wearing a waistcoat of deep claret-coloured leather and a Marjoribanks riding coat. His breeches are chocolate brown, cinctured by a black leather belt with a buckle that looks like a trap for small animals; his boots are glossy black. His eyes are covered by a pair of silvered aviator sunglasses in steel frames.

The ocelot looks at Josephine, its nostrils flaring slightly. Its eyes narrow in the hazy light spreading from the tall windows of the old hotel. It looks bored.

Josephine rolls onto her side. Her breasts shift heavily, Leonard shuts the door, comes and kisses her.

'Where are the boys?' she asks.

He kisses her again, thoughtfully. 'I swapped them,' he says. He takes her chin in his hand. 'You haven't put your blindfold on.'

Josephine reaches up and folds him in her arms, kissing him with a passion. After a moment, he breaks free. He kisses her neck. Her heart beats faster as she confesses, 'I wanted to see you.'

Leonard withdraws. He says. 'What you want is of no consequence. Obedience is the law. Absolute obedience is the law absolute.'

He folds his glasses. His serene eyes survey her nakedness.

'I am glad to see you are at least prepared. I may extenuate your punishment, by some degree.'

He gives the ocelot water and settles it on a couch, petting it until it lies quiet. Then he returns to Josephine.

He lowers his head and kisses the black tattoo between her magnificent breasts.

'Turn over, slave,' he tells her.

Then he blindfolds her and stretches her out on her face, across a pile of pillows to raise her hips. He ties her to the corners of the bed with the silken purple ropes he finds there. The management of the Hotel Medusa is very thoughtful in providing such things.

In total darkness Josephine hears him open the large cupboard in the wall beside the bed.

'What have you been doing in my absence, slave?' he asks. As she often does when she cannot see his face, Josephine thinks how much older his voice sounds. She rejoices that he is so young, and yet knows so much, so much more than anyone. When she was his age, she knew nothing.

146

'This slave has been making free with Yvette,' she confesses. 'And also seeking pleasure with her own hands.'

She hears him rattling equipment in the cupboard, then shutting the door with a soft click.

'I shall beat you until half past,' he tells her. 'Then I shall have some good news for you, I think.'

He begins with a ruler, snappy plastic rather than sharp wood. He smacks her lightly but freely with it, all over her bottom, warming her up. Josephine's bottom prickles and stings.

Then he pauses.

Blindfold, bound, stretched out face down with her smarting bottom on a pile of pillows, Josephine can sense very little of his movements around the room. She drifts in a state of suspense.

She hears the cat snuffle and make a tiny high-pitched moan.

'I tested your darling,' says Leonard suddenly, above and behind her; and before she can think the belt lashes down.

It is no ordinary belt, Josephine can feel that already. The second and third strokes confirm it. It is a Scottish taws, split into two tails along more than half its length. When it falls the split pinches and squeezes a ridge of Josephine's flesh with stunning suddenness and force. She bites the bedclothes and watches the inside of her eyelids explode red.

'She looks fine in bondage.' he continues, spacing his words with three more strokes. Josephine's plump bottom gives him plenty of room to play the taws about, up and down, across from either side. 'It's not hard to see why you find her so – fascinating,' he adds, placing a cut so the tips of the tails land inwards, curling in between her bottom cheeks.

Josephine arches her back with a squeal of anguish.

She wants more than anything to know what has happened to Cadence.

'A less romantic eye,' says Leonard, spanking her low, across the vent of her backside, 'could easily see she would only benefit from a longer period under Suriko's tuition. Your insistence on bringing her away early was impetuous,' he says, spanking her again, 'and foolish,' he says, with another spank, 'and *wilful*.'

Josephine shouts.

Leonard kisses her neck. He trails his lips softly down her back.

Josephine moans.

The mantelpiece clock chimes once, the half hour.

147

Leonard dangles the end of his strap between Josephine's stretched thighs.

'May I continue, slave?' he asks.

'Yes, master! Yes!'

He does.

'Jacqueline is bringing her,' he says.

Josephine convulses with pleasure. Her bottom and the tops of her legs are awash with barbed fire. To have Jackie bring Cadence to her, initiated in the mystery of obedience and ready for thorough training — that is the wish that has sustained her through the boredom of Ile de Porquerolles, the eternal sunshine and inactivity, managing the dreary novices, inferior substitutes for her California girl.

Through the rest of her correction she imagines she is Cadence Szathkowicz, and that it is her own hand administering punishment. To raise a healthy glow on that sleek bottom, those sweet golden thighs — what keener pleasure could the world hold?

Nor, whatever her master says about impetuosity and haste, has she any doubt about Cadence's suitability. She remembers how remarkable Cadence's powers are, once aroused and properly motivated.

Leonard unfastens his mistress's bonds and turns her over on her back. She succumbs to a violent need to lift her burning legs up high off the bed, one in each hand. He kisses the marks of his own imposition. He slips his penis into the inflamed portal between her throbbing thighs and slides it home.

He orders Josephine to stroke herself while he thrusts wetly and vigorously between her legs. She feels a silver, singing bolt of pleasure consolidate and burst amid the pain. Then he pulls out his cock and mouths her for a while, punctuating his approach with sudden unexpected squeezings of her ravaged flesh. When she howls, he laughs, and spends himself quickly in her mouth.

Many clutching, sliding, melting orgasms later, Josephine rises, dripping with sweat, and returns to the shower.

Later they dress for dinner. Moving carefully, sitting on a cushion at the dressing table, Josephine arranges her hair. She has on a long black sheath in stretch velvet by Jane Roarty, its plunging neckline chosen to make the most of her wonderful cleavage. Leonard arranges it to frame her tattoo, for she wears no brassière. He kisses her throat. Patting his back, she raises her chin and lifts her collar to her neck; a black strip of kid set alternately with silver studs and diamonds.

148

|12|

The MG roars through Calumet, turning onto 57. Cadence sees the car as a little green zipper, unzipping the windy night. The buildings rise ahead like glowing stacks of light, like sequinned penises, wow.

Cadence came tonight, the trained tip of Jackie's tongue caressing her, one lick soft, the next hard, soft hard soft. It was amazing. That wasn't the end of it either. In this world, orgasms are stepped, like escalators, each one rising under you to take you up to another floor.

Sometimes you take a long time to pass from one to the next, sometimes you're on your way before you know.

There don't seem to be any down escalators.

Hang on, Cadence tells herself. She wriggles her bare bottom on the seat, working on the strapmarks, pressing them against the seat so she can feel them sting.

'Sit still, Cadence,' says Jackie.

'Are we going where Suriko and everybody went?'

'No,' says Jackie briskly. 'Be patient.'

Cadence exhales a tiny sigh. She mutters something distracted, Jackie can't hear. 'What was that?' she demands.

'I never got to sleep with her,' Cadence repeats. 'With Madam Suriko,' she amplifies.

Jackie seems amused. 'Maybe you didn't earn it,' she says.

Cadence looks concerned. She touches her collar with an unconscious finger. 'I graduated, though, right?' she persists.

'Be quiet, Cadence.'

Cadence is sitting there in just her collar and a tracksuit top, to stop her running away. The seatbelt squeezes her left tit. She thinks of the harness available for the discipline and restraint of slaves, in the long room at Madam Suriko's. She sits with her hands in her lap and

149

watches the city slide past them, concrete, a scary park, a dark metallic-looking river.

A local exit sign passes overhead. Jackie flips her indicator. 'I'm going to get a coffee,' she says.

They run into town, looking for an all-night drive-through place Jackie knows. She fancies a boy who works there, a high school kid. It's off the main drag, though not out of their way. There's no one in front of them at the window.

The server is a jock with straight black hair, the same colour Cadence's is. He manages to behave like a robot, the way they're trained to, but can't keep the grin off his face when he looks down into the crazy green European sportscar and see two beautiful babes, one in just a tracksuit top, the other dressed as a nurse. The one in the tracksuit top is just sitting there with her hands on the seat, not even trying to cover herself up.

'*Welcomta Bengo's, my name is Frank, howmy I help you thesevening?*'

'Two coffees,' says Jackie into the mike.

'*Creamansugar?*' says Frank. Jackie says yes. He presses his keyboard and turns to the coffee machine.

Cadence looks at the back of his head. His shoulders look nice. She doesn't mind that she's being displayed to him. She knows it doesn't matter whether she minds or not, but she doesn't. She wonders if the sight of her crotch has given him an erection. She hopes so.

They pull across into the parking lot to drink their coffees.

'Is that him?' Cadence asks.

'Him?' Jackie's eyes are very green in waves of harsh light coming across from the street. 'Good God no, girl. Give me credit for some taste, Cadence, please, do.'

'Oh.' Cadence sips her coffee, scalds her upper lip. 'I think he's kind of cute.'

'It doesn't matter what you think,' says Jackie.

'I know, I was just thinking that, only I just thought, well, you know –'

Jackie holds her coffee on the wheel with one hand, puts the other on Cadence's cheek, turning her face gently towards her. She kisses Cadence on the mouth.

'Do you want him?' Jackie says.

'Me? No.'

Jackie turns, leaning her elbow on the sill, looking back at the lighted window. 'We haven't time anyway,' she says.

Cadence wonders if the guy saw them kiss. She wonders if he gets off on that. She sips her coffee again, more carefully. She looks at Jackie's face, choosing her moment.

'We're going to the airport, right?' she says.

'That's right.'

Cadence has no baggage, no clothes, nothing but this tracksuit top and her collar. Her funny credit card and her passport are back in her purse, in Missouri.

'We going to England?'

'No.'

Cadence's heart sinks. She's been hoping. Trying not to, but hoping anyway.

Cadence starts to cry.

Shocked, Jackie strokes the back of her head. 'Cadence! Now Cadence!' she says, softly but reprovingly.

Cadence sniffs, wipes her eyes with her fingers. She looks into her coffee. She won't look at Jackie.

'Is she really dead?' she asks.

'Who?'

From that Cadence knows at once she isn't.

Unless Jackie is being cruel and lying to her.

She looks warily at Jackie, then back at her cup. 'Josephine,' she says.

'Whatever gave you that idea?'

'He said she was dead.'

'Who did?'

He had no name, not for Cadence to hear. He had a domino mask and a young body like a Michelangelo sculpture. 'The Supreme Master.'

Jackie says, 'Did he now.'

'I didn't believe him,' Cadence says immediately. 'I knew it wasn't true. I mean, how could she be dead? He was only wanting me to think that so he could have me. Have all of me, I mean. You know what I mean,' she says.

The sadness sweeps out of her like dirty water down a shower drain.

Unexpectedly Jackie says, 'They're full of it sometimes, the Supreme Masters.'

Cadence knew she wasn't lying. They're in this together. Like sisters,

151

Cadence imagines. She never had a sister. Like players in a rock and roll band. Like the women at Crystal's bar.

Cadence sighs. 'Why do we let them? Why do we let them spank us and screw us and push around?'

In the darkness of the car Jackie slips her left hand onto Cadence's bare thigh and strokes her fingertips lightly over it, up towards her groin. Her hand is warm from the styrofoam cup. 'Oh, Cadence,' she says. 'I thought you knew better now than to ask such a question.'

Her fingers grip Cadence's thigh, commandingly.

'You're all in a muddle, aren't you? Come on over here now,' she says. 'Come on across my knee.'

Cadence gets up, puts her foot on the tunnel where the gearshift is, kneels on the edge of Jackie's seat. It's very hard, leaning over like this. She puts her head over Jackie's shoulder, her hand on the sill for balance. She feels Jackie pull her top up to her waist, baring her bottom to the night.

Cadence looks at the drive-through window, at the jock server, who is staring across the parking lot at them, open-mouthed with delight, surrounded by the faces of the kitchen staff. She has this weird *déjà vu* thing. Then Jackie spanks her.

She looks down at the pavement while Jackie spanks her again, avoiding the eyes of their startled audience. This really is pretty humiliating for her. Maybe Jackie is counting on that.

She only gets six spanks, then Jackie is ordering her to sit down again, to buckle up. She wants to get to O'Hare. The wheels of the car spin, the empty cups topple off the dash, the two crazy lesbians in the green sports number rocket off towards the freeway.

At the airport Jackie heads into long-term parking, and finds a bay on the top floor between a panel truck and a grey Mazda. She gets out of the car, goes to the trunk, and hands Cadence a bundle.

'Get these on,' she says.

Cadence opens the door and sticks her bare legs out of the car. She pulls on the tracksuit bottoms and the sandals. She leans back into the car to look in the rearview mirror, and adjusts her collar. She wishes she had a pair of earrings, big gold loops, no, silver with this colour hair.

'You know what I need?' she says.

'You'll get it in a minute if you don't hurry up,' says Jackie.

But she kisses her and briefly fondles her tit while Cadence squeezes past her between the vehicles.

They check in fast, Jackie's carry-on their only baggage. They're booked on a redeye to Boston, then an early morning flight to Orly, Cadence doesn't know where that is.

Jackie looks Cadence over. Her eyebrows flicker, her lips part in a knowing smile.

Cadence comes very close to her. Tentatively she takes her arm.

'Is that where Josephine is?'

Jackie shakes her head.

'But we're going to see her, though?'

Jackie nods.

Cadence kicks her heels up, then she throws her arms round Jackie and kisses her on the mouth, right there in the check-in area. A tired-looking woman emptying ashtrays grins, scandalized to see them kiss.

Cadence takes Jackie's arm.

'I want to buy her something,' she says.

'You haven't any money,' Jackie points out.

'Will you buy it for me?' Cadence asks. 'Please? Please, Jackie?'

'Shall we see what it is, first?' Jackie suggests, primly.

They find a gift shop still open. The radio is playing some easy-listening music, an instrumental arrangement of 'When I Fall in Love' for a zillion strings. The young woman at the register looks tired, her face is white with dark smudges under the eyes. 'Hi,' she says, trying to sound bright and failing. She's covertly eating a giant chocolate chip cookie from the display. She is the only person in the place.

Jackie starts making suggestions. 'How about this box of fruit liqueurs? Or some perfume?'

Cadence is searching the shelves for a particular gift. Not looking at Jackie she shakes her head. She moves away along the aisles. The checkout girl is watching them, supervising them as they shop.

Jackie pulls a sleeve out from a rack of clothes. Acrylic sheer white, with a fine slinky finish. 'Look at this blouse,' she says.

Cadence glances, already saying 'No.' She spins a rack of cosmetics, then moves quickly to a shelf just beyond.

'Is theranything special I cn help you find thesevening?' asks the checkout girl, who trained with the same system as the boy at Bengo's.

But Cadence has already found what she's looking for. She turns and shows it to Jackie. She offers it to her.

It is a wooden hairbrush, in a cardboard and cellophane package.

Jackie takes it. She looks at the price tag, hefts the package in her hand. 'For Josephine?'

Cadence nods earnestly.

Jackie feels the brush through the plastic. 'Real bristle,' she comments.

Cadence lowers her voice. The clerk is listening. 'Not that side,' Cadence says.

Jackie feels the wooden back.

She looks Cadence sternly in the eye.

'It's quite unsuitable,' she says.

Cadence takes the brush back. She looks at it, she looks at the woman who's been spanking her all day, it feels like.

'No it isn't,' she says. 'In fact it's real good.'

Jackie takes the brush out of her hand. 'Cadence, behave,' she says. And she puts the brush back on the shelf.

Cadence snatches it off again.

The salesgirl is watching them, looking dazed.

Jackie seizes Cadence's hand. 'Come on, Cadence, put the brush back, we'll go and see if they're boarding yet.'

'I want this brush for Josephine,' says Cadence.

'Cadence, put it *back*.'

'Ask her if we can try it out.'

'Cadence —'

Cadence turns to the salesgirl. 'Can we just take this out of the box?' she says.

'Uh-uh,' says the girl. 'I'm afraid I can't let you do that. We have a full refund policy if your gift proves unsatisfactory. All you have to do is bring it back.'

'We're not going to be back,' says Cadence. 'I just need to look at something here.'

She opens the box and takes the brush out.

'That would be fine, nurse, look.' She gives the brush to Jackie, back up. Jackie refuses to take it. Cadence puts a hand on her arm, imploringly. 'Please, nurse, look. Don't you want to try it out?'

'I can't let you do that, ma'am, I'm sorry.' The salesgirl is getting louder and louder. 'We have a hygiene policy in this company. I mean I'm sure your hair isn't dirty or anything —'

'Who said anything about hair?' Cadence asks.

Then she takes down her tracksuit bottoms and sticks her butt out.

154

The clerk's mouth falls open. Unhygienic chocolate chip cookie crumbs fall out. 'Oh my *God*...' she moans, softly.

Cadence's bottom is well striped already. A slight flush from her brief punishment in the parking lot is barely visible between the darker stripes, like a deranged tartan, left by the strap. Further treatment with a hairbrush does not look necessary, exactly. Jackie is about to push the brush back inside the box, but she hesitates, holding the box in one hand, the brush in the other.

'I have to have this,' Cadence assures the salesclerk. 'She has to do this for me. It's like therapy. It doesn't hurt, really.'

She bends over and screws up her eyes.

'Okay, nurse, I'm ready,' she says, very loudly.

Jackie looks around the mall outside. The redeye passengers are arriving. People are passing the store, slowing down, looking in.

'Cadence, pull your trousers up at once. It's not our brush. Whatever are you thinking of, girl?'

But she is smiling. She thinks Cadence's idea is all right. If you can spank a woman in a parking lot, you can spank her in an airport. Even if you can't make a fast exit afterwards.

Jackie appeals to the salesgirl. 'Please,' she says. 'Do you have somewhere private?' And she points the brush to the door behind the counter, marked *Private*.

'Ma'am, I have to call security now,' says the girl.

'Oh don't trouble yourself,' says Jackie, with a confidential smile. 'I'm all the security you need. Trust me.' She pats the snowy breast of her apron. Then she pats Cadence's bottom. 'Come on, Cadence, come along with me to the ladies' room.'

Cadence looks around her hip at Jackie. 'You have to give it to me here and now,' she says. 'I choose it. You said I had to choose, remember, when you went down on me this morning.'

She hears someone gasp. A small crowd has gathered now. They're pressing as close as they can outside the doorway. A kid with his cap on backwards has come inside, grinning appreciatively at the sight of the lady with her ass all bare and shiny red.

'All right, Cadence , you win,' says Jackie. She speaks to the girl. 'We'll take the brush. How much is that, please?' She is looking in her holdall while she speaks. She pulls out a bill and goes up to the register to pay, leaving Cadence posed where she is, displaying her bottom down the length of the store.

There is a murmur of amusement from the onlookers. They sound impressed. Someone whistles.

Cadence doesn't move. She ignores them. Inside she is in the big dark castle she heard them whispering about at Madam Suriko's. She is wearing not these stupid sport clothes but a long dress of pink and purple silk. Her hair is long, braided. She is chained by the neck to a heavy iron ring, one of half a dozen set in the wall beside the fireplace. She is being stripped for the cold-eyed inspection of a splendid nude woman with fierce eyebrows who stands there tapping the side of her riding boot with a riding crop. Josephine is watching from a tall armchair, the fingers of her hands steepled together.

Wow. Sometimes Cadence amazes even herself.

'Ma'am, you can't do that here,' she hears the salesgirl protesting stupidly. 'You can't do that.'

'You be quiet or you're joining her,' says Jackie, and she comes back to Cadence, brush in hand. She sets her free hand in the middle of Cadence's back and lifts the brush.

The crowd falls completely silent.

The brush lands with a sharp *crack*! low on the patchy red hillock of Cadence's right cheek.

The buzz of exclamation and conjecture begins again. 'Anyone got a camera?' someone asks, and as the second smack falls, a little higher and around towards the hip, a flashgun flares. The clerk clasps her hands in distress. 'Oh, God, oh, God, oh, God . . .' She bounces up and down, she has to call security but she can't *move*. She can't stop watching.

The third stroke Jackie places higher again, and the fourth above that. She is working her way over the purple places where the end of her strap curled round.

This must be very painful, not to mention embarrassing. Yet Cadence hasn't let out a peep; not so much as a sigh.

Jackie shifts her attention to the left cheek. She finds the skin somewhat less marked there, probably because she gave her her strapping from that side and didn't walk around the way you have to to make it really thorough. The way Suriko always does; or Dr Hazel. Jackie spanks her harder on the whiter skin, though not a lot of Cadence's bottom is white now, really.

'God, please, stop, God, please, stop,' chants the salesclerk, leaning out from her stool like a buzzard from a branch.

156

'I'll make you sorry you suggested this, you wicked girl,' says Jackie. And she repeats the pattern from the right cheek.

Cadence's flesh bounces satisfactorily under the hard wooden back of the brush. First there is a white, oval patch, then the red floods in, pink, scarlet, crimson, deeper and deeper.

Still Cadence makes no sound.

Jackie swings the brush back as far as the shelving will let her and delivers a fast spank on the crown of the left buttock.

That, at least, get a grunt out of her; and another whistle out of the crowd, a yell from someone at the back. Jackie straightens, turns to face them down the aisle.

'Be quiet will you there, please. You're disturbing the patient.'

She plants the equivalent spank on the right buttock, where Cadence is reddest. She spanks back and forth, back and forth, little short strokes, faster and faster.

Cadence pants through her nose, makes little choked whinnying noises. She jogs up and down, flexing her knees with the pain. There's a smattering of applause from the spectactors.

Not ceasing to spank her charge, Jackie leans her head back to survey the target area. Conditions on those twin blushing hillocks are starting to look severe. Where else is there to go? Only downwards, she is forced to conclude. She presses down on Cadence's spine. 'All fours now, Cadence, please.'

Cadence tips forward, catching her weight on her outstretched fingers. She wobbles painfully and inelegantly forward, spreading her hands, keeping her backside in the air. This too is a popular move.

The salesgirl is silent now. She's sitting hunched on her stool, her head down as if she can't bear to look.

But in fact she can't bear not to. Worried, she peers up through her bangs like a deer through a hedge.

Jackie gives Cadence a half-dozen even-handed smacks with the brush, as if driving her into position. 'Open your legs,' she instructs her.

Cadence's feet creep apart.

Her cleft widens. Her crotch opens, tilted up for the nurse's inspection, and the audience's. It shows as a pale valley of soft flesh and wet brown hair between two blazing, ravaged hills. Cadence quivers with pain, with the tension of her muscles in this position. Her anus is a dark brown wrinkled eye, her vagina flushed and seeping.

157

Anyone might have her now. Covertly, Jackie glances at the crowd, speculating. Then she sends three completely callous, full-blooded spanks slamming into the taut underside of the crimson cheeks.

Cadence shouts and loses her balance. She falls flat, her cheek hitting the floor. Jackie crouches over her, sees swiftly she is not injured. Cadence's eyes shine, begging.

Jackie half-straightens, hitching up the skirt of her uniform dress. She squats over the sprawling slave, mercilessly spanking her bottom with the brush. The tops of her stockings are on display to the crowd, a flash of white thigh, more. She starts in on the backs of Cadence's thighs. Cadence is crying now. Or is that the whine of a service vehicle approaching up the mall?

It must be security. Someone must have called them. Jackie stands up, steps away from Cadence, who rises shakily to her hands and knees, head hanging. Two teenage boys come running up the aisle of the shop to help her up. One grins, shakes her hand, over and over again. The other crouches behind her with his head between her thighs, marvelling at the fiery heat of her, the rich aroma. The boys' parents come to claim them, shouting, shouting louder as the humming noise grows nearer. The boys are dragged off Cadence, who leans on the counter with one hand, pulling up her pants with the other. She looks at Jackie.

Jackie pushes through the crowd as if they weren't there, ignoring their compliments and complaints. She strides out into the hallway.

A passenger transport car comes into view. At this time of the night it is empty, but for its elderly driver, who looks into the store window with a curious frown. Jackie steps forward in her uniform and throws out her arm, hailing him. 'Injured woman here! Hurry please.'

On Jackie's arm Cadence limps out of the store, into the car, lies full-length along the bench, face down, clutching her seat. Jackie sits down and strokes her head. The driver starts a klaxon and a flashing light and away they roll, heading for the departure gates.

The kids start to run after the car, but their parents restrain them. People shout and laugh. They pile into the gift store as if an invisible force field had been switched off. They argue over the empty hairbrush carton, tearing it in their hunger for a souvenir.

Then the salesclerk faints and they start helping themselves to the stock.

|13|

From Toulon we drive east and south to Giens, and over the hills to the coast. Lunch at Le Pilou Encarré is no less expensive for the obscurity of its situation, though sometimes distinguished enough to justify the cost. Note the piratical relics on display in the bar. Theatrical as they may look, they are all perfectly authentic.

Having dozed away the heat of the day here over an aromatic glass or two of Bandol, the traveller sets out to clear his head by walking the rest of the way around the coast to the ferry. The road passes the ruined Fort de la Tour Fondue, about which Richelieu was so enthusiatic. Dismayed as the cardinal might be were he here today to see the sad state of its tumbled walls, we can scarcely conceive the horror with which he would view the chattering tourists, immodestly clad, that cluster and dawdle on the quay, or the boats that bob buzzing and stinking alongside.

We too descend to the shore, at a more circumspect pace; for we are tired, we have come a long way; and we are conscious that for some at least, the journey across the strait will be more than a simple pleasure trip.

Dreaming of more elegant days, of steamers with funnels pink as sugared almonds and *vieux garcons* playing chess beneath the palm trees, we step down into the *Alouette* or the *Cigan*. If there are no excited children already running about the forecastle, perhaps one takes a seat there, among the languid and the tanned. Blazered arms lean on the gunwale, binoculars are produced.

The water is a deep, reassuring blue; but also black, iridescent with sump oil, spattered with white gobbets of expanded polystyrene. The bay too was finer, purer, once.

When the jowly attendant bangs the gate shut, the engines rev. The *Cigan* leaves, the noise of its passage blaring back from the water to assault the delicate green shore. Startled, as they must be almost hourly at this time of year, the herons take to the sky and wheel, complaining, above the saltflats of Giens. As the launch curves out into the strait, we see the sunlight flash from the high, crystallized white mounds.

We are bound for the Iles d'Hyères, which some call the Iles d'Or, either, as Baedeker prosaically presumes, for their mica-flecked rocks, or because there is gold to be gained from the tourists who visit them. But lest we be thought too cynical, let us add at once that they are indeed worthy to be gilded in name, as one of the most beautiful corners of the Mediterranean.

In antiquity a haven for sailors from the thunderbolts of Zeus and the wrath of Poseidon, the archipelago was first settled, archaeologists tell us, by seekers after spiritual peace and natural bounty: friars and farmers. Thereafter the fragrant wooded hills and deep, mysterious inlets recommended themselves to buccaneers, whose numbers were augmented by the very ex-convicts François I sent to domesticate Porquerolles and defend his realm from piracy. With his characteristic diplomacy, the poet Saint-John Perse wrote:

> The snakes
> (Because there are always snakes),
> The king preferred to fling
> Far from Paris, even if into Eden.

Later devils, in the shape of Nazi troops and artillery posted on Port-Cros and Levant, were disabled by American forces in the closing years of the Second World War. Levant and Porquerolles still support French garrisons; cynics along the Côte have been heard to remark on the excellent taste shown by the military in securing locations for their bases.

No such martial concerns need trouble us today. The sun blazes down on the *Cigan*; below decks, the engines throb, pushing us through the tainted waters to the island. A delicate salt breeze alleviates the swelter of the afternoon. In these conditions the skin of young women takes on a wonderful moist sheen of vitality and health. Look at those two in the bow, one with long copper hair, the other jet-black, cropped against the heat. Apart from that difference of the hair, they could be sisters. Watch them as they come past us now, their dresses brushing the end of our bench. They move with the thoughtless harmony of intimate familiars.

160

But for each other, they have no discernible companions. They are in their twenties, let us hazard no more closely than that. One, most likely the elder, has a fair complexion that must take some protecting from this semi-tropical sun; the other is golden-brown, freckled, animated by an eagerness she is scarcely suppressing. They wear halter-topped sundresses, similar but not matching, in shades of caramel, light tan and creamy pale orange; bare legs and elegant sandals; and (and this, among a score of bare-armed, beautiful women, is what has truly caught our eye) black leather chokers, rather like the collars worn by performing animals or expensive pets. The elder's is hidden beneath a beige Rabanne scarf, but the breeze betrays it. It seems an unusual accessory for such a lightweight, casual outfit; and even stranger that she seems to be trying to conceal it: as though she were constrained to wear it. Her sister's collar is narrower, an undecorated strip of soft leather as black as her hair, and not hidden at all. The women murmur, too softly to be heard above the loud engines. They stand very close together at the rail amidships.

The elder, in the neckscarf, looks out to sea with a small smile expressive more of satisfaction than mere sensual pleasure. The younger, as we have observed, keeps her lovely lithe head turned to gaze along the bow towards our destination, the harbour of Porquerolles. It is clear she has not been here before. She asks a question. Her companion observes her over the top of her sunglasses, reprovingly. Chastened by the merest glance, the younger woman lowers her eyes, abashed. The elder touches her casually and almost caressingly, on the inside of the elbow where the skin is so delicate and sensitive. Sisters they must be.

The afternoon breeze stirs the skirts of their thin dresses to and fro, now flapping them against their long thighs, now ballooning them up tantalizingly, but alas never satisfyingly, into the air. All the men aboard are secretly watching, comparing the curved forms of the delicious bottoms to which the fabric intermittently clings. Is the elder sister's appreciably more trim, more alluring? or is the swell of the younger's simply more succulent, more full of promise to the eye and hand?

The younger woman leans out over the side, offering her high firm bosom to the sun. Her hips swivel, her bottom tilts upwards as she spreads her arms wide, sliding her hands along the white rail. You look away for fear of staring too frankly. And yet there is something odd here. You are convinced the girl has assumed this abandoned posture in obedience: you believe you heard her sister tell her to.

It is easy, sitting here with half-closed eyes while the glazed, turbid water rushes by below, to dream about such women, the younger dressed perhaps in the unbecoming costume of the chambermaids at the hotel in Toulon, the turquoise nylon overall, black tights and flat black lace-up shoes. Returning unexpectedly to your room you find her with a drawer open, leafing through certain papers, letters of a highly personal nature addressed to you and notes you have made, on the subject of other women in other ports.

She slams the drawer shut. Her light green eyes, her moist pink lips are round with surprise and guilt. Oh my god, she says, in a voice that is husky, surprisingly deep for her age and size, I didn't know you were here. I mean, I thought you'd gone out for the day. I was just tidying your room, I hope you don't think I was reading your private correspondence here. I was just putting these papers away for you, is all. I hope you don't mind. I mean, I'm sorry.

You say nothing, closing the door behind you. It locks with a quiet but firm click.

The chambermaid is still speaking. Oh god, she says. Oh god, you're angry. You're angry with me now, I can tell. Please don't tell the manager. Please don't, I'll lose my job. I wasn't going to take anything, honestly.

It is scarcely necessary for you to speak. The chambermaid is convinced that you intend to report her, that it will take desperate measures on her part to prevent this. You sit on the bed, adjusting the creases in your snowy white trousers. She stands before you, running the tips of her fingers nervously through her bristling hair. It is the unconscious gesture of a different woman, one with longer hair; perhaps hers has been cut recently. You wish she would stand here like this forever, the broad sunlight of the Côte d'Azur shining revealingly through her thin uniform from behind; looking into your eyes with an expression of apprehension and compliance on her face. Her teeth are white and straight and perfect, her skin innocent of make-up. What are you going to do to me? she asks.

You tell her.

For some reason she is not surprised.

She bites her soft lower lip as if suppressing a nervous smile. She looks at you questioningly and starts to hitch up her overall.

162

You stop her and tell her to remove it.

Large eau-de-nil plastic buttons run down the front. She unfastens them. Whens she opens the overall you are surprised and pleased to see that the black tights are actually nylon stockings, clipped to a plain black suspender belt; that her panties are plain white cotton, very clean; and that she is wearing nothing else under her overall.

She slips her arms out of the sleeves and turns to deposit the ugly garment on your bedside chair. Her breasts are not large, but sweetly pointed and evenly tanned, the nipples dark brown. She has shaved her legs and beneath her arms, but not, you can already tell, between her thighs. She has been sweating beneath the overall. The smell of her is sweet and heady.

Without waiting to be told, her hands go to the elastic waistband of her panties. She raises her eyes, looking for your approval.

You nod, slightly. Her lips part again as she leans forward from the hips to slip her panties down.

Her bottom is golden-brown as the rest of her. It flexes adorably as she straightens up, her hand worrying her hair again.

You tell her she must bend over.

Yes, master, she whispers, and scrambles across your lap.

Master. You remember the collar. You have forgotten to include it in your daydream. At once you open your eyes.

The boat has nearly arrived. You can no longer see the women. A party of strollers has come between you and them. It would be churlish to get up and pursue them, pushing without a reason through the idling throng. Unless you truly intend to strike up a conversation, to make their acquaintance. You think not. Later, perhaps, ashore. L'Ile de Porquerolles is not so large, its cafés not too numerous. You breathe deeply and look out to sea once more, the breeze ruffling your hair in a way both annoying and pleasant.

But your mind is dark, like a room with waxed paper blinds drawn down over tall windows. You do not see the hot blue blur of sea and sky. You see the other young traveller, dressed in white with her hair coiled up, a little starched cap on the top of her head. She comes smartly into your room to examine her sister, to make sure you have done her no damage. She purses her lips. She is cross, cool, imperious. With a crook of her finger she beckons you to rise from the bed. Her deft, professional hands unfasten your belt, unzip your fly. Your erection does not impress her. She goes down on one knee to pick up one of your slippers from beneath the bed. Your underpants are around your ankles. We'll see how you like it, shall we now? she says; quiet, inflexible, terrifying.

You shake your head, rousing yourself from the dream. The ferry is bumping against the fenders of the jetty. All around seabirds skim and turn, riding the thermals. Jolly music is playing from a cracked transistor radio. People are jostling to be the first ashore. Irritated, you lift your head and look up over the rooftops. Your eyes fill with tropical green.

It is believed by all authorities that, like its furthest neighbour Levant, Porquerolles is the property of the French government, which bought the island on the death of its ancient proprietrix in 1971. The presence of the garrison seems to confirm this; or, if not, the records can be easily examined at the Forte de Sainte-Agathe, which overlooks the village.

Unfortunately, the records are untrue. The true, secret owners are content to leave the derelict forts unrestored, having much better fortresses elsewhere, elaborately equipped and constantly in service. They enjoy other properties here, some discreet, others remote, and all of them utterly exclusive. For example, this beach house, perfectly visible from the path behind impenetrable thickets of abandoned vine, is scarcely recalled by any of the locals, yet it is wholly and minutely familiar to some visitors, voluntary and involuntary.

The women have evaded the throng and taken another boat, a private launch, around the headland to this otherwise inaccessible beach. They have waded through the shallows. Now they stand ashore on a slab of worn brown rock, trying to wipe the water and the clinging sand from their legs. The younger starts to put her sandals back on.

'Carry those, Cadence,' says her companion, her guide.

Together they walk up between the rocks, following a neglected path of flat rocks. Gnats whine, dancing around them. The house appears on a rise above them: low, peeling white walls, a roof of orange shingles. Steps cut in the bank lead up to a heavy door of golden, varnished wood. The varnish is dull, faded, scoured by sea air; no one has polished the brass knocker recently. There is no one about, no signs of life.

In the porch the novice stands, flexing her arms, pulling her shoulder blades together as though displaying her cleavage to an unseen spectator. 'Do we knock or what?'

164

'It's not necessary to speak,' says her companion, sternly, and she reaches for the knocker. Inlaid in the brass is a domino of yellowed ivory, the double six.

The boom of the knocker echoes inside the house.

The women stand waiting, in the shade of the porch, listening to the sea breaking on the rocks at their backs.

Inside the house, the hallway is red-tiled, dim, shuttered against the light and heat. A door creaks open at the back of the house, bangs shut on a spring. In a moment a young woman appears in the hallway, coming to answer the door. She wears an old-fashioned housemaid's dress: plain black frock and white pinafore. Her legs, in black woollen tights, are skinny as a bird's; on her feet she wears button-strap shoes. This outfit, and her meagre waiflike figure conspire to give the impression, in the shadowy hallway, that she is only a girl, though she is scarcely younger than the novice waiting outside the door. Her eyes are a watery hazel, her eyebrows thick as a man's. Her name is Yvette. She opens the door and frowns out into the bright sunlight.

Cadence thinks she is frowning at her.

Yvette ignores Cadence. 'Mam'selle,' she says to Jackie, with a slight curtsey.

Jackie has taken off her sunglasses. She folds them and slips them into her handbag. 'Please tell the master that the new slave is ready for inspection,' Jackie instructs her.

Yvette curtseys again, submissively. She stands and holds the door open for the women to step inside the house. Then she closes it, turns, and walks quickly back along the hall.

Leonard is in the dormitory, supervising two of the novices. 'Come,' he calls. He is speaking to the maid at the door, not to Alexandra or Peter. She enters and curtseys, bobbing her head.

The master is absorbed in his work. His eyes are intent, his hair dishevelled. He shakes it back from his face. His cheeks are pink. He wears a black leather waistcoat, criss-cross lacing up the front revealing his hairless chest, the black tattoo imprinted there. Skin-tight black leather trousers are tucked into scuffed black calf-length boots. Around his neck he wears a broad black collar set with blunted steel spikes.

When he speaks his voice is calm, like the voice of a much older man. 'What is it, Yvette?'

Alexandra and Peter are on the bed. Ahmed is with Francis. The

165

chauffeur has been given use of him for the day. At seven this morning he led the young man off up the beach to a convenient cave. There are certain practices and disciplines in which Ahmed needs to be trained. This leaves Leonard free to concentrate on Alexandra and Peter.

Peter, whose infatuation with Alexandra continues to overwhelm him at the most inconvenient moments, is being taught a measure of self-restraint. Under Leonard's instructions, Alexandra has tied the Dutch boy by his wrists and ankles to the four corners of his bed. He lies there spreadeagled, face up, blindfold, naked. Alexandra, also naked, kneels between his legs, sitting back on her heels. She has been set to torment his loins with a feather. She is not allowed to speak to him, kiss him, or touch him in any way but with the long white feather.

They have been at this a long time, the pair of them. Poor Peter's prick is quivering, twitching, like a blind animal seeking to fuck thin air. It is swollen hard, and sore red with hyperstimulation. Sore red too are poor Alexandra's plump bottom and thighs, blotched and striped with red, for every time Peter ejaculates, Alexandra receives more punishment. Peter can't see but hears the dull blows of the slipper, the snap of the lash, Alexandra's squeals and pleas. Belatedly, the hapless pair are learning how much kinder their mistress is than their master.

The boy is whimpering. Next time, Leonard thinks to himself, he will lay the girl face down across the boy's body and punish her in that position. Or perhaps set them end to end, the girl's face in the boy's sticky crotch, and order her to lick up the spilt seed while Leonard spanks her bottom, her own wet quim shuddering an inch above her beloved's straining mouth.

The maid has come to tell Leonard that Sister Jackie has arrived, with the new slave, the American. Leonard remembers her, spilling apples all around him in the hallway. Josephine's pet from Dominica. He smiles.

'Where is your mistress, Yvette? On the terrace?'

'*Oui, m'sieu.*'

Leonard stretches, flexing his wrists. 'Send them out to her. Then come back here.'

The door closes, and the button shoes patter quickly away up the hall.

Leonard reaches out languidly and touches Alexandra's anus with the tip of his finger. She is soaking wet. She inhales, sharply, tilting her crotch towards him as he probes.

Her fat little cunny smells strong and inviting. Later he will reward her for her obedience and console her for her punishment. He will make Peter watch.

The maid returns. He goes to the door and lets her in. She seems reluctant, as if she would rather have conducted Jackie and the new slave to Josephine herself. She looks up at him, frowning, her dull straight hair held back with hairgrips over her ears. '*Je peux retourner à la maîtresse, maintenant?*' she requests.

'No, Yvette. Not yet.'

Leonard returns to his seat on the bed across from Peter. He unzips his trousers, takes out his erect cock and gives it to Yvette. She squats obediently between his legs, the master's cock encircled by her thumb and forefinger. She masturbates him lightly, the way she knows he likes.

Leonard leans forward and kisses the top of her head. As she fondles his cock, he reaches behind him on the bed, takes up the small domestic whip and puts it in her other hand.

Meanwhile Jackie and Cadence have come out onto the terrace. On the terrace they see a monumental grey-greeen olivewood table, stained with use and time. On it stands a lamp, a bottle of suntan oil, a jumble of miscellaneous equipment. The terrace is half in sunlight, half in shadow of the house. Asleep in the sun, stretched out beside the table across a velvet cushion, lies an ocelot in a scarlet collar. Asleep in the shade, on her back on a sun-lounger, lies a majestic figure.

She has stripped off her Carol Henri blouse and lies there in white panties and slave sandals, flat tan soles laced halfway up her calves. Her body is oiled and sleek, her hair short and shaggy, straw blonde gone almost white in the Mediterranean sun. On the floor beside her chair lies a broad, fraying straw hat with a batik scarf for a ribbon. Her lips are raspberry red, her changeable eyes masked by a large pair of cheap Italian sunglasses. Her splendid breasts loll heavily, her thick, dark nipples pointing at the sky. Sweat trickles down her neck, through the valley between them, where some careful hand has inked a small black tattoo of a domino mask. Her belly is flat, the angles of her pelvis like knives beneath the bronzed and shining skin. The cotton panties hug the ripe cheeks of her bottom, concealing her groin, the profusion of her pubic hair. Sweat seeps through them in blots.

Around the lovely throat is a heavy black leather master's collar, silver studs alternating with diamonds.

Jackie steps up to the reclining form, profferring Cadence before her, guiding her by the elbow.

'Your Majesty,' she says. 'Your new slave is ready for inspection.'

Josephine says nothing. If she is awake now, she gives no sign of it.

Jackie steps back towards the door, stands with her hands clasped behind her, her head lowered.

Cadence stands by the lounger, gazing down at the woman she has crossed two continents to find. The sun dazzles her eyes, gleaming off Josephine's perfect skin. Cadence's heart bangs painfully in her ears. She moistens her lips.

'Do you want me to take my clothes off?' she asks. 'Your Majesty?'

The Domino Queen makes no reply. Cadence looks at Jackie, who is obviously not going to be any help. She looks down at the red lips she longs to kiss.

'I guess I'm kind of late,' she says, 'I'm sorry. I mean, you were really hard to find, you know? If it wasn't for Jackie, I don't even know I'd be here at all. I'd still be back in California, probably, with my head on backwards, making movies, letting a bunch of men screw me around. Either that or turning tricks for Louie at the Bluewater Lodge. Did you see I put that ad in the *Times*? And I sent the photo, just like the guy said, only I don't really know if he ever got it. I got it taken at my mom's place, Crystal's Bar, Turkey Flat, Arkansas, I don't know if you know it. It's a real nice place. Topless.'

Cadence stares at Josephine's breasts.

Josephine does not move.

Cadence shifts from foot to foot. She runs her finger round her collar, unsticking it from her skin. She flaps at the neckline of her dress, trying to let some air in.

'Jackie has a nice place too,' she says. 'Oh, oh, and Madam Suriko, I guess you know her, right? In Chicago? There was this one master, a real awesome blond guy, he said you were dead.'

Cadence sniffs.

'I cried all night, you know?' she says softly.

Across the terrace the ocelot yawns.

Cadence feels a clamour of panic in her breast. She has lost her heart to this woman. Beneath her sundress she is already moistening at the familiar odour rising from Josephine's hot bare skin. But she isn't moving, she isn't answering. Maybe she really is dead. Only no,

168

she's breathing, deep and quiet, her breasts are moving slightly as her ribcage rises and falls. Through the dark green lenses of the shades, Cadence can see her eyes are still closed.

She feels deflated, disappointed. She swings around helplessly, looking at Jackie again, but Jackie hasn't moved. She strokes her own hair. They said she was going to be inspected, like at Madam Suriko's, only Josephine doesn't seem to be interested. Cadence thinks she's going to cry.

She leans over the recumbent form, one hand reaching down, hesitantly.

'Josephine? Your Majesty?'

Her eyes still closed, so there's no way she could have seen, Josephine opens her mouth and says: 'If you touch me, I shall whip you.'

Cadence smiles. Her heart fills with love and adoration and relief. She puts her hand back behind her back, clasps her hands together. Then she bends down and kisses Josephine's tattoo.

Josephine smiles.

Cadence kisses her again, lower, kisses her solar plexus, the top of her diaphragm, her navel. The fragrance of Josephine's panties fills her nostrils.

She kisses Josephine's crotch, lightly, and again, touching her lips to the swell of the vulva through the warm fabric. She licks Josephine's odorous sweat from the cotton. One sip heals all her wounds, alleviates her torment. She feels refreshed and new, burning now only with love and desire.

Josephine lifts her hips a fraction from the canvas of the lounger. 'Afterwards,' she promises Cadence, 'I shall whip you. Do you understand?'

Cadence understands.

She kneels at the feet of her queen, where the shade of the house does not reach, and she pulls Josephine's panties down. Josephine spreads her thighs. Cadence presses the lips of her mouth to the lips of Josephine's quim. She feels the Mediterranean sun on the back of her neck. But Josephine's desire is hotter. It feels like forever since they last met like this, since Cadence touched the tip of her tongue to the proud, tender bud of Josephine's clitoris. Yet also it feels like only yesterday.

Cadence licks. Josephine shifts her body, lifting her wonderful legs

169

up either side of Cadence's head, pressing it between the cheeks of her bottom. Cadence drinks. Josephine murmurs, directing her attentions. Cadence obeys without difficulty or delay.

Josephine shudders. The sinews of her thighs are like taut cable along the planes of Cadence's cheeks. Thoughtfully, Cadence inserts her finger into Josephine's puckered anus, presses it suddenly deep and hard.

Josephine cries out, arching her back. The sky falls, heaven and earth are made anew.

She lies there a moment, pressing Cadence's head to her warm belly, stroking her damp hair. Then she rises, pulls up her panties, goes to the table and collects some things.

On its cushion the ocelot lifts its head, inquiringly. Josephine quiets it by stroking behind its ears. She puts on a domino mask, black velvet lined with midnight blue silk, and a bikini top that supports her breasts while leaving her nipples exposed. Then she comes back to Cadence and clips a lead to her collar.

The Domino Queen leads her barefoot slave down from the terrace and a little way into the tangled grove. There is a device on a pole there, two hinged planks of wood with half-moons cut in them for neck and wrists. Cadence stoops, enters the pillory. Josephine locks the frame across her shoulders. Then she grabs the neck of the thin, damp sundress and rips it straight down the back. She rips off Cadence's panties. Cadence stands there, bent, in tatters, her back and bottom bare. There is no trace now of any of her recent spankings. It is as if they have melted from her body at Josephine's touch, leaving her skin clear and smooth and ready for whatever treatment it pleases her mistress to administer.

Josephine raises a short whip of black snakeskin with a platinum handle.

She summons Jackie, who comes down from the terrace. 'Make sure she doesn't get bored,' orders Josephine.

Jackie gets down on her knees in the dirt. She shuffles under the stooping Cadence, positioning herself between her sagging legs. She kisses Cadence's trembling thighs and moistens her lips with her tongue. Expertly she parts Cadence's flossy pubic hair and takes the clitoris, tense, swollen beneath its hood, between the tip of her tongue and upper lip.

Cadence gasps.

Josephine uncoils her whip.

Epilogue

Night on the Ile de Porquerolles is made luminous by the moon. The sand glows and the sea stirs, black and silver, in its nets of shivering light. Night birds call from the trees and tiny creatures dart through the rustling thickets of vine. In the solarium of La Lointain the ocelot stretches, flexing its claws.

Naked, Leonard crouches to fondle the cat, squeezing the back of its neck and shaking it slightly in a way it loves. It slits its eyes and menaces the air, slowly, with one stiff forepaw. Leonard strokes its fur.

The room smells of greenery, of sandalwood and cat. Windchimes of copper and pottery swing by the window, too heavy to sound in the faint draught that sways them.

The cat turns its powerful neck, sniffing its master's groin. He bats its nose away with a muttered oath and scratches it under the chin, whispering. He pulls on shorts and a towelling top, and stretches an elasticated sweatband around his temples. The cat washes itself.

Leonard goes to the door and opens it. The windchimes tinkle. Leonard clicks his tongue, softly. The cat rouses, scenting the air that slides gently into the room. On velvet pads it follows its master out into the hallway, clawtips clicking on the tiles.

They go down to the beach.

The tide is out, the glowing sand strewn with jetsam, driftwood, seaweed, each limp accumulation black and unidentifiable in the uncertain light. The ocelot noses about, trotting from one clump to another. Down on the wet foreshore lugworms suck air with tiny pops.

Leonard starts to run.

His bare feet pound the packed, wet sand.

The ocelot streaks past him. It swerves and vanishes from sight between the rocks.

Leonard runs on, following the line of the sea. The moonlight silvers

171

his golden hair. The island is asleep. At this season he prefers the night, when the air is cooler; he prefers the light of the moon to the blaze of the sun.

A week has passed since Jackie arrived, bringing the new slave. Soon the master intends to go north, taking the household with him. He thinks of a certain castle in the Swiss Alps, of the night hunt that rides by torchlight, slaves with flaring torches running ahead through the forest of black firs. Even as he runs, his prick begins to swell, bumping against his driving thighs.

He reaches a rock outcrop and stops to rest, panting hard, leaning his bottom against the rock, his hands on his knees, his head hanging down. He feels his heart thud, the blood coursing through his hungry muscles.

There is a crack of twigs, a scuffle in the forest. Leonard raises his head. A bird starts to shrill in alarm.

Leonard leaves his resting place and strolls up the beach, picking his way over the sharp stones.

He sees the cat, suddenly, perfectly camouflaged among the undergrowth. One second there is nothing, the next there is a cat, silver and black, only its haunches visible, its head down, chewing something. Prey. The prey flaps frantically, squeals, falls silent.

The ocelot looks briefly over its shoulder. Its ancient eyes flash in the moonlight.

Leonard knows better than to approach it now.

The cat dips its head again. There is a distinct crunching sound.

The ocelot's master squats on the sand, waiting, recovering his breath.

His head is full of spires, midnight processions down steep mountainsides, dark clearings in the forest, cool fountains where virgins wait, tethered, ready to open their pale thighs for inspection.

Across the black water the lights of the Côte d'Azur shine like filigree of amber and gold.

The cat browses among the undergrowth.

Leonard clicks his tongue, softly, louder. The cat comes and stands, three metres off. It stares at him with its cold eyes as though it has never seen him before.

Leonard snaps his fingers, holding his hand low to the sand. The cat lopes up, nosing. It licks its jaws. There is a smell of blood.

The ocelot nuzzles Leonard's open hand.

172

Leonard gets up and starts to run, back along the beach the way they came. The cat runs after him, less urgently now. It darts ahead, crosses and recrosses his path. It stops and gazes out to sea, ears pricked. Leonard reaches down and pats its rump as he passes.

Back indoors, the Supreme Master strips off shorts and shirt and showers in hot water. He dries his body roughly, anoints his throat and beneath his arms with subtle musk, drapes the towel around his neck and leaves the bathroom. He goes wearily to open the back door, letting the cat out onto the terrace. He is tired now, and ready to sleep. But first he will make a final check on the members of the household.

The doors of the private rooms at La Lointain are equipped with spyholes; or perhaps there are no private rooms, only walls and doors and degrees of license and restraint. Fondling himself absently, Leonard looks in on Francis, the chauffeur, whose room is at the back of the house. He is sleeping on his back, his face in shadow, a light sheet pulled over him. A dark mound curled on the floor at the foot of his bed is Ahmed, Leonard presumes. Moonlight through the blinds picks out the links of a stout chain.

The other pair of the curious trio are in their dormitory. They sleep without covers, naked but for their collars and wristbands, chained to the rings in the wall at the head of their beds. Even in sleep, their pale bodies, one soft and rounded, one elfin and childlike, yearn towards each other.

Leonard smiles. He wipes his hair with the towel. Tomorrow perhaps he will reintroduce Ahmed to their games, make him vie with Alexandra for Peter's attention. His new attachment to Francis is amusing, and useful, but his spirit is still proud. He must learn the true humility of slavery, to be constantly and instantly available to everyone who wishes to command his dark-fleeced loins.

Leonard goes down the hall to look in on Yvette. She too is sleeping chained, and in harness, presumably as a discipline, or in correction for some earlier infringement or disobedience. She sleeps face down, the pale cheeks of her skinny bottom proffered to the indifferent moon.

Leonard reflects. During his absence Yvette was given a considerable portion of power and freedom in the supervision of the novices. It may be time, as a preliminary to her induction to the Château des Aiguilles, to remind her of her true status and humility. Perhaps he will start by including her as another element in the intriguing triangle of Peter, Ahmed and Alexandra. To take them all headlong through the sharp confusions of jealousy to self-abasement, the loss of self, the profound peace of submission to the will of all and any masters, or those to whom a master may give them. Leonard gazes at Yvette's bare bottom, bisected by the black crotch strap of her harness, and imagines four of them, in a line, legs spread and chained, locked to the legs of their beds, none of them knowing whether, in the next second, they will be punished or penetrated; and learning to welcome and exult in that freedom from choice, and knowledge, and will.

Leonard is erect. He crosses the hallway, his cock swinging in the night air. Jackie and Cadence are sharing a room on the west side of the house. Their shutters are closed, the moon does not reach their window. It takes Leonard some time to make out the shape of Jackie, sleeping peacefully on her side, her hand on the pillow by her head. Jackie is an angel, versatile, quick-witted, trustworthy: a perfect servant. After the Château, Jackie might well be given Yvette to train. There is a clinic in London where technique is taught and practised. The Shepard woman is still most resourceful and reliable.

Leonard imagines Jackie, after a hard day, changing out of her nurse's uniform, letting down her long, fine hair, brushing it until it shines. She wears a long nightgown of plain white cotton, nothing else. A quartet by Haydn plays sweetly in the painted room. He embraces her, kisses her cheek, her throat, the swell of her breasts. The smell of her is like honey and clean linen. She might lift her leg, pressing her crotch against his pelvis, kissing his face.

The Supreme Master shudders, alone in the lightless corridor.

But what of Cadence? What of her?

He cannot see her at all, cannot even see where her bed is in the black room.

Cadence is a special case, deserving of the very best treatment, the finest leather, the most exquisite clamps and ties. Cadence's powers are, as several people have remarked, quite extraordinary; she has lived high on the world and broken the hearts and emptied the loins of men without a thought, yet her mind is still, after her long odyssey of love and a week with them here on the island, perfectly virgin, wholly untutored. Her appetite and her obedience alike spring from a heart of quite unprecedented purity. She is as fearless as the Mediterranean wind; and as helpless as the birds that sail on it. Cadence kisses the whip; but the whip cannot touch her.

Leonard blesses the invisible Cadence in her nest of shadows and goes into his own room, the master bedroom.

Where entering he stops short, and almost laughs.

The American girl is not in her room at all. She is in his, and in his bed.

Josephine, his queen, is in her arms, gasping at the working of her fingers.

She caresses the dark head huddled against her breasts. She arches her back. Her splendid breasts assault the night. She kneads the silvery hillocks of Cadence's spine.

Leonard strides across the room and whisks the sheet from their straining bodies. The room reeks of the wild ferment of sex. The fatigue is all gone from him, sliding from his back with the towel, falling away. He is drawn by the yearning of his cock for the musky, fecund heart of that viscous mystery. Both women are naked but for their collars: mistress, slave, which is which? He will bind them together with a chain and punish them both, long and slowly. He will fetch locks and a chain from the cupboard. But first he will separate them.

He clasps hold of the cheek of Cadence's bottom, digging his fingers into her cleft. She cries out. Her fingers are still at Josephine's crotch, working, working.

With his free hand Leonard seizes Josephine's thigh. He prises the two women apart like the two halves of a clam.

Josephine growls in her throat like an animal. She reaches for Leonard's cock.

Cadence falls back against the pillow, laughing. She embraces Leonard, pulling him down between them. Her breasts quiver in the moonlight.

Between them is imprinted, like a black kiss, the insignia of the domino tattoo.